## 'Angel?'

His eyes searched ... ...
awareness as his a... ...
before sliding down to where her breasts would
be if she had not bound them.

Pippa pushed him gently down on the pillows.
'Calm yourself,' she murmured. ''Tis only me,
Pip—Pippen.' She had almost said her own
name, she was sure because of his blatant regard.

Dev's eyes lost their startled look and his gaze
fell away from her face. 'For a moment I thought
you were someone else. A...a woman.'

'What would a woman be doing in here?'

**Georgina Devon** began writing fiction in 1985 and has never looked back. Apart from her prolific writing career, she has led an interesting life. Her father was in the United States Air Force, and after Georgina received her BA in social sciences from California State College, she followed in her father's footsteps and joined the USAF. She met her husband, Martin, an A10 fighter pilot, while she was serving as an aircraft maintenance officer. Georgina, her husband and their young daughter now live in Tucson, Arizona.

**Recent titles by the same author:**

SCANDALS
UNTAMED HEART

# BETRAYAL

## Georgina Devon

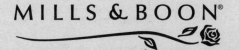

MILLS & BOON®

*MILLS & BOON and MILLS & BOON with the Rose Device are registered trademarks of the publisher.*

*First published in Great Britain 1999*
*Harlequin Mills & Boon Limited,*
*Eton House, 18-24 Paradise Road, Richmond, Surrey TW9 1SR*

© Alison J. Hentges 1999

ISBN 0 263 81810 1

*Set in Times Roman 10½ on 12 pt.*
*04-9910-79368 C1*

*Printed and bound in Great Britain*
*by Caledonian Book Manufacturing Ltd, Glasgow*

# Prologue

*Waterloo, 1815*

*W*ar *is* hell.

Major Lord Deverell St Simon ran his hand over his face, smearing rain water and mud across his nose and jaw. It was hot and muggy, and he hated Napoleon Bonaparte's guts. His troops were demoralized and he was close behind.

Damn Napoleon. Damn him to *hell* for starting this war with his plans of world rule. Damn him.

If it were not for Napoleon's escape from Elba, they would not be here. But the Little Emperor never quit.

Even now, there were occasions when Dev could see Napoleon just over the next hillock as the bastard urged his troops to victory. Because of him, Britain's finest were ready to give up their lives. He was the reason they had been fighting for four days, and the massive losses on both sides were devastating.

Smoke lay like fog over the churned, bloody dirt. Death was a miasma Dev waded through while stifling the urge to vomit. Bodies, human and equine, littered the ground, grotesque in their death dance.

The rain started. Again.

Still, Dev made himself grin at his fellow officer and friend, Captain Patrick Shaunessey. 'We are almost through this, Pat. Don't give up now.' The words were for himself as much as for his comrade, and he was honest enough to realize it.

Pat grimaced, his carrot-colored hair sweat stained. 'Never say die,' he said, bitterness tingeing the words.

Dev shrugged and shook his head like a dog, sending drops spattering out from his light brown hair. 'You'd say the same, Pat, except you are more tired than I.'

For the first time that day, a smile quirked up one corner of Pat's mouth. 'And I didn't stay at the Duchess of Devonshire's ball until there was no time to change into my uniform.' His blue eyes gleamed as he looked pointedly at Deverell's gunpowder-stained evening shirt.

Dev grinned, knowing his friend needed the bantering to ease the strain of battle and death. He needed it too. 'They don't call me Devil for nothing. I had no intention of leaving the Duchess's ball early and cutting short my pleasure.' His teeth formed a white slash in his exhaustion-lined face. 'There were any number of ladies ready to console a man about to face war.'

The Captain's snort of amusement was lost in the roar of wind ripping through the poplars. Rain pelted down, turning the already muddy ground into a morass that would impede anything that tried to move. The artillery, with their heavy guns, would have a devil of a time.

Glancing behind and to the right, Dev caught sight of the Duke of Wellington. The Duke was mounted on Copenhagen, his chestnut gelding, and wearing his familiar dark blue coat, white breeches, white cravat and cocked hat.

'Wonder what the Iron Duke wants?' Pat muttered, raising up just enough to see over the ridgeline of Mont Saint Jean, the place Wellington had chosen for his final stand against Napoleon.

'We'll know soon enough,' Dev said.

The sun broke through the clouds, turning the damp ground into a mist-shrouded enigma. Dev considered taking off his black jacket, but thought better of it. White made as good a target as the typical British red uniform coat.

'Dev, Pat,' Lieutenant Colonel Sir James Macdonell yelled, 'come here. We have orders.' Both men exchanged a telling glance as they rose.

Macdonell was a large Highlander, with a reputation for accomplishing what no one else could. His mouth was grimly tight. 'Wellington has ordered us to hold the Château de Hougoumont.'

'With what?' Dev asked, realizing that the château's open position made it a hard place to defend.

'He has given me command of the Scots and Coldstream Guards, the best we have. The château occupies a strategically important place. As long as we hold it, Napoleon must split his forces in order to get to Mont Saint Jean.' Macdonell made eye contact with each man. 'It's our best chance to defeat Napoleon. We must hold it or die trying.'

A *frisson* of excitement ran up Dev's spine. He had never been one to ignore a challenge, not even one such as this. 'Then we will do it.'

'I knew I could count on you,' Macdonell said. 'See to your men and supplies. We have to be in place before Napoleon realizes what is happening.'

After Macdonell left, Dev turned and winked at Pat. 'This is it, old friend. We are about to earn our place in the history books.'

Pat's face was pale but determined, his blue eyes clear.

'You always were one for action. I hope this isn't your last.'

Dev clapped Pat on the back, ignoring the uneasiness his friend's words created. 'I'll stand you to a bottle of Brooks's finest port when we're through this.'

'And I'll hold you to that,' Pat said.

Dev sobered as he saw the fear return to his friend's face. Dev knew his eyes mirrored Pat's. 'Good luck and God go with you,' he said quietly before turning away.

Dev made haste to round up his troops and get them positioned. Coming from the east, they passed through an orchard before entering the walled portion of the property where the château, a chapel, and a barn stood. In reality, Hougoumont was barely more than a farmhouse, its grey stone walls bleak under a sky that had suddenly turned leaden.

The men broke loopholes into the buildings and walls for their Brown Besses to shoot through and then set about cleaning the rifles. Next, they built small fires in an attempt to dry their clothes, which were soaked from the earlier rains.

Dev made his rounds, uncomfortable in his wet jacket and breeches, but unwilling to stop long enough to dry them. Macdonell counted on him, and he would not let the man down. They would be prepared for Napoleon's on-slaught.

Once, he passed Patrick and grinned. Pat gave him a brief salute and continued his preparations.

It was after eleven in the morning when they saw the French. The enemy stormed through a hedge and into the fifty feet of barren ground that stood between them and the château. Dev ordered his men to fire. The French dropped, good British lead in their chests.

Time was a blur to Deverell. His men loaded and fired,

loaded and fired. Dev paced amongst them, shouting encouragement, giving direction.

Without warning, a group of Frenchmen reached the gate of the château. A gigantic French lieutenant swung a sapper's axe at the gate. The gate splintered.

Dev rushed forward, knowing that if the French breached the gate the battle was lost. He swung his sword in sweeping arches, using it like a machete. Around him other British soldiers did the same.

From the corner of his eye, Dev saw Colonel Macdonell put his shoulder to the gate and begin to push it closed. Dev followed suit. Men leaped to help.

Somehow the gate was closed. Dev only knew his existence had become a red haze of death and blood and survival.

The French trapped inside Hougoumont were killed or taken prisoner, the château secured once more.

The excitement that had held Dev drained away. He moved toward the grey stone wall with the intention of resting.

*'Merci.'* A weak voice caught his attention. It belonged to a French drummer boy. He had been slashed in the arm and blood ran in a red rivulet down his sleeve. He was only a child.

Dev yanked the cravat from his neck and tied it securely around the boy's arm, then yelled for one of his men. 'See that this soldier is kept alive.'

The British ensign who took the prisoner was not much older than the Frenchman. Dev shook his head in resignation. Death and dying.

The day wore on. The French artillery pounded the château. Afternoon was well progressed. Ammunition was low.

Dev wiped sweat from his brow and prepared to exhort his men further, when smoke arose from the building be-

hind him. The French artillery had hit a haystack. The
flames spread to the barn where the wounded lay. Horses
ran into the flames. Men and animals screamed.

Dev felt hot, then cold. 'Pat,' he yelled to his comrade,
'see to our men. I must help those poor devils.'

Dev ran toward the fire. Another man joined him.

Dev plunged into the barn, grabbing the first person he
reached. The man's moans were pitiful, but Dev ignored
them. Better to cause him pain than to lose him to the fire.
He deposited him outside and went back.

Where was the French drummer? He had been near the
door.

'Boy?' Dev yelled in French.

The answer was a ragged cough, but it was enough. Dev
turned left. A figure staggered toward him, and Dev caught
the slight youth. Smoke curled around them and burned
Dev's lungs as he sped toward the door.

Overhead the timbers crackled. A large snap reverberated
through the murky air. A hand grabbed Dev's leg. He slung
the drummer boy over his shoulders and gripped the fingers
still clinging to his leg. With a grunt, Dev pulled the other
man to his feet and propelled the lumbering figure forward.

Noise reverberated through the building.

A large overhead timber gave way, crashing to the floor,
bringing a curtain of fire with it. Dev threw the youth forward at the same time he shoved the older soldier toward
the doorway.

Pain ripped through Dev. His right leg gave way and he
tumbled to the ground. Smoke filled his mouth and burned
his lungs.

His last conscious thought was: *this* is hell!

# Chapter One

Pippa's gaze darted around Brussels's crowded, stinking streets. Wounded men lay everywhere. She could only be glad she was here. The times she had helped the local midwife and the county surgeon had given her skills which might save lives, or at least ease the passing.

Her twin might even be here. Wellington's letter saying Philip was dead had been sent from here. Philip might be amongst the British fighting Napoleon, and Wellington might not even know.

Her mouth twisted. It was a far-fetched idea. The note was dated weeks ago, and everything pointed to her twin being dead. But she knew her twin was alive, she felt it, and this was the only place she had to start.

A cry of pain caught her attention. It was from a man, his head wrapped in bandages turned brown by dried blood. Flies buzzed around him. His cracked lips opened, and his tongue ran over them, searching for moisture that was not there.

Pippa rushed to him. Kneeling, she felt the heat of fever emanating from him. She took a dipper of tepid water from a nearby bucket and, supporting the soldier's head with one arm, tipped the liquid into his mouth. He gulped greedily.

'Thank ye, lad,' the man said, his voice a hoarse whisper.

''Twas nothing,' Pippa murmured, for the first time regretting her decision to disguise herself as a youth. She had done so because young men were allowed in many places where women were barred, places where there might be people with information regarding her brother. Nothing mattered more than finding Philip.

Yet, if she wore skirts, she could tear off her petticoats and make a new bandage for the man's wound. As it was, she wore a pair of Philip's old pantaloons and one of his shirts, her breasts bound by linen to give her the appearance of a man. She had nothing she could take off without exposing herself.

'Blast,' she muttered, putting aside her wish for petticoats. Steeling herself, she made the decision to remove the filthy bandage. The man would be no worse without it, and probably better.

'Hey! Boy! What do you think you are doing?'

Pippa heard the voice as background noise. She was still too new at her masquerade to realize she was the 'boy'.

'You, boy,' the gruff voice said angrily as a beefy hand gripped her shoulder and swung her around so she landed on her knees.

Pippa did not like being touched. She liked even less being interrupted when she was with a patient.

'Unhand me,' she said, lowly and furiously.

'Touchy for a mite of a lad,' the man accosting her said, dropping his hand.

Scowling, Pippa stood and dusted the dirt from the knees of her buff pantaloons.

The officer looming over her—and she was not small—was a bull of a man, with a scowl the equal of hers. A shock of dark brown hair fell over equally dark eyes.

His frown deepened. 'Leave the men alone. We have

enough problems without your meddling.' He squatted by the soldier. 'And this one is sorely hurt.'

Pippa's anger seeped away as she watched the surgeon gently tend to the man's wound. 'I can help, sir. I've trained with our county surgeon and know many of the local midwife's pain remedies.'

Disregarding her, the surgeon soaked the bandage with water from the nearby bucket and then carefully unwrapped it. 'He would be better off without this.' Dismay moved across his craggy features, followed quickly by stoic acceptance.

The surgeon took off his coat and made it into a pillow, which he carefully laid the soldier's head on. Next, he washed his bloody hands in the water and dried them. Only then did he deign to give Pippa a critical once-over.

'You are naught but a boy, dressed in his older brother's clothes. I'd sooner trust yon private—' he jerked his head in the direction of a man who was going around giving the hurt soldiers water '—with an amputation before I'd let you treat these injured men.'

His callous words bit into Pippa, but she held herself straighter and met the other's hard gaze with one of her own. 'I know enough to realize you have ruined the drinking water by washing your hands in it. Now you must send someone to fetch a fresh bucket.'

'Any fool knows that.'

'You should also consider giving him a tincture of henbane to ease the pain and promote relaxation and sleep. You could do the same with opium or laudanum, but I doubt there is enough of either to go around.'

The surgeon's eyes narrowed. 'How old are you, boy?'

The barked question took her by surprise. It should not have. Only very young boys have downy cheeks and slim shoulders. She had tried to pad her shoulders, she could do nothing about her cheeks.

Going on the offensive, a trick her twin had taught her early in life, she met the surgeon's eyes boldly. 'Old enough to be here.'

For an instant the man's wide mouth quirked up. 'Plenty of spunk.'

Two moans pierced the air, each from opposite sides of the street. The surgeon glanced from one wounded man to the other, his face torn by indecision. The hook of his nose seemed to turn down.

'All right, boy. This is your chance. I cannot tend both men simultaneously.'

Anticipation made Pippa's hands shake. She looked from man to man and found her attention drawn to a bright brown thatch of hair. Her twin had hair that color, not black as her own because they weren't identical. Could it be Philip?

She took a step toward the man, saying over her shoulder, 'Yes, sir.'

The surgeon didn't stop her. 'Mind you don't do anything that will harm the bloke,' he stated, his dark eyes boring into her back. He raised his voice. 'Or I shall have you thrown out of the city on your arse.'

'Ingrate,' Pippa muttered under her breath as she hastened to the patient who might be her twin.

She knelt beside the man, disappointment clenching her hands. He wasn't Philip. But he was sorely injured.

The man's moans increased in volume, and his arms and legs thrashed about, throwing off a dirty blanket that had been draped over him. His right calf was a mass of torn muscles and protruding bone. If she did not act quickly, putrefaction would set in and he would lose the limb. The moans stopped the first time she probed the wound.

She glanced at his face to see him watching her with pain-racked hazel eyes. Rivulets of sweat poured from his high brow. He was more handsome than she had ever imagined a man could be. Pain twisted his features and furrows creased his forehead and carved brackets around his mouth, a mouth that might have been wide and sharply defined if it were not flattened by agony. His jaw was square and clenched. His cheekbones were high and flushed with fever. Perspiration slicked his hair.

'Don't cut it off,' he said, his voice a deep, dry rasp that made her fingers shake even more.

In some ways he reminded her of her brother; strong and clean of limb, with the exception of his right leg, and similar in colouring. But the feelings this man aroused in her, in spite of his helplessness, weren't sisterly. Nor were they welcome under any circumstances, much less these.

Forcing her attention back to his wound, she saw that amputating the limb was his best chance, and yet she found herself agreeing with his command not to remove it. This man had a fierce light in his eyes and a muscular wiriness that spoke of activity. He would not appreciate living without his leg.

By the time she pulled the last fragment of bone and the final piece of torn cloth from the wound, perspiration drenched her shirt. His piercing gaze bent on her face as she worked did not help. Never had a man stared at her so intently, and never had a man's attention affected her so completely.

She dared glance at him again, only to wish she had not. His face was creased in agony, and she knew it had been a supreme effort of will that had kept him conscious during the cleaning.

'That leg will have to come off,' the surgeon said in a gruff voice.

Pippa had not heard him approach. Starting, she twisted around in her squatting position and looked up at him. 'I think I can save it.'

The surgeon shook his head. 'If we were in a small town or he was the only patient, I might agree. But 'tis not so, lad. If the leg stays, it will fester and kill him. Better he lose a limb than lose his life.'

Pippa frowned. She had heard the surgeon at home say similar words, but...

Perhaps the surgeon was right.

The man's broad shoulders shook and the leg beneath Pippa's fingers twitched. His eyelids fluttered, their thick sandy eyelashes creating a sharp shadow against his pale skin. His eyes caught and held her attention, commanding her.

'Don't let him take my leg,' the man whispered, his voice coming hoarse through cracked lips. His hand gripped her wrist and squeezed to emphasize his order. 'I would rather die.'

Even as he said the words, his eyes closed and Pippa realized he was trusting her to do as he ordered. He did not have the energy to fight the surgeon. It was up to her to save his limb.

Her twin came instantly to mind. Philip would not want to lose his leg. He would call himself half a man. This man would do the same. She knew it with a certainty she did not want to question for fear that she would find herself gone insane; that she would find herself more involved with this man than she had any reason to be.

Chewing her bottom lip, Pippa stood and faced the surgeon. 'You heard him. He would rather die.'

'You would risk his life on a whim?' The surgeon's bushy brown eyebrows formed a bar across his wide face. 'I was right not to entrust anyone's care to you.'

Pippa flushed, half-embarrassed at her statement and half-angry at the surgeon for doubting her skills. 'The way a man feels about his life is as important as whether he has one.'

The surgeon's scowl deepened, his attention going to the patient. 'You did a thorough job of cleaning the flesh. Can you set the bone?'

Pippa nodded, sensing that she had won.

'You,' the surgeon bellowed to a nearby soldier, 'bring an eighteen-tail bandage and splint.' Turning his frown back on Pippa, he said, 'If this man dies, you will have to live with your conscience. Now, show me what you can do.'

Pippa bit her bottom lip and studied the surgeon. He met her gaze squarely. He was laying a heavy burden on her, but one doctors and healers faced every day of their lives. She could and would accept that burden.

Reaching into her herbal pouch, she withdrew some garlic oil and mixed it with fresh water. She poured the mixture over the wound to protect against putrefaction. Her patient flinched, and when she looked at his face she saw he had bitten his bottom lip until it bled. But his eyes were open and watching her.

Conscious of his gaze on her, she flexed the leg to straighten the bone for setting. Without a sound the man flinched and then went limp. He had finally passed out. She breathed a sigh of relief for his sake. Quickly and competently, she set the bone, put on soft lint to absorb the drainage and crossed the eighteen tails of the bandage so that the leg was completely wrapped. Lastly, she applied the splint.

By the time she was done, her hands shook and sweat ran in rivers down her spine. It was a hot, muggy day, but she knew it was the fear of failure that had worn her down.

She did not want this man to have his leg amputated. She wanted him to awaken a whole person, wanted to see the fierce determination and fire in his hazel eyes once more.

'You know he will limp—if he survives.' The surgeon's gruff voice intruded on her thoughts.

'And it will pain him most in damp, cold weather,' she added, standing and taking a deep breath to steady her nerves.

'Perhaps we can use you after all. I could not have done a better job of cleaning and setting the leg.'

It was a concession she had begun to think would never come. Pippa released the breath she had been unconsciously holding and broke into a radiant smile. 'You won't regret it.'

He looked at her from the corner of his eye and shook his head. 'You are as pretty as a maid. See that you watch yourself. Some of these men are none too particular.'

Pippa turned red. 'Yes, sir.'

Her attention flitted to the unconscious man. What would he think of her as a woman? It was a question she was fearful of having answered.

'I'd be doing you no favors if I didn't warn you, lad.'

'Thank you,' Pippa muttered, trying to deepen her voice.

The surgeon looked at the patient. 'This one is your special case. See that you let me know when gangrene sets in and the limb must be removed. You have until then to try and save the leg.'

'I will do all I can,' Pippa vowed, watching the steady, shallow rise and fall of the hurt man's chest.

'Meanwhile, there are others who need your services and your herbs.' Turning from her, the surgeon bellowed, 'Jones, stay with this lad and see that you get him what he needs.'

A tall, thin, battle-scarred sergeant ambled up. 'Knew we

was robbin' the cradle for the fightin', Major, but thought we wasn't in need of babies to tend the sick.'

'This young man has just performed as well as any army surgeon I know,' the older man said. 'Don't go giving the lad trouble or I'll have you confined to the hospital.'

Jones shuddered. 'Horrible place. Dark and hot and stinking.'

'A living morgue,' Pippa whispered, her stomach churning. 'Those poor men.'

'Ah, Lord.' Jones rolled his eyes. 'The boy has that fervent look in his eyes. Now he'll want to go nurse the bastards there.'

'You are absolutely right,' Pippa said firmly, squaring her shoulders and jutting out her chin. 'Show me the way, Jones.'

'What about this one?' the surgeon said, stopping Pippa in her tracks. 'Do you intend to leave him here, exposed to the elements?'

Pippa's gaze travelled over the patient. He was tall and well-formed, with broad shoulders and narrow hips. He was a spectacular man. She didn't want him going to the filth and squalor of the hospital.

*He is your patient,* she told herself. Patient and nothing more. He might not even live.

With difficulty, she forced her concentration to his medical problem. Because of the bands of muscles in his legs, it had been difficult for her to relax his calf enough to open the wounds so she could clean them. It was a good sign because of the strength it showed he had, but he had already been exposed to the wind, sun and rain too much. For the benefit of his limb, he should be sheltered.

'If you can spare the men, Major,' she addressed the surgeon the way the sergeant had done so, 'I'll give them directions to my lodgings. He…he can stay there. 'Tis a single room only, but all that could be had.'

'It'll be done,' the Major said. 'And see if anyone recognizes him. He must have rooms of his own somewhere.'

It took some time before they found men to transport the unconscious soldier to Pippa's lodgings, but when that was done, she set off for the hospital. She knew the men in the confines of the hospital would have less chance of survival than the ones littering the streets. Contagion spread easily in the crowded, dark places and probably the worst of the patients had been taken there.

She was right.

Loud moans woke Pippa from an exhausted sleep. Her head still ached from too many hours over the past weeks spent in the small, smelly quarters of the hospital, and it took her some time to become reoriented.

The room was dark except for a sliver of moonlight entering through the single window, which she had opened in an attempt to get any slight breeze. It had not helped. Heat and humidity hung over Brussels like a pall, and she was sticky and miserable.

The moan came again.

It was her patient. Pippa rose from her pallet on the floor and hurried to the single bed where he lay. A sheen of moisture lit his forehead and the sheets were damp. His linen shirt clung to him, outlining the muscles of his chest and shoulders.

Pippa bit her lip and forced her attention back to his face. Even in the silvered light of the moon he looked flushed. She poured a small amount of bark into some water and knelt beside the bed. Gently she lifted his head and put the mixture to his lips. He swallowed thirstily.

'That will ease the fever,' she murmured to him, not

expecting an answer. He had yet to regain consciousness since having the leg set, and she did not expect him to do so now.

'Nothing will ease hell's flames,' he muttered, opening his eyes.

Their intensity held her spellbound. Although she knew they were bright from fever and sickness, they seared to her soul. She reached to put the empty container back on the nightstand and missed. It crashed to the floor.

'Oh!' Exasperation coloured the word. Now she would have to clean up the mess before she stepped or sat on a piece of glass.

'Unless 'tis a goddess,' the man whispered, continuing his confused train of thought. He caught her hand and brought it to his lips.

Pippa's attention snapped back to him. His gaze was roving over her face and down to the nightshirt she wore. The muslin sheath was loose, but the material was thin enough to show the swell of her bosom. She had removed the confining linen wrap because of the heat and now regretted the comfort that one action had given her in the moist heat. His intimate perusal was making her heart pound. She told herself it was fear that he would discover her charade.

'You are mistaken, sir. I am a youth, not a maid.'

'And I am the Prince Regent,' he muttered, his mouth curving into a rakish grin. 'No man of my acquaintance has such translucent skin. Nor eyes of such lustre. Green as new grass in a summer meadow. Or are they silver?' he muttered, his voice turning querulous as he sought to focus in the dim light. Giving up, he closed his eyes. 'God, but I hurt!'

'You have been grievously injured,' Pippa said, forcing her voice down an octave. 'I...I have been tending you.'

Her subterfuge was wasted. He had passed out again.

Her worry of exposure was immediately replaced by worry for his leg. Was it worsening? Lighting a candle, she quickly examined him. The wound had finally scabbed over several days ago, but the bandage needed changing. Thank goodness there had been enough materials for her to have extra. She changed the dressing quickly and efficiently. Next, she had to lower his fever.

She soaked a cloth in water, wrung it out, and wiped it across his brow and cheeks and down his neck. Hopefully this would bring the fever down while the bark worked from inside. The water was warm, but it was better than doing nothing. She dipped and wrung the cloth again.

If he were not so well muscled and completely inert, she would move him and change the bedding, but she had learned early that he was too heavy for her. Instead, she lifted up his nightshirt as best she could and ran the cloth down his chest and across his ribs, tempted to follow the trail of brown hairs that led beneath the covers. Intellectually she knew that cooling his groin would ease some of the heat from his body, but just the idea of doing so made her stomach knot.

She did not know what was wrong with her. She never had reacted to a patient this way. Never.

She was a healer.

Eyes averted, Pippa carefully peeled back the cover. Soon she would have to look at him, but first she could moisten the cloth. She did so with meticulous care. The last thing he needed was to have sheets wetter than they already were from his sweat, or so she told herself.

Taking a deep breath, she turned to face him. Her gaze travelled slowly down his body, past broad shoulders and flat belly—lower. He was lean and narrow. She gulped and turned hot and cold and hot again.

He was magnificent. Everywhere.

She was a healer. It was her duty to sponge his flushed skin until it cooled, and she would do exactly that.

It seemed a long time before his fever began to break, and every minute was alternating pain and pleasure. Was he as wonderful a person as his body was perfect? She almost feared he would be. He was definitely charming. No man had ever kissed her hand.

He was very likely a rake.

Her hands moved automatically while her mind raced. Perhaps when her quest for her twin was over, she would go to London for a Season. She had refused to do so these many years because she had no wish to find a husband. Now, to her chagrin, she found the idea had some interest. But that was the future. First she had to heal this man and then she had to find her brother. After that would be time enough to think further.

Resolutely, she covered her patient and returned the cloth to its bowl. Next she cleaned up the broken glass she had forgotten about.

When she crawled back into bed, she felt as though she had been riding to hounds and all her energy was spent. All because of him. The way he affected her made it hard to breathe and even harder to think impartially.

Never had she been this attracted to a man, much to her grandfather's irritation since Earl LeClaire wanted her married. All she had ever cared about was her healing. Now she had found a man who stirred her blood—and she was impersonating a male.

It was a situation she could do nothing about, and morning would come soon enough. She needed rest as tomorrow would be another busy day.

But sleep eluded her. And when it came, her dreams were of a tall, smiling rake who pursued her down a tree-

shaded lane. Spring filled the air with the scent of freshly
scythed grass; grass the colour of her eyes.


Dev woke slowly, his head spinning, his leg throbbing.
Heat was a palpable blanket of discomfort, so he tossed
aside whatever was covering him, only to discover he was
still twisted in something.

'Bloody hell,' he muttered, frustration and pain increasing his normal impatience. Where was he? Why did he
hurt? Why couldn't he move?

Hougoumont. Flames. Pain. The woman.

Memories roared back, bringing agony instead of comfort. But he was alive, he had survived that battle fought
in hell. Was it over? Had they defeated Napoleon? What
of Patrick?

He tried to sit up and pain shot from his right leg to his
groin and up his spine. He fell back, cold sweat breaking
out on every part of his body.

Slowly and carefully, he lifted his head only and gazed
down the length of his body. He wore a nightshirt that
reached down to his thighs, ending—

His right leg was encased in a wooden splint from foot
to knee.

He groaned and let his head drop. He vaguely remembered someone saying it would have to come off and him
telling a lad not to let it happen. It seemed the youth had
done what he asked. Relief washed over Dev.

It was instantly replaced by anxiety. He was alive and
whole. Was Patrick? Had he saved the French lad?

And what about the woman? The one who had cared for
him. Or had she? The memory was not solid. It seemed to
float in and out of his mind. Maybe it was a dream. Perhaps
it had been the lad, if there had been a lad. He was delirious.

Yet, the image of a beauty with ebony hair and green, green eyes haunted him. Her face was an oval with high cheeks, a wide mouth and flawless skin. Unless there was no woman, and his mind was playing tricks with him— which was quite possible under the present circumstances.

Perhaps he was even crazy. He would not be the first to go insane after a battle. His older brother, Alastair, had suffered nightmares for years that made him relive the battles against Napoleon in Spain.

Wearily, Dev rubbed a weak hand over his brow. If only someone were here to tell him what was going on.

The sound of an opening door caught his attention. Turning, he saw a youth pause in the act of entering the room.

# Chapter Two

Pippa stopped flat. Her patient was awake and alert, his gaze fixed on her. Taking a steadying breath, she stepped into the room and closed the door behind her.

His cheekbones were rouged with fever or exertion, but his eyes were aware and intelligent. 'Who are you? Where am I?' he demanded in the tones of one used to being obeyed.

She smiled in spite of herself even as she bristled at his order. He reminded her much of Philip, her twin. Moving to the bed, she said, 'My name is Pippen LeClaire, and you are in my room.' At his frown, she added, 'No one knows who you are, and I am the only one with room for you. I could not leave you in the street or have you taken to the hospital with the other wounded.'

The scowl faded from his face when she laid the back of her hand lightly on his forehead to feel for fever. He had none.

'Then I have much to be grateful to you for. And my name is Deverell St Simon.' His brow furrowed again, and his eyes took on a faraway look before coming sharply back to her face. 'Are you the lad who saved my leg from amputation?'

She nodded.

'Then I owe you my life,' he said gravely. 'I would not have wished to live a cripple.'

'You owe me nothing,' Pippa said hastily, feeling uncomfortable at his solemnity. 'I am a healer and helping others is something I must do. Besides,' she said as matter-of-factly as possible while her heart pounded in discomfort, for she had known exactly how he would feel and that scared her. 'You will never move comfortably and most likely that leg will plague you until you die.'

He attempted a shrug that made him grimace. 'Much better than wearing a wooden peg.'

Pippa, seeing the stubborn set of his jaw, forbore comment and hoped fervently that he would continue to think so. 'You have been unconscious and delirious for nearly a fortnight and must be ready to eat a feast. If you will lay quietly, I will ask the landlady for some gruel.'

'I won't eat pap!'

Instead of arguing, which she knew from past experience with her twin would be fruitless and only end in a fight, Pippa turned away and left the room. He was weak enough and hungry enough that he would eventually eat whatever she brought him.

Dev watched the youth leave. The boy had an odd feminine look about him, with a face that was free of beard and hips that were a trifle too wide for his shoulders and moved a tad too much for masculine purpose. Pippen reminded him of the woman he had seen in his delirium—a ridiculous thought.

Exhaustion ate at him. Sighing, he fell back on to the cushions and told himself Pippen could not help that he was made the way he was. It was not as though the lad was the only man ever born with more female traits than was good.

Dev promptly fell into a restless half-sleep where cannon and musket shot echoed in his ears, and the stench of burning flesh swamped his nostrils.

A short time later Pippa re-entered the room with a tray. Warm tea and a steaming bowl of beef-flavoured gruel would do wonders for her invalid.

Putting the tray on a nearby table, she saw her patient—Deverell St Simon, she told herself—had slipped back into a troubled sleep. Sweat dotted his brow and his hands clenched the sheet in bunches. The urge to soothe him was as overpowering as it was bewildering. All her life she had felt the need to help others, but never had the desire to care for another made her body shake. Why, she knew nothing about this man except his name, and that meant nothing to her.

She took a controlling breath and laid a hand on his shoulder. He jolted awake.

'Who—?' He broke off, his eyes wide, his body jerking upward. 'Angel?'

His eyes searched her face, bringing a blush of awareness as his attention lingered on her mouth before sliding down to where her breasts would be if she had not bound them.

Pippa pushed him gently down on the pillows. 'Calm yourself,' she murmured. ''Tis only me, Pip—Pippen.' She had almost said her own name, she was sure because of his blatant regard. She must be more careful, constantly on guard. It would not be easy. 'I have brought you some food.'

His eyes lost their startled look and his gaze fell away from her face. Some of the tension left his body. 'For a moment I thought you were someone else. A…a woman.'

Pippa kept her countenance smooth, showing only mild interest. 'What would a woman be doing in here?'

He turned away. 'I don't know. I thought a green-eyed lady cared for me while I was unconscious.' He looked back at Pippa. 'She had your face. Only I would swear, she had the sweet curves of a female.' He sighed. 'But enough of daydreaming. Right now I could eat the landlady's entire larder.'

Pippa chuckled, letting the relief she felt at his change of topic ease the tightness that had mounted in her shoulders during his talk of a strange woman. He was remembering the time she had sponged him. 'You will eat lightly. I don't want you throwing everything up no sooner than you get it down.'

He grimaced.

Pippa put her fists on her hips, feet shoulder width apart, and looked at him. Belatedly she realized what she was doing. The pose was natural with her when dealing with her brother, and invariably it put her twin's back up. It would probably do the same to her patient.

With a sigh at her own mishandling of the situation, she quickly sat down on the only stool the room had and ladled up some of the gruel. She put the spoon to his lips. Instead of opening his mouth, his nose wrinkled in disgust and he scowled at her.

'Please,' she said. 'You need food to get well, and you need food that is easy on your digestion. Later, when you are better and your stomach can handle mutton, I will allow you a complete meal.' When his face softened, she added the clincher, 'I don't have the time or energy to care for you longer than necessary. I'm already late for my shift at the hospital.'

She watched his countenance as irritation warred with consideration. Consideration won. Pippa had been right about the way to handle him. It was the way she would have dealt with her twin.

Dev swallowed the gruel quickly, and Pippa was sure that if he had the energy and the bad manners, he would pinch his nose closed. Afterwards, she sponged off his face as professionally as she could when his nearness made her stomach knot. That finished, she tucked the covers around his chest to protect him from a draught.

Her face flamed at the familiarity of the gesture and the feel of his muscled shoulders under her fingers. It was a relief to turn away and prepare a draught.

'Take this,' she said, pivoting back and tipping the glass to his lips.

'I'm not an invalid,' he groused, wrapping the fingers of one hand around the glass Pippa still held.

Mind-startling awareness travelled from where they touched to explode in Pippa's chest. She stepped abruptly away and chattered, 'The drink is laudanum for sleep and pain and bark for the fever and inflammation. When I return, I will change your dressing, but 'twill not be until late tonight. If you need anything, ring this bell and the landlady will come.' She laid a brass bell with wooden handle by the bed.

'Thank you,' he said solemnly. 'I won't ever forget what I owe you.'

''Tis nothing,' Pippa mumbled, grabbing up her coat and heading for the safety of the hospital.

The less time she spent in her handsome patient's company now that he was awake, the better for her peace of mind. She was here in Brussels to find her twin, not get herself embroiled with a man who might be anyone. But even if he was the Prince Regent himself—which he wasn't because he was much thinner than that corpulent royal—she would not be interested. She was going to dedicate her life to healing.

Best, when she returned, to find out if he had lodgings

somewhere and arrange for him to be moved there. Surely there was someone who could look after him. That decision made, Pippa found herself alternately unsettled at the thought of him alone and relieved that he would no longer be a constant temptation to her.

Arriving at the crowded hospital, she set to work with a vengeance. There was always so much to do and not enough people or supplies to do it with.

Bent over the ripped arm of a sergeant, Pippa concentrated on removing the dressing with as little pain as possible. Gangrene had set in.

'How is it?' the man asked, agony etching furrows in his brow.

Pippa looked from the arm that would need to be amputated to the man's face. It was all she could do to keep tears from slipping down her face. 'You will need the surgeon to look at you,' she said calmly, quietly, hoping the sergeant didn't see the truth in her eyes. 'For now, I am going to clean it and let it lay unwrapped. The air will do it good.'

What she didn't tell the man was that it would not matter what she did, and the surgeon would be glad of the time saved by not having to remove a bandage. Too many soldiers needed operations. Sighing, Pippa stood and knuckled the kinks in her lower back.

'You, young man,' a French-accented female voice said imperiously. 'Come here.'

Pippa was getting used to being called a boy and turned to see if the woman was speaking to her. A small, blonde Pocket Venus with the biggest, bluest eyes Pippa had ever seen, knelt less than ten feet away with a soldier's head in her lap. The woman was dressed in the height of fashion in a sprigged muslin dress, all of which was covered by a voluminous apron. Definitely a lady, but the accent was wrong for a British hospital.

Pippa strode to her. 'Madam?'

'Lady Witherspoon.' She motioned Pippa down. 'This man needs a bath and I cannot give it. The water is right here and a piece of soap.'

Pippa nearly choked. This was one of the few duties she had managed to avoid. 'Ah, milady…'

Before she could finish her explanation, the lady had gone on to the next patient. Pippa stared after her, feeling awkward and trapped. Luckily, she saw Sergeant Jones and waved him over.

'I cannot lift the man properly,' she gave him her regular excuse, one he'd heard frequently.

Jones gave her his great lopsided grin that showed a missing canine tooth. 'Then you take that bloke over yonder. Has shrapnel all in his head. Them head wounds are the bloodiest nuisances. Turn my stomach with all their weeping they do.'

Pippa agreed willingly, but before going asked, 'Who was that lady? Her accent is all wrong.'

Jones didn't even bother to look where Pippa indicated. 'Frenchie. Married to our Marquis of Witherspoon. Several of the men have spit on her, but she never says a harsh word. Almost as though she's doin' this to make up fer somethin'.' He grunted as he rolled the patient on to his side. 'She's been helpin' regular as clockwork. Not as good as you, mind, but then she's a woman—and Quality.'

Pippa suppressed a grin at his lumping her with the 'men', while she digested the information. 'Then why have I never seen her?'

Jones slanted her a knowing look. 'Fine woman, but not fer the likes of me 'n' you, lad. Besides, she comes in the late afternoon. You're with the Major making rounds.'

Accepting Jones's assumption and explanation, Pippa went to her next patient. At least her disguise was perfectly safe. If the man she spent the most time with, and who did all the really personal care of the wounded, thought she was male, then everyone else did too.

Many hours later, Pippa walked the darkened streets of Brussels. Her back ached, her feet hurt, and she'd cried enough tears to float one of His Majesty's ships. The man had lost his arm, screaming in pain in spite of all the rum she and Jones had forced between his clenched teeth. She hated it when these things happened.

Her reaction made her question her commitment to healing. She should be strong and not cry. She should be able to focus on doing what was necessary and go on. The local surgeon had said she felt too much of her patients' pain, that she needed to distance herself emotionally—and that was before she came here and saw all this carnage.

She raked her fingers through the short length of her hair, her hand running on even after the strands ended. A month since she'd whacked off her waist-length hair, and she still tried to comb it as she had for many years. Another tear slipped.

Pippa stopped in the middle of the road and stomped her foot. She was acting like a watering pot. This would never do. She had things to do. Sick men to help and a brother to find.

Philip.

Somewhere her twin still lived. Instead of spending all her time worrying about the man lying in her bed or crying over things that had to be done, she should try again to see Wellington. Last week was the most recent time she'd sought an audience with the Iron Duke, and last week was the most recent time her request had been denied. Tomorrow she would try again.

Finding Philip was her sole reason for being here in Brussels, disguised as a boy and unchaperoned. Nothing else mattered.

Her grandfather thought she was here with Aunt Tabitha, but Aunt Tabitha was in London, blissfully unaware that Pippa was supposed to be under her chaperonage in Brussels. That was the way Pippa wanted it.

She had cut off her hair and taken the clothes Philip had worn as a youth. They were no longer in fashion, but a country man might still wear them. Disguised as a boy, she had booked passage on a packet crossing the channel and made her way here.

A young woman would never be told anything but what was proper, and she had a funny feeling that what had happened to her twin was less than respectable. Nor would a woman have been allowed the freedom to come and go as she had been while asking about her twin in the hopes that some clue to his whereabouts would emerge.

But if someone ever found out what she had done, her reputation would be gone. No one in Polite Society would ever receive her. No decent man would ever ask for her hand, no matter how wealthy she was. Not that she wanted to marry. She wanted to heal the sick and had turned down numerous offers from Aunt Tabitha to come to London for the Season. Still, she did not want to be beyond the pale.

She sighed. She had to stop this useless worrying, it did her no good. Shaking her head to clear the melancholy thoughts, she squared her shoulders. Spirits somewhat under control, Pippa strode purposefully to her lodging.

She paused just inside the door of her darkened room, allowing her eyes to adjust. The moon shone through the lone window like a silver flame in a big lantern. A splash of white light fell across the bed where Deverell St Simon lay, his face flushed and glistening from sweat.

'Patrick! Damn it man, where are you?' His anxious words cut through the night. 'I can't see you!'

A nightmare. Pippa forgot her earlier resolve to have him gone as soon as possible and rushed to his side.

She put a hand to his forehead. Fever. She should have prepared another draught of bark and left it with the landlady with instructions to give it to him. Instead, she had let her attraction to him make her careless. Guilt twisted her stomach even as she wrung a damp cloth in the nearby bowl of water which she had placed just for this type of occurrence.

Remorse brought still more tears. She dashed them away with the heel of her hand and concentrated on cooling and soothing her patient. She was overly tired and needed a good night's sleep, something she would get shortly.

'Deverell,' she murmured, 'everything is fine. You're in my bed, not on the battlefield. Patrick is not here.'

Her voice seemed to calm him. He stopped thrashing and no more words came.

Pippa crossed to her bag of herbs, lit a single candle and prepared more bark. Kneeling at the bed, she dripped it into her patient's mouth.

His eyes opened, catching her in their brilliance. 'Angel,' he whispered. 'My angel of mercy.'

Pippa started, nearly dropping the half-full glass. 'No! That is…' She took a deep calming breath. He was delirious. ''Tis me. Pippen. The boy who is taking care of you.'

'Pippen?' Bewilderment replaced the admiration in his eyes. 'Oh, yes. I remember now.'

Pippa lifted his head and tipped the rest of her concoction down his throat. 'That will help you,' she said as he sputtered.

'Choke me, more like,' he said with a faint smile that did dangerous things to her equilibrium.

She let his head fall. 'Some laudanum will ease the pain in your leg and help you sleep.'

'You should take some for yourself, Pippen.' His hazel eyes, full of compassion, held hers. 'You look exhausted. I'd wager a monkey that since I've been here you have not gotten a decent night's sleep.'

His words were too close to the truth for comment. Instead, she held out the opium.

'I need to go back to my own rooms,' he said. 'There is no reason you should have to give up your bed and your privacy for me.'

He took the small glass from her. Pippa didn't fight him, understanding that he needed to show he was not completely helpless. His hand shook, and he very nearly spilled the contents before getting it to his mouth. The small act exhausted him, and she grabbed the empty glass as his arm fell.

'You will get stronger every day.'

'Can I be transported to my rooms?'

'Most probably. But it would not be comfortable.'

His eyes darkened. 'I can stand pain, Pippen. I am not a milksop to be constantly coddled. I am a man who has taken care of himself for many years.'

'Tell me where your rooms are, and I'll find out tomorrow if they are still available.' Now it was her turn to frown. 'But I'm not sure this is a good idea. You need someone to care for you.'

He grinned. 'You can check on me. It isn't right that I have taken your bed. Where have you slept while I've been here?'

Pippa nodded to a screen. 'Behind that is a pallet. It's big enough and comfortable enough.'

Dev gave the tiny room a cursory look. A single window provided what cooling breeze there was. There was a plain oak wash-stand, a small stool and table. A single candle illuminated the area around the bed. Nothing was expensive, but it was utilitarian. The screen took up space, but he understood why Pippen would want it. No one, not even family, liked living this close together.

'This room isn't big enough to house my father's hunting dogs, let alone two men,' he said.

'Your father must be very grand, indeed.'

'The Duke of Rundell.'

Pippa sat abruptly on the stool. 'The Duke of Rundell?' Even she had heard of the most powerful duke in Britain. That meant Deverell was definitely an officer. He might know her twin. Excitement clenched her hands and made the breath catch in her throat.

'Do you…do you know Philip LeClaire?'

His brow furrowed. 'No. I've heard of the LeClaire name, but that's all.' He gave her a narrowed look. 'Why do you want to know?'

She took a deep breath and plunged into her rehearsed lie. 'He is a distant cousin and we were told he was dead, but I know better.' For once the words came easily to her tongue. 'I am searching for him because his grandfather— my great uncle—is ill and needs him home.'

'Who told you he was dead?'

'The Home Office sent a letter two months ago saying Philip was dead. But it isn't true. I know it.'

'Steady,' Dev said.

Pippa took a deep breath and just barely kept her voice from catching. 'Earl LeClaire suffers from apoplexy. He had a seizure just six months ago, and the letter nearly brought on another. The doctor has ordered complete bed rest. I fear that if I cannot find my t—cousin soon, the Earl

will have another. One that might be the end.' Only sheer
will power kept her from more tears. 'I have to find Philip.
I have to.'

'I will help you,' Dev promised. 'When I am able to
walk we will go see Wellington. If anyone knows where
an officer is, and I assume an earl's grandson is an officer,
the Iron Duke will.'

Gratitude overwhelmed Pippa. 'Do you know Wellington?'

A lopsided grin eased the lines of pain around his mouth.
'Not really. But he's a crony of my father's and my commanding officer. I think he will see me.'

'Thank you so much.' This man would finally get her
into the illustrious hero of Waterloo. The barely checked
tears flowed. 'You must think me a sissy to be crying like
this.'

'I think you a young man who has carried too much
responsibility and needs a good night's sleep. Something I
doubt you'll get on that pallet.'

Pippa gave him a watery smile. 'That's where you are
wrong. I am so tired I could sleep on a heap of rocks.'

'Then go to bed,' her patient said, 'and let me get my
rest.'

Pippa went behind the screen and sprawled on the blan-
kets. Excitement made her pulse speed. Deverell was going
to do for her what she had been unable to accomplish. He
would get her into Wellington. But tonight she had to put
the hope aside and rest.

The room was close and humid. The discomfort from the
heat was intensified by the binding she wore around her
breasts and the fact that she was still in her shirt and
breeches. She had slept this way since Deverell had regained consciousness, but the lack of rest was finally wearing her down.

This constant crying was not like her, and she realized that if she did not get some rest, she would not be able to keep going. It was a thought she could not bear. Too many people needed her healing skills.

She had to undo her breasts and sleep in less restrictive clothing in the hopes of being cooler. But what about Deverell? Did she dare? What if he needed her in the night? She sighed. She could give him more laudanum.

'Deverell,' she whispered, 'are you awake?'

'Yes,' he whispered back. 'You need to sleep. I need to think.'

'You are fighting the laudanum,' she scolded gently. 'I can give you more. You need rest.'

He snorted. 'You have already given me enough to fell an opium eater. No, thank you.'

She heard him shift. 'Do you need help getting comfortable?'

'No, thank you again,' he said. 'Will you take a message to Wellington's headquarters tomorrow? Tell him I'm alive and find out where Patrick is? Ask him to meet with us.'

'Of course, if that will make you sleep tonight.'

'It will certainly help.'

'Consider it done.'

Now perhaps he would sleep so she could put on her loose nightshirt and be able to rest herself. Within minutes she heard his light snoring, a sound that strangely enough did not bother her.

She gave him several minutes more before acting. Freeing her breasts from their restraint was like taking a deep breath of fresh air. Comfort eased some of the ache in her back and legs as she laid down.

She would feel better in the morning. Tomorrow she would be her old self.

* * *

The next day, Pippa wondered how she ever thought she would be her old self while Dev still lived with her. Even taking off his bandage was an ordeal she dreaded nearly as much as he seemed to. Most patients faced anxiety when bandages were removed, and normally she dealt with their emotions better. But this was Dev. She was beginning to realize that when he was uncomfortable so was she. And for some reason she did not understand, he was very upset about this. There was no underlying excitement or joy as she was used to seeing.

She looked down at his strained face. 'This shan't take long. And it should be relatively painless.'

He nodded, his mouth white around the edges. 'Pain isn't the issue, Pippen.'

She stopped unwrapping the linen bandage that covered his lower right leg. 'Then what is?'

'Nothing.' He turned away.

Dev gritted his teeth to keep from telling Pippen all his fears. The boy had no idea what it was like for a man to look into his future and see himself as an invalid. He was used to being active and doing what he pleased when it pleased him. Much as he might tell himself differently, he knew his wounds would make a difference. The knowledge was like a sore that ate at his peace of mind.

'Dev?'

Pippen's enquiry pulled Dev from his melancholy thoughts. There was no reason to burden the lad with his problems. Pippen was doing more than necessary for many British soldiers here in Brussels. He was just another one of the youth's patients—or would be if he hadn't ousted Pippen from his bed.

Dev released the breath he'd unknowingly held. 'Never mind, Pip, just unwrap the blasted thing so I can see just how ugly it is.'

Pippen's too green eyes darkened in something suspiciously like pity. 'It will be like any other wound that's healing, but not completely well.'

It was an effort not to snap at the boy. With carefully measured tones, Dev said, 'I don't need your pity, lad. Your skill as a sawbones has been more than sufficient.'

Pippen nodded, refraining from a response.

Under the bright afternoon light of a hot Brussels afternoon, Dev's leg was slowly revealed. In much less time than Dev had thought possible, his limb lay stretched out on the sheets. Vivid red lines slashed across his flesh, interspersed with splotched welts where the skin was healing after being burnt.

'Not a pretty sight,' Dev said softly.

'No worse than many others I've seen. You are fortunate that it has healed cleanly and you still have your leg.'

Pippen's gentle words did nothing to assuage the bitterness knifing through Dev's gut. Exhaustion smashed into him, and he fell back on the pillows, one arm flung across his eyes. The last thing he wanted to see right now was his deformity.

'The swelling is almost gone.'

Dev nodded.

'I think it looks fine,' Pippen stated.

Dev ignored Pippen's attempts to gloss over the wound. He didn't want to talk about his leg. Maybe in a couple days, after he got used to the looks—like he'd got used to the pain and then later the constant ache—he would be interested in talking to Pippen about what the scars would look like after the redness went away. Maybe. Not now.

He said nothing while Pippen bathed the leg.

'I think we can stop wrapping it,' Pippen said, his tone thoughtful. 'The fresh air will be good for it.'

Dev grimaced. Without the bandage he would be able to

see the carnage that was his leg. When it was wrapped, he
could fool himself that it would return to normal. Even with
the discomfort, he had been able to tell himself the leg
would be fine when it healed. But seeing it, with the scars
and puckered flesh, would be a constant reminder that it
would never be normal again.

He stared at the dingy wall, wishing Pippen would go
away.

'Dev?'

'Go away, Pippen. Go see if you can get a message to
Wellington. See if anyone knows what happened to Captain
Patrick Shaunessey.' He managed to keep from saying, Go
away and let me wallow in my self-pity.

For long moments, the lad said nothing and Dev could
feel his gaze. 'As you wish, Dev. I shall tell the landlady
to bring you something to eat. Stew, if you like, and a big
chunk of fresh bread.'

Dev forced himself to smile and meet Pippen's eyes.
'That would be more than welcome. Now, please go.'

He heard, rather than saw, the door close. With a grunt
of pain, he pulled himself up in bed. His leg lay spread out,
immobile and stiff. He looked his fill, willing himself to
accept the disfigurement. He bent at the waist and carefully
ran one finger along the line of the worst scar. The welt
twisted and buckled, the angry red trail ending just above
his knee. He barely felt his touch.

Growing braver, he ran his palm along the damaged skin,
noting the roughness. Little pricks of pain darted along the
length of his leg. At least he could feel something. That
had to be good.

Exhaustion ate at him. This was more movement than he
had done since regaining consciousness. Yet he gritted his
teeth and continued to study his leg.

He had always been active. The army had been the ideal

place for him. As the youngest son, many had expected him to join the clergy, but he was too energetic. Knowing he would never be happy in so sedate a position, his father had bought him a commission. Dev had never regretted that decision. Not even now.

He could have crippled himself riding to hounds or in a coaching accident. At least he had gained his wounds by fighting for his country, by protecting something he felt strongly about, by defending England.

Determination clenched his fists and tightened his shoulder muscles. He would heal. He would do everything he always had. He would ride a horse. He would dance the night away. He would bed a woman.

So help him, he would not waste away into the life of a cripple. He would not.

# Chapter Three

Deverell's previous landlord shrugged his ample shoulders, that perennially Gallic motion expressive of great regret. 'I am sorry for it, but Monsieur St Simon never returned from the battle. I am a businessman. I rented his rooms.'

Pippa felt like crumbling. This was the second piece of bad news today. Just minutes before, she had been denied access to Lord Wellington and anyone else who could have answered Deverell's questions. The setback would not please Dev.

Now she was being told that Deverell would have to stay in her small, cramped room. He would continue to disturb her in ways she was unaccustomed to. Desperation gnawed at her. 'Do you have any other rooms available?'

'*Non*. The English are coming like the droves of sheep they raise.' A grin split his thick, wide lips. 'Very profitable, to be sure.'

Pippa nodded. She had spent all morning preparing herself to move Dev. She had told herself it was for the best. Being the son of the wealthiest duke in Britain, he could easily pay someone to watch him around the clock. She didn't have to be that person. She had squared her shoulders and girded her loins, so to speak. And now this.

She felt an inexplicable mixture of emotions. Regret, apprehension…elation. As much as she had known closer proximity to Deverell would not be good for her peace of mind, she found herself glad that he would have to stay with her. At least, for a while longer. This way she would know he got expert care, and she wouldn't have to worry about someone harming his leg, which was not entirely healed. Why, he couldn't even use a cane yet, so could not walk.

They were paltry excuses for the real reason she was glad, but she refused to acknowledge any other.

'Well,' she said briskly, 'do you still have his things?'

The portly landlord drew himself to his full height, which was several inches shorter than Pippa. 'But of course. When I let his rooms, I had all his belongings packed away in case someone came to claim them. I have, also, a note. Sent from London,' he finished, a sly, curious gleam in his dark eyes.

'From his family, no doubt,' Pippa said. 'I would like his possessions, please.'

It was a short matter of time before Pippa's errand was completed, and she was back in her room. With Dev's possessions, her meagre space was more cramped than ever. Having been raised on a country estate where all of the public rooms were large enough to train horses in, and the private chambers were not much smaller, Pippa found herself feeling claustrophobic. There was too little space and too many objects in this single room. Not to mention Deverell.

Trying to stow his gear under the bed, she accidentally knocked the mattress. Dev opened his eyes, their usual bright clarity muddy from sleep. His light brown hair lay

like thick satin across his broad forehead. He grinned and
Pippa thought her knees would fail.

'You're back from the hospital early,' he said, grimacing
as he pulled himself up in bed until he lay propped up
against the pillows.

'You should not do that yourself,' Pippa scolded, rushing
to help him get comfortable.

'I have done this before.' His gaze darted to her, his
knuckles white where he gripped the sheet. 'Did you find
out about Patrick?'

Pippa gulped. He wanted so badly to find out what had
happened to Patrick. 'I know you're eager for information,
but no one I could reach knew anything. I couldn't get into
Wellington or even his aide.' She sighed and added softly,
'As usual.'

Dev frowned, but his grip on the sheets eased. 'Well, no
news is good news, or so the saying goes. Patrick is very
likely doing better than I am.'

'I would not be surprised,' Pippa said, wanting to ease
his anxiety about his friend. 'I understand how it is when
you are worried about someone.'

He smiled at her. 'I know you do, and we'll do something about that. Wellington will see me. I promise you
that.'

She returned his smile, her stomach doing funny things.
'I know. I wish I could have helped you today.'

'You helped by trying. How about my rooms?' He gave
her a devilish grin. 'If I remember right, that was another
errand I asked you to do for me.'

Chagrin pulled her mouth down. 'And again I have no
good news. The innkeeper gave your rooms away.'

Dev fell back into the pillows. 'That is not surprising. I
shall just have to find others.'

Pippa shook her head. 'There are none to be had. Brussels is filled with every Englishman and woman who wanted to travel to the Continent in the past years but could not because of Napoleon.'

'I should have thought of that,' Dev said. 'Oh, well. We will make do.'

'That we will,' Pippa said, picking up the concoction of bark and water she had left on the table by the bed and giving him a purposeful look. 'You were supposed to drink this.'

He returned her gaze complacently. 'It tastes bitter.'

Without conscious intent, she assumed her position of hands on hips. Exasperation made her voice breathy. 'You are like a child about this medicine. If you don't drink this for the pain, you won't be able to rest. If you don't rest, you will be longer healing.'

Dev cocked one devilish brow. 'You fuss like an old woman, and you're not even old enough to grow a decent beard. And speaking of which…did you get my gear? A shave would be the very thing to make me feel human again.'

Pippa's heart, which had speeded up at his reference to an old woman, eased as her patient's thoughts turned to his grooming. 'I have all your things, and a heavy load it was. Most of it is in your trunk in *Madame*'s cellar. Only a portmanteau is here. Are you one of those dandies who must dress to perfection for everything? Although you certainly weren't dressed correctly for the battlefield.' She shook her head in private amazement at the fact that he had fought in evening dress.

Dev smiled, a rakish baring of perfect teeth. Memories of enjoyable times sparkled in his eyes. 'I dare say I wasn't the only one out of uniform. A group of us went directly from the Duchess of Devonshire's ball. And I'd do it again.'

Pippa left him to his memories while she pulled his portmanteau from under the bed and rummaged through it, looking for his shaving equipment. She found his razor, a small mirror, a lathering brush and finally a tin in which she found his soap. The exotic scent of bergamot, an ingredient for perfumes distilled from the rind of certain oranges, surrounded her. It was a very distinctive smell, and Pippa found herself entranced by it.

'Is this what you use to shave?' she asked, holding the soap out to Deverell.

Dev's attention came back to the present. 'Yes,' he said, the bergamot bringing back memories.

He had first worn the scent the night he met Sam. She had seemed like a goddess on the stage, all aflame with the passion of her role. Losing her to his oldest brother, Jonathan, Marquis of Langston, had been the hardest thing in his life. Until now.

He sighed and forced his thoughts back to the present. A good cleaning would make him feel better.

'Help me sit up higher, Pippen, and then bring a tray with hot water and towels.'

Pippen gazed at him, doing nothing. 'I'll help you sit straighter, but you cannot shave yourself.'

This boy to whom he owed his life had a very definite way about him. Any minute now he would spread his feet and plant his fists on his hips, a stance he took when he was determined to have his way.

'I can shave myself very well, thank you,' Dev said in his chilliest tone. 'You cannot do it.' He gave the youth a once-over that made the boy blush. 'You have probably never wielded a razor in your life. And you aren't about to start on me.'

The lad drew himself up and assumed the pose. 'What

if you slit your own throat? You are still weak and shaving is a very precise art.'

Dev felt his lips twitch. 'Are you a valet when you're not healing? If so, tell me and I will let you clean me up.'

Dull red spread over Pippen's unfashionably tanned skin. The boy was in the sun too much. 'No, but I have done the service for…for Earl LeClaire. Upon occasion.'

Much as he was inclined to argue, Dev found that his small store of energy was fast depleting. 'Show me how you sharpen the razor.'

With methodical motions, Pippen stropped the razor over the sharpening strap. He had a grace of wrist that Dev could not remember seeing in any man other than his middle brother's valet. But then Alastair was a Corinthian and well thought of in the *ton*, so his man was the best to be had.

When the razor glistened in the bright sunshine pouring through the single window, Pippen gave him a 'what now?' look. Dev sighed.

'Proceed as you would with Earl LeClaire and if you falter, I will stop you immediately…if I am not mortally injured.'

The words were as autocratic as he could bring himself to be with the boy. Pippen looked too vulnerable for his own good, and when his chin trembled like a child caught with his hand in the toffee, it made Dev wonder how the lad had got to Brussels on his own, let alone how he had been so successful as a healer for Wellington's victorious army.

Then there were the boy's soft looks. Dev very nearly shook his head in wonder before catching himself. Pippen had taken off the hot towels, which had been wrapped around Dev's face to soften his beard, and lathered his cheeks, jaw and upper neck. Now he was applying the razor to Dev's skin with a look of complete concentration.

Yes, his saviour looked almost like a madonna. The boy's hair was pitch black and too long for fashion, with curls that sprang in all directions. Some lady of Quality would want Pippen for ulterior motives. But some man of questionable virtue would want the youth for even more nefarious schemes.

Pippen's long, slim fingers firmly guided the razor up Dev's neck in one smooth motion. A slight line drew Pippen's ebony brows together and accentuated the pure green of his eyes. They were the colour of the emeralds Dev's mother had set aside as a wedding gift for his bride. The jewels would suit Pippen.

The thought was a leveller.

Dev closed his eyes. What was he thinking? He had never been a lover of boys. His last love had been Samantha, who was decidedly female and several years his senior. Since losing her, he had flirted with every eligible girl in Brussels and shared less acceptable activities with the ineligible ones.

No, these wayward thoughts were due to exhaustion and the fact that Pippen was too feminine and delicate. A state no man should enjoy being. He would do his saviour a favour by telling him to toughen up and get to Gentleman Jackson's for some bouts with the great man. Perhaps, when he was recovered, he would take Pippen there and introduce him. He might even stand as a mentor to the youth during the Season and get the lad some town bronze. He owed Pippen much.

Bit by bit, Pippa slid the razor over Dev's bergamot-scented skin. Some patches were difficult because of the length of his beard. She had shaved him with a borrowed razor early in his illness when he had been too weak to know what she was doing and then a couple weeks later before he regained consciousness. Now she was unbearably aware of him and did as little grooming of him as possible.

The exotic smell of bergamot seemed lodged in her senses and locked in the tiny space of the room they shared. It was an unusual scent. Her brother used sandalwood or, when he tired of that, lemon. Even as she toweled away the remains of the soap, Pippa knew that every time she came into contact with bergamot she would remember these moments and Deverell St Simon.

To divert herself from this dangerous track, she said, 'There was a missive for you at the inn. I forgot until just now.'

She dug into the pocket of her jacket and withdrew the cream-coloured sheet of paper that had been folded into a screw and handed it to Dev. He took it eagerly and read it while she put away his shaving gear.

'What day is it?'

'The twenty-ninth of July. Why?'

'My mother is here in Brussels. Her note says she expected to arrive the first week of the month.' His voice was full of joy and lightness. Genuine pleasure eased the lines around his mouth that were threatening to become permanent. 'She gives her direction and orders me to come to her when I get her letter.' He smiled. 'That is just like her, assuming that, no matter what the carnage of Waterloo, I would survive.'

'She is an optimist.' Pippa wished she had the Duchess's unfailing faith. In a way she did. Everyone thought her brother dead, but she would not believe it. That was very like the Duchess's determination that her son would live through hell.

'Very much so. Do you have paper and ink? I need to send her news.'

'*Madame* will have something, although not as grand as that your mother used.'

'Mother won't mind. She is not a snob.'

Pippa fetched the writing materials and tried not to watch Dev as he jotted down the note. Such joy lit his features that seeing it made her glad. He had come to mean so much to her. It was disturbing.

When he was done, she took it herself. 'I will go straight away and deliver this.'

'Thank you. Stay for a message,' Dev ordered, grinning like a boy about to take his first pony ride. 'And don't be surprised if my mother sees you herself and then instantly orders her coach brought around. She is very impulsive.'

Pippa nodded. Her grandfather and brother often accused her of jumping before she looked. There was the time a labourer's small daughter had dropped her puppy into the trout stream. Pippa had plunged into the icy water without a thought for her own safety. The mountain snows had melted, and the stream had been nearly a river. The current had caught Pippa's skirts and dragged her hundreds of feet until she had managed to grab an overhanging tree branch. Later she had caught an inflammation of the lungs, but she had saved the puppy. That more than compensated for a week in bed with the sniffles and a fever.

If Dev's mother was equally rash, she could deal very well with her ladyship.

Dev was not far off the mark, Pippa found out thirty minutes later. The butler had barely shown her into the salon when a petite, vivacious woman burst through the door.

'Where is Deverell? Is he all right? Why did he not come with you?'

Alicia, Duchess of Rundell, was strikingly beautiful.

Shorter than Pippa, she was willowy thin. Her thick black hair was cropped fashionably short in front. The glossy waves shone blue in the late afternoon sun that poured through the large double windows. Her irises were the clear grey of polished silver and ringed by ebony lashes that were so abundant as to make her eyelids appear heavy. Her full, red lips were parted in a welcoming smile as she came to Pippa and grasped her hands.

Taking a step back and studying Pippa, the Duchess said, 'Why, you are nothing more than a child. What is Dev doing to rob the cradle for his minions?'

Pippa squelched her first impulse to curtsy and instead did the best bow she was capable of with the Duchess still grasping her fingers. 'Your Grace, I am all of four and twenty.' The Duchess gave her a quizzical look and Pippa realized her mistake. 'That is, I am a late bloomer. My entire family matures slowly. That is—'

'I understand perfectly,' the Duchess said, releasing Pippa's now clammy hands. 'You don't want anyone to know how young you really are.' She patted Pippa's arm. 'I will keep your secret, child. Now tell me where my son is and how he is doing.'

Before Pippa could speak, the door opened again. 'Excuse me, your Grace,' the butler intoned, 'but I thought you and your guest might like refreshment.'

'Goodness, yes, Michaels.' The Duchess gave Pippa a rueful smile. 'My staff endeavour to keep me from making too many *faux pas*.'

Pippa grinned. Yes, she could like this woman whose concern for her child superseded all else. In as few words as possible, Pippa brought the Duchess up to date. The last word was barely out of her mouth when the Duchess jumped up and rang the bell.

When the butler once more entered the room, Alicia,

Duchess of Rundell, said, 'Have the carriage brought round immediately, Michaels, and prepare two rooms. I am bringing Lord Deverell back, and his young friend here—' she waved a graceful, manicured hand at Pippa '—will be staying with us indefinitely.'

Pippa nearly choked on the tea the Duchess had poured and liberally laced with cream and sugar. 'Your Grace, I cannot impose on you. I have my own room and am quite happy.'

'Stuff! I dare say you will be much more comfortable with us, child. Brussels is a wonderful city, but after the battle and with all the riff-raff, you will be safer here.' She turned a stern look on Pippa's rebellious face. 'Don't argue with me, young man. You did not say so, but I believe you are responsible for Deverell being alive today. You will come to us.'

Pippa carefully set her cup down. 'Your Grace, I am perfectly happy and safe where I am.'

'Not another word.' The Duchess stamped her foot. 'I swear, you are as difficult as my own boys. Now, come along.'

Without a backward glance, the Duchess exited the room. Her muslin skirts swirled around her fashionably clad feet, and the perfectly coiffed back of her head led the way. Pippa followed.

She would go with Deverell's mother to fetch him, but she would not move here. 'Twould be too easy for her deception to be discovered in a household like this. Servants were everywhere and they saw everything. No, she would not be coming to stay with Deverell and his mother.

Several hours later, chagrin filled Pippa as she explored her new room in the Duchess of Rundell's town house. How Deverell's mother had got her here she still did not know. It must be from raising three boys that, if the Duchess were correct, had been hellions before growing into wonderful adults and husbands and fathers. According to their mother, they were everything that was admirable, with a few perfectly understandable flaws.

Pippa shook her head.

A discreet knock on the door caught Pippa's attention. She opened it to find a footman. He bowed and said, 'Pardon me, Master Pippen, but Lord Deverell requests your presence.'

Instant fear that the move had been too much for her patient sent Pippa flying to her bag of herbs. She should have never left him. She should have made him wait another day before relocating. She should have stayed by his side instead of coming to see her room. The admonishments twirled in her brain as she hurried after the servant.

Deverell's room was down the hall and to the left. In all, it was not very far. Pippa was winded by anxiety when she entered the chamber and came to a standstill.

Dev lay propped up on copious pillows, laughing at something his mother was saying. There was no sign of pain or discomfort that she could discern from this distance.

'Ah, Pippen,' he said, waving her forward. 'My mother thinks I am suffering, and I am trying to convince her it isn't so. You tell her.'

Pippa moved to the bed and looked from the Duchess's worried countenance to Dev. On closer examination, he had the tiny line between his brows that always intensified when he was hurting. And his eyes looked strained around the corners. But he wanted her to assure his mother that he was fine. She looked back at the Duchess.

Many aristocratic parents left the care and raising of their children to servants. Often that meant the ties between them and their children were not great. She had been lucky in

having her grandfather. He had taken care of her and her
twin after her father's death in a coaching accident. Grandfather had given them over to nannies and tutors, but he
had also spent time teaching them about the estate and their
place in the world. He had played children's games with
them, and he had read to them. Church on Sunday had been
a weekly activity he had insisted they share as a family. It
seemed that Dev had had similar care from his mother.

Consequently, Pippa knew she could not lie to his
mother. Not even for him.

Pippa chose her words carefully. 'Your Grace, Deverell
has been grievously wounded. He's mending now, but
'twas nip and tuck about his leg.' She glanced at her patient
to see him frowning fiercely at her. She decided to ignore
him. 'We were able to save it, mainly because Deverell is
strong and stubborn. He didn't want to lose the limb. That
can be a powerful motivator for recovery. He weathered
the infection that set in and the leg will heal. Still, he is
not fully recovered. Even now he is in pain.'

'Blast you, Pippen. See if I ever cover for you.'

'Deverell St Simon,' the Duchess interposed, 'how dare
you talk so to the young man who saved your life? Now
be quiet while *Pippen* tells me the truth about your injury.'

Pippa took another deep breath and looked from her patient to his parent. 'He will always be plagued by the leg
and may not regain complete movement in it. He would
help himself…' she slanted him a reproving glance before
turning her attention back on the Duchess '…by taking the
draughts I prepare for him instead of leaving them untasted
on the nearest table. They would ease the discomfort and
promote restful sleep.'

'Do you have one prepared now?' the Duchess asked.

Pippa hid her smile behind a cough. She had hoped
Dev's mother would ask that question. 'I can prepare one

quickly, your Grace. A bit of laudanum will help him sleep tonight. He needs rest after being moved.'

Dev glared at her as she prepared the mixture, his pointed regard making her hands shake just a bit.

''Tis for your own good,' she told him firmly when the preparation was done. She handed him the glass.

'I know that well enough,' he growled. 'But I don't like the feeling of helplessness the drugs give me. Even though they dull the pain, they remind me that I have a deformity.'

Pippa stared at him. She had known he was headstrong, but until this instant she hadn't realized why he disliked the medications. He was going to find it hard going when he was healed enough to move around, but not well enough to do as he saw fit.

'I am sorry for that,' she murmured, wishing she could do something for him besides give him the painkillers. Noticing that the Duchess had moved away from them, she added, 'I am sorry that I had to spoil your plan to shield your mother. Your sentiments toward her are very admirable, but she deserves to know. This way, when you don't bounce out of bed in the next couple days, she won't be surprised and worried.'

Dev grunted. 'You're right, Pippen, but all of us have got in the habit of protecting her from the harsh things of life—if we can.'

His words brought a rush of warmth to Pippa's heart. Would she have been so protective of her mother, had her mother not died birthing her? The question brought back all the old guilt over being the death of her mother and the determination to atone for that deed. Even though no one had ever blamed her for her mother's death, Pippa had occasionally blamed herself. She knew death in childbed was common and that her mother's demise was not her fault, but still her mother's death was the reason Pippa had first wanted to learn midwifery and later medicine. She wanted to help others and hopefully prevent parents from dying and leaving behind their children.

She shook her head to clear it of the old memory. A long time had passed since she had last had these thoughts. They were probably brought on by watching Dev with his mother. That the two loved each other was obvious. That she was getting maudlin was even more obvious. She needed to go to her own room and do exactly what she was telling Dev to do—rest.

Resisting the urge to smooth the hair back from his forehead, Pippa stepped away from the bed and packed her herbal bag. 'He should be fine now.'

'Thank you, Pippen,' the Duchess of Rundell said, coming over and taking Pippa's hands. 'I will never be able to thank you enough.'

Pippa felt awkward and embarrassed. She didn't want anyone's gratitude. She just wanted… She glanced at Dev and saw his roguish grin. She just wanted things she had never wanted before, things she couldn't have. Not now.

'You don't need to thank me.' Pippa gently pulled her fingers from the Duchess's grasp. 'I am glad I could help Dev.' She stepped back. 'If you will excuse me, I am very tired.'

'Of course, child,' the Duchess said. 'Sleep as late as you need.'

'Sweet dreams,' Dev added, his hazel eyes twinkling with devilry.

And what type of dreams did he expect her to have? Pippa thought sourly as she made her way back to her room. As far as Dev was concerned, she was a young man who couldn't even grow a beard. She knew from living with her twin that not being able to grow facial hair was tantamount to being a baby.

Pippa closed her door behind herself and looked around the room she had been given. It was masculine in its simplicity. A large oak four-poster bed took up the centre while a matching armoire hogged one entire wall. A Turkey rug covered most of the wood floor, and blue drapes that echoed one of the rug's colours hung from the high ceiling to puddle fashionably.

What would Dev do if he knew she was a girl, and her room at home was done in peaches and soft greens? He would be scandalized. If she was unmasked, she would be beyond redemption. Dev's liking would turn into loathing. It was a thought she could not bear to contemplate for long.

Deverell St Simon's admiration and friendship meant too much. To lose them would be unbearable.

# *Chapter Four*

Pippa shifted the very fashionable hat she had just bought to cover her too short hair. Then, with a determined tread, she pushed open the bank's door and entered the cool interior. The sprig muslin morning gown that would have been better for a good ironing left her arms and much of her neck bare to gooseflesh.

She had packed the gown, reticule and kid slippers in her portmanteau for just this occasion, and had had a devilish time of it keeping the women's clothes hidden. The Duchess of Rundell had assigned a maid to put her clothes up, and Pippa had had to shoo the girl out any number of times, telling her she had already unpacked.

Her letter of introduction that would allow her to draw funds on her father's account was in her reticule. Nearly all the money she had brought with her from England was spent and tomorrow Dev was taking her to meet Wellington. From there she would continue her search for her brother, and that would require more blunt.

The use of blunt, a cant word Philip had taught her, brought a smile to her lips. She would find her brother. She would.

'Pardon—' a French-accented woman's voice intruded on Pippa's vow '—but have we met before?'

Wariness tightened the muscles between Pippa's shoulders as she turned to face the speaker. The Marchioness of Witherspoon stood not less than two feet away, studying Pippa like a naturalist studies a bug pinned to a specimen tray. The Frenchwoman must have noticed the similarity between Pippa and Pippen from the hospital.

A shiver skated down Pippa's spine as she forced a smile. 'I don't believe so. I would have surely remembered if we had.' She made a slight curtsy and tried to edge around the woman. The sooner she was away, the sooner the Marchioness would forget the memory.

*'Non, non,'* the Marchioness said, her small white hand shooting out and coming to rest on Pippa's arm. 'Do not run, *chérie*. I mean you no harm, only…' Her head cocked to one side and her blue eyes studied Pippa. 'I could swear I have seen you before. In Brussels, perhaps?'

Pippa shook her head. 'No, milady. We have never met.' She moved her arm so that the woman's hand fell away. It was like having a chain opened. 'Excuse me, but I have an appointment.' That was not the truth, but she hoped to soon have an appointment.

Before the Marchioness could detain her further, Pippa spurted forward. The last thing she needed was for someone to penetrate her disguise.

Even as her palms turned clammy at the possible ruin, an image of Dev as she had left him formed in her mind. Her step slowed and her gaze saw nothing in the bank. For the first time since she'd met him, Dev had been dressed to go out, his tall, lean form shown to advantage by buff-coloured buckskins that fit his legs to perfection and a bottle-green coat of superfine that showed his broad shoulders to advantage. Smudge-free Hessians had hidden the scars on his right leg—not that they mattered to her. She sighed.

Would he find her attractive dressed as a woman? She berated herself immediately.

Whether Dev would be interested in her was not an issue. Deverell St Simon was not her reason for being here. Nor would he want to be, considering how she was flaunting the conventions of their society. Best to put all thought of him from her mind.

Suiting action to thought, Pippa presented her letter of introduction to a clerk. While she waited, she watched the people around her. To her surprise, the Marchioness was still on the premises. She seemed to be depositing a large sum of money which was causing a stir with the young man taking it.

Briefly, Pippa wondered why the woman would be depositing money when the normal course of action for an Englishman or woman while in a foreign country was to draw on their British bank. Before she could dwell long on the problem, she was approached by another clerk and escorted to a large desk where the bank manager smiled benignly at her.

The Marchioness's actions quickly slipped her mind as she concentrated on her transaction.

Her task done, Pippa retraced her footsteps to the small closet in the hospital where she had stashed her boy's clothing. It was a matter of minutes before Pippen emerged, carrying a wicker basket, the letter of introduction safe in the breast pocket of the jacket. Her first instinct was to dump the basket and revealing clothes in the nearest heap of trash.

It had been safe to bring the dress with her and keep it in her portmanteau until she had moved into the Duchess of Rundell's town house, where servants were constantly cleaning and straightening her belongings. The dress would have to go. The letter of introduction was much easier to hide and irreplaceable. She could always buy another dress.

On her way out of the hospital, she saw a woman kneeling by one of the patients. From the threadbare look of the woman's dress it was obvious she didn't have much money. Yet love shone from her eyes as she gazed at the man whose head lay in the pillow of her lap. Tears tracked down the woman's cheeks even as happiness made her face glow.

'Hush, darling,' she said. 'All that matters is that you are alive. I love you no matter what.'

Using the only hand he had left, the soldier gathered his love's fingers to his lips. Moisture blurred Pippa's vision. Another couple weathering the horror of war.

Without another thought, Pippa crammed a pound note into the basket and edged toward them. Unobtrusively, she set the wicker container beside the woman and slipped away.

Outside, the August heat quickly evaporated the moisture from Pippa's eyes. The sunshine was golden and warm on her skin, easing the tightness in her chest. The brisk walk to the town house lifted her spirits.

'Master Pippen,' the butler said, bowing her into the house. 'Her Grace wishes your presence in the morning room.'

Pippa grinned at Michaels. Since moving here, she and the old retainer had become fast friends. Michaels had taken her under his wing and endeavoured to remind her of the proper behavior for a young man of Quality, as he did the Duchess when she failed to do the proper thing. Pippa would be sorry to leave him.

She gave the butler her hat. 'Thank you. I suppose that means I must go there immediately.'

'It is customary.'

Pippa's too large Hessians, which she padded with socks in the toes, clumped on the polished black marble floor as she made her way. A footman opened the door and announced, 'Master Pippen, your Grace.'

'Fustian, Jones,' Her Grace said. 'There is no need to introduce Pippen.' The footman nearly smiled before catching himself and closing the door. 'Come here, child.'

Pippa nearly shook her head. The staff was completely devoted to their mistress, but her lack of formality was often a burden they did their best to correct.

'Good afternoon, your Grace,' Pippa said, making a leg before taking the outstretched hand the Duchess held to her.

'Call me Alicia. How many times must I tell you that? You saved my son's life, we won't stand on formality.'

'Yes, your Grace.' Alicia was too familiar. When Dev's mother frowned, Pippa said, 'I am sorry, milady, but as much as I know you would like it, I cannot bring myself to be so familiar with you as to call you by your Christian name.'

Michaels might often think Pippa lacked correct manners, but 'twas not so. Her grandfather had drilled her and Philip in the behavior required by their stations. They did not call duchesses by their first names. Not unless they had run tame all their lives in the lady's household, which was not the case here.

'Child, I shall surely lose my temper with you if you persist in this stubborn adherence to polite manners that is not necessary between us.' She pulled Pippa down to sit beside her on the pale blue silk-covered settee. 'Why, I begin to feel like a mother to you. And the first thing we need to do is get you some evening clothes. I am having a small dinner party tomorrow to let our close friends know that Dev is fine.'

Pippa's face blanched. The very last thing she needed was a male tailor taking her measurements.

'Thank you, your Gr—Alicia.' Using the Duchess's given name was a desperate attempt to make Dev's mother more accepting of the following refusal. 'But I cannot put you to the trouble. Besides—' she brightened '—I won't be here much longer. Right this moment, Dev is making arrangements for me to meet Wellington. When I find out where my brother was last seen, I will head there.'

'Nonsense. No matter what you learn from the Duke, you won't be leaving here in the next couple of days.'

The door slammed open before Pippa could remonstrate. Dev strode into the room, his brown hair awry and his hazel eyes wild.

'Bloody swine!'

'Dev!' Pippa jumped up without thought and ran to him. 'What is wrong? Are you hurt? Sit down and let me see.'

She wrapped one arm around his waist and urged him to the nearest chair. As soon as he sat, she fell to her knees in front of him.

'Is it your leg? Help me get this boot off so I can examine it.'

'Leave me alone,' Dev snarled. 'I deserve to feel this pain.'

Pippa rocked back on her heels and stared up at him. The wild look was still in his eyes, but the skin around them was dark and bruised looking. His full lips were thin. He looked in pain.

'What is this all about?' the Duchess demanded, coming over and taking her son's hand. 'There is no excuse for your rudeness to Pippen.'

Pippa watched the emotions battle across Dev's face: anger, hurt, contrition and back to anger. Something was terribly wrong.

'That damned Napoleon. May he rot in hell. May the ship taking him to St Helena sink and take his carcass to the bottom of the sea for fish bait.'

Pippa reached up and smoothed the tumbled lock of hair from his brow before she realized what she was doing. The motion was so revealing, she dropped her hand, stood and paced away. The more distance between them, the harder it would be for her to do another action so unlike what one man would do to another.

The Duchess cast her a quick, appraising glance before turning her attention back to her son. 'Calm down, Dev, and tell us what has happened.'

''Tis Patrick.' The words were torn from his throat and sounded like a raw wound. 'He's…damn it. He's dead.'

Patrick was the friend whose whereabouts had been the first thing Dev wanted to know when he regained consciousness. All Pippa's resolutions fled. She rushed to him and gathered him close. His head fell to her shoulder.

'I'm so sorry. So sorry,' she crooned.

For long minutes she rocked him, trying to absorb his anguish. She could give him a sleeping draught, but that would do nothing for the grief. She knew. This was the ripped-apart feeling she'd first had when the letter had arrived saying Philip was dead. Nothing but time would ease what Dev was going through now.

Finally, Dev pushed away. 'I'm all right. You can stop coddling me.'

'Of course,' she muttered.

Pippa released him immediately and stepped away. Her face flamed at what she had done. The best interpretation anyone could put on her action would be that she cared for Dev as a brother would. The worst was that she was a woman in disguise. Best that she get away and let his mother comfort him.

'Please excuse me.' Without waiting for a reply, Pippa rushed from the room.

Alicia, Duchess of Rundell, watched the slim figure of her guest fly out before turning a worried look on her son. 'I am sorry about Patrick. He was a good man and a good friend.'

Dev stood and limped to the wall of windows that overlooked an extensive garden that was in full bloom. Rosebushes mingled with iris and sweet alyssum. The beauty did nothing to ease the tightness in his chest or the urge to smash his hand through the glass.

'His death was a waste. I was glad before that we defeated Napoleon. I am ten times gladder now.'

Alicia followed him and put a comforting hand on his arm. 'You are right.'

Dev gripped her hand. 'And what am I to do with young Pippen, Mother? You saw the way he comforted me. It was more intimate than I would have expected.'

Alicia met his troubled gaze squarely. 'What are you going to do? You are the one who laid his head on the... lad's shoulder.'

Dev sighed. 'So much sorrow and so much confusion. The boy is too soft and too compassionate for his own good.'

'Perhaps,' the Duchess said with a strange smile. 'But right now, you need rest.' When his mouth opened on what she knew would be a protest, she put one finger over his lips. 'Don't argue with me. Do as I say for once. You will feel better for the sleep.'

To her surprise, Dev did as she urged. That, more than anything else, told her how devastated he was.

And what was he going to do about 'Pippen'?


Nearly three months after arriving in Brussels, Pippa finally stood outside the door to the Duke of Wellington's

office. She owed this meeting to Deverell who lounged in
a chair along the wall, his wounded leg straight out in front.
A brass-handled cane leaned against his thigh.

His mouth was a thin line, the residue of yesterday's
news about his friend. He had not come down to dinner
last night, and her heart had ached for him.

Outside the day was hot and humid, a storm moving in.
Every once in a while, Pippa caught Dev frowning and she
knew the weather change was causing his leg to ache—
although it could as easily be the grief over Patrick. This
was something he didn't need right now. He was not fully
healed. But then, none of the people suffering from the
battle of Waterloo needed the pain.

'When we return home, I'll get you some laudanum. Just
a little to ease the pain.' She was mildly surprised that she
had called the Duchess's town house home, but it felt that
way.

He looked at her and forced a smile. 'My leg is nothing,
Pippen. I will be fine. I don't like waiting, that's all.'

She nodded even though she knew that was only a small
part of his discomfort. In the last weeks, she'd learned that
Deverell St Simon was impatient but he was also kind to
others. He'd had his outburst yesterday, and now he was
not going to subject anyone to his feelings. He was protecting her the same way he protected his mother.

A lightheartedness that was out of place in the current
situation suffused her. The emotion was scary. As soon as
she found out where Philip had last been seen, she would
leave. She had to. It was better that way. For everyone.

Dev was so handsome. His brown hair had grown longer
in the past weeks and brushed the bottom of his jacket
collar. One shank of it fell attractively over his high forehead. Pippa had long since lost count of the number of

times she'd wanted to smooth it back, but the gesture was too intimate for a lad to do to another man or a maiden to do to anyone. Yet, she had lost control yesterday and done exactly that. The emotions she felt for Deverell St Simon were overwhelming.

She sighed and looked away.

'A penny for your thoughts?' Dev asked, bringing her gaze back to him.

'Nothing that would interest you,' she muttered.

'Lord Deverell,' a young, eager aide to Wellington said as he stepped into the room, 'the Duke will see you now.'

Dev grabbed the cane in his right hand and used it to lever himself up from the seat. Pippa bit her bottom lip and resisted the urge to rush to him and help. That was the last thing a proud man like Deverell would want.

'Your companion, too,' the aide added.

'Thank you, Peter,' Dev said, motioning Pippa to precede him.

The office was as spare as the man it housed. The Iron Duke, the hero of Waterloo, sat behind a large desk, all his papers in neat piles. His dark hair was cut short, his dark eyes drooped at the corners and his long nose was the epitome of the aristocratic British ideal. He was neatly dressed with no creases visible.

Dev went to attention. Pippa stood several steps behind, studying the most famous man in the world.

'Lord Deverell,' the Duke said, 'take a seat. You, too, boy,' he added without glancing at Pippa.

'Thank you, sir,' Dev said, sinking into one of several plain wooden chairs. He stretched his hurt leg out and hooked his cane on the back of the chair where it would not be in the way or seen.

Pippa took another seat, sitting on the edge. She clasped her hands tightly in her lap to stop their shaking.

'What do you need?' Wellington asked in his abrupt, down-to-business manner.

'Sir, I'd like to introduce Pippen LeClaire, a relative of Earl LeClaire. He's in Brussels looking for the Earl's grandson, Viscount Staunton. Supposedly, the Earl received a letter from the Home Office saying the Viscount was dead. The news nearly killed the Earl, and he sent Pippen here to find out what was going on.' Dev cleared his throat as though what he intended to say next made him uncomfortable. 'It seems the Viscount has a twin sister who does not believe he is dead.'

Wellington looked at Pippen. His gaze was so penetrating, she felt pinned to her seat. For a brief moment she even thought he could see through her disguise.

'What precisely is your relationship to Philip LeClaire?'

She held his disconcerting gaze without flinching. 'I am a distant cousin. The closest male relative besides the Earl, his grandfather.'

Wellington asked several more questions in an effort to establish her connection. 'Do you have a letter of introduction?'

Pippa gulped. She did, but it gave her real name and said she was accompanied by her aunt Tabitha. 'No, sir. The Earl was too upset to think about such a thing. All he wanted was for me to sail immediately.'

Wellington studied her for several more long minutes. 'Major St Simon, do you vouch for this person?'

Dev sat straighter. 'I owe Pippen my life, as do many of your men. The lad has worked in the hospital for the last five weeks. Ask Major Smythe, the surgeon.'

Wellington looked from one to the other. 'The Home Office sent that letter because Viscount Staunton is believed dead. We don't know that for sure, but he dropped from sight two months ago. He was last seen in a Paris tavern.'

*No one had actually seen Philip die.* The tension that had built in Pippa burst. She jumped to her feet. 'Thank you, sir. Thank you. If you will tell me the name of the tavern, I'll go there immediately.'

A slight smile curved the Duke's thin lips before disappearing and leaving his face grim. Wellington was not known for his friendliness or social abilities. He was a general.

'I need to speak with Major St Simon now. I will tell him the information you need.'

The urge to fall into a curtsy, as though leaving royalty, was strong. Instead, Pippa bowed deeply. This man had given her a place to start her search and renewed her hope.

With a spring that hadn't been in her step for weeks, Pippa left. She would wait for Dev outside in the sunshine that matched the sudden lifting of her spirits. Nothing could mar her optimism now.

Dev watched Pippen leave. The lad had a lift to his walk and a smile on his face that had not been there before. Once more, the boy looked almost feminine with that glow in his eyes. He shook his head. This constant thinking that Pippen was too much like a woman was not good. He had been too long without female companionship, something he would remedy shortly.

'Major,' Wellington said, breaking into Dev's thoughts, 'you have been promoted to lieutenant colonel for your bravery at the Battle of Hougoumont.'

Dev suppressed the shout that came to his lips. Even though his father had provided for him, initially buying him a captaincy and setting up a trust fund, and his maternal grandmother had left him a small inheritance which allowed him to live like a man about town, he was still a younger son whose future was the military. This advance before he was thirty put him well on the road to success in his chosen career.

'That is great news. But I didn't do anything unusual. Every man there showed bravery.'

'True. But you lived. The others who survived have also been rewarded.'

Dev sobered. Yes, he was still alive. Unlike Patrick. The memory, so recent and so raw, felt as though someone had grabbed his wounded leg and squeezed. It was an effort of will over heart to keep his sight from blurring. His head bowed.

'Damn Napoleon,' he swore softly. 'Damn that Corsican to hell.'

'We have,' Wellington said. 'For a man of Napoleon's ilk, St Helena will be like hell on earth. He won't escape again.'

'Thank God, and all our men who died.'

'Quite right,' Wellington said. 'And because of this, I have a mission for you.'

Dev's head snapped up. He grasped at something to do that would keep his mind from Patrick.

'I want you to go with Pippen LeClaire and find Viscount Staunton. I believe Staunton is a traitor.'

Dev stared, his mind a riot of conflicting thoughts. 'Why?'

'We thought Staunton was spying for us, but he was last seen by one of our men talking to a known French agent. Later that evening, another one of our men was found dead. Someone had to reveal his identity. I think that person was Philip LeClaire.'

Anger boiled in Dev. 'A British peer betraying his country. That is the worst type of treason. The man should be shot.'

'Precisely. We want Staunton found and brought to London, but…' a thin smile stretched Wellington's mouth '…to be tried and hung as a traitor to the crown. Had we caught him during the battle I would have had him shot.'

'I will find the scoundrel, sir,' Dev said, his earlier anger still roiling and making his gut twist.

'I know you will. Because Staunton is the grandson of a respected and liked Earl, not to forget a very powerful man, you will report directly to me. While I am nearly a hundred per cent sure that Staunton is the traitor, his family is too influential for this type of action to be bandied about. No one—and I repeat, no one—is to know what you are doing.'

Wellington picked up a sheet of paper and began reading what was written on it. Dev knew he was dismissed. He eased himself up and resisted the urge to rub the ache in his leg. His disgust and fury over a British peer betraying the country that had made him everything he was gave him the strength to walk out of the room without limping.

As soon as the door closed behind him, Dev used the cane. One look at Pippen's radiant face told Dev the up-coming journey was not going to be easy. In fact, it was going to be the hardest thing Dev had ever done. He was going to betray Pippen's trust in him, and he owed Pippen his life.

Sudden exhaustion made Dev's shoulders slump and his leg hurt even more. Using the cane, he made his way to the chair he had used earlier and nearly fell into it.

Pippen did a jig on his way to stand in front of Dev. 'Is this not exciting? 'Tis the best news I've had in over a month. I am leaving tomorrow for Paris. I won't be coming back to Brussels.' The words babbled out of the boy's smiling mouth. 'Oh, yes. I must send a message to Grand— Philip's grandfather to tell him the latest information.'

Dev groaned.

Pippen fell to his knees in front of Dev, concern wrinkling his brow as he began to gently massage Dev's lower leg through the thick leather of the Hessian boot. 'Oh, you are in pain. Let us go home and I will give you something.'

Dev stared at the boy, his gaze going from the black hair to clear green eyes and on to lips that were too full and too pink and finally to Pippen's slim fingers that were surprisingly strong. They eased the discomfort of his wound. Lying was not going to be easy.

'I am going with you,' he said. 'Wellington promoted me to lieutenant colonel and told me to take some time to heal my leg. I am going to use that time to help you, as I promised I would.'

Joy filled Pippen's face to be instantly followed by another emotion Dev could not name. 'Don't feel that you have to do that, Dev. I know you're trying to help me as payment for the care I have given you. You don't need to. I am a healer, and I would have done the same for anyone.'

'But you didn't,' Dev said quietly. No, Pippen had saved his life, and now he would use Pippen to do what must be done. Patrick and others were dead because of men like Viscount Staunton. A jolt of remorse shot through Dev, quickly followed by sorrow over Patrick and renewed determination to find the traitor.

If there was one thing Dev had learned in the past six months, it was that life is never easy.

# Chapter Five

'Don't work too hard,' Dev said, forcing himself to tease Pippen as the lad took off for the hospital. The boy grinned over his shoulder. 'Damn!' Dev swore softly. He was going to destroy that happiness.

But he had no choice. Not really.

An image of Patrick as he'd last seen him rose in his mind. Patrick had been hot and tired and scared. As they all had been. He was exhorting his troops to hold Hougoumont.

Dev's breath caught.

Damn. Damn. Damn.

He could do nothing for Patrick now except bring to justice one of the men responsible for the carnage. But he could find out about the French drummer boy he'd tried to save from the fire. The lad had been younger than Pippen.

Hours later, Dev found himself on his mother's doorstep with the French boy, named Raoul, in tow. The lad had been in one of the makeshift prisons for Napoleon's army.

The door opened and the butler's imposing body met them. 'Lord Deverell.' Michaels's gaze roved over the French boy. 'And friend.'

Dev rolled his eyes. Leave it to Michaels to be droll. 'Take Raoul here to the kitchen and see he gets a good meal. Then find something for him to do.' He cast a wicked look at the appalled servant. 'He knows how to do a drum roll.'

'Just so, milord. But does he know anything else?'

'How should I know?' Dev entered the house and handed his cane to a waiting footman. 'I don't know the boy. And he doesn't speak English.'

Michaels drew himself up to his full height. 'And I do not speak French.' Under his breath he muttered, 'Bloody frogs.'

'I heard that.' Pippen's voice came from the salon doorway. 'Shame on you, Michaels,' he said, striding into the foyer. 'Who is this?'

'A boy who lost out in the war,' Dev said, his good humour replaced by a tinge of bitterness.

'Poor child,' Pippen said, moving to the boy's side. 'For he's no more than that.'

'Obviously,' Dev said. He turned his stare on the butler. 'Well?'

'Yes, milord,' Michaels intoned, reluctant to do as ordered.

'Now.' Dev's voice brooked no further delay.

The butler bowed and shooed the French lad away. Over his retreating shoulder, the boy said, *'Merci, monsieur.'*

Pippen turned to Dev. 'You have saved that boy's life. Did you stumble on to him or what?'

Dev ran his fingers through his once immaculate hair and headed for the salon and the decanter of port he knew reposed there on a sideboard. He poured himself a glass and drank the entire thing down.

'That boy was in the burning barn.' Images of the inferno crept along the edges of his memory, images that had eaten along the edges of his dreams but not yet busted through. He broke into a cold sweat.

Pippen stepped up to him and put a hand on his arm. 'The barn where you were injured?'

Dev stared into nothing. Flames dazzled his eyes. 'Yes.'

He broke free and turned to pour himself another glass of the strong wine. He gulped it.

'Did you rescue him? Was he one of the people you were cited for bravery for saving?'

Pippen's fingers bit into Dev's arm, drawing him from the past back into the present. 'I don't know. I tried.'

'Then you did,' Pippen said decisively. 'And you've saved him once again.'

Dev shook his head to clear the thoughts away. 'Perhaps. Only time will tell.'

'Time will tell that you went to the trouble to find that boy. Most would not have.' Pippen's voice brooked no argument.

Dev shrugged and turned away. 'I had to. I had to help someone. Patrick is...' he choked on the finality of the word he had intended to use and substituted others '...Patrick is beyond my help.'

Before Pippen could offer the comfort Dev saw in the youth's green eyes, Dev twisted away and left the room. He didn't want comfort from a lad who was barely out of the school room. Most particularly when the admiration in Pippen's gaze would soon turn to hate and disgust.

'Child.' The Duchess of Rundell's voice stopped Pippa from entering the salon where tonight's few guests mingled. The Duchess, as usual, was late.

Pippa turned and made a leg. 'Your Grace...ah, Alicia.' The Duchess smiled her wonderful, warm smile that never failed to elicit an emotional response in Pippa. Dev had his mother's smile.

'I see you did not go to the tailor I recommended,' the Duchess said, taking Pippa's arm. She slanted an amused grey gaze at her guest. 'I am not really surprised.'

'You aren't?' Pippa had thought Dev's mother would be irritated at her for attending the dinner in the same clothes she wore everywhere. But going to a tailor had been out of the question.

The Duchess chuckled softly. 'No, child, I am not. Dev may be blind, but I am not.'

Pippa stiffened. Surely she could not mean what Pippa thought she meant. After all these weeks, no one had hinted that they had the least suspicion Pippa was not what she claimed to be. Not even the maid who cleaned her room seemed to know, and that was nothing short of a miracle.

Before Pippa could probe her hostess's enigmatic comment, the Duchess signalled the butler to announce them. In the grand manner that only a woman secure in her position as the wife to the most powerful duke in Britain can achieve, Alicia swept Pippa into the room. No easy feat considering that Pippa's feet dragged.

Pippa had not wanted to attend this dinner, but when the Duchess had cornered her at breakfast and reminded her of the occasion and how having a friend nearby would help ease Dev through his first social engagement after his wound, Pippa had wavered. Dev had walked into the room just then. He had limped to the table and rested his cane against the back of a chair.

'I heard you two talking,' he'd said, turning to eye Pippa. 'You will come. If I have to attend my mother's little gathering, then so do you.'

'But—'

'Your clothing won't be correct, but that's nothing.

Don't want the frippery these continental tailors produce anyway. We will get you the best from Stultz when we're in London.' He'd gone to the sideboard and loaded a plate with eggs, kippers and toast. Before sitting, he'd poured himself a tankard of ale.

'But I don't want new clothing,' Pippa had declared.

He'd taken a mouthful of eggs. 'Going to get you some. Stultz does all the military men's coats. You aren't exactly army, but with all your healing and doctoring, you might as well dress like the men you're helping.' He took a bite of kippers and washed them down with the ale.

Pippa'd glared at him.

'Now, children,' the Duchess had intervened, 'stop this arguing. Pippen is old enough to do as he wishes. As for you, Deverell, you need to try on your evening attire to see how it fits after the weight you've lost.'

A persecuted look crossed his face. 'Did. The jacket is loose, but fits the shoulders. Horton is having the breeches taken in at the waist.'

'Good,' Alicia had said. 'You will be the most handsome man here tonight.'

Something like anger had lit his eyes, but was quickly extinguished. 'Wish you hadn't done this, Mother.' As soon as the words were out, Dev had flushed as though he regretted them. 'That is, with Pippen and me leaving early tomorrow...'

Pippa had known he didn't want to attend this dinner in his honour any more than she did. Probably less. Everyone would be watching him, looking for differences, expecting to find them. His heroism and subsequent wounds were well known.

She could not leave him to face the curious stares on his own. Even knowing the Duchess would be with her son had not been sufficient. Pippa had needed to be with Dev.

The strength of that emotion was something Pippa had refused to study. Tonight, as she pulled herself back into the present and walked into the room where the Duchess's dinner guests mingled, she once more refused to analyse why she had to be with Dev in his first foray back into society.

Even realizing that some of the people here tonight might know her grandfather had not kept her from Dev's side. The guests might even know more about her family tree than Dev and his mother did, and, if so, they could expose her. The danger was not exhilarating. But she had to be here, to stand by Dev.

Meeting face to face with the Marchioness of Witherspoon and her husband upon entering the room did nothing for Pippa's peace of mind. The Marchioness was as beautiful and dainty as ever. Her blonde hair curled fashionably about her rosebud face. Her evening dress of pale blue muslin, overlaid with a silvery gauze material that echoed the cool brilliance of her crystal-speckled turban, showed her figure to perfection.

Her husband was a complete contrast. At least forty years her senior, his coat was peacock blue superfine, but the waist was tighter and the skirts fuller than men wore today. He echoed, in a mild way, the style of his youth. His heavy-lidded brown eyes and long nose conspired to make Pippa feel he looked down on her, even though she was his height.

'Jane. George,' Alicia said, pulling Pippa forward, 'I want you to meet the young man who saved Deverell's life. Pippen, the Marquis and Marchioness of Witherspoon.'

Pippa made a hasty bow to each.

'Alicia, *chérie*, I have met your paragon. Only...' the Marchioness's blue eyes took in Pippa's unfashionable clothing and hair before smiling kindly '...I did not know

the pride and joy of the hospital surgeons was your pro-
tégé.'

'Jane, I owe him everything. Without him, Deverell
would have died on the streets of Brussels.'

Flushing uncomfortably, Pippa demurred. 'No, no, your
Grace. I only cared for him. Nothing more.'

'Such modesty in a young man,' the Marquis said, his
dry, soft voice feathering over Pippa's already raw nerves.
'The youth of today is too often loud and full of themselves.'

He was of an age with her grandfather, but while the
Earl had a joviality about him and an interest in others, this
man was cold. His words were more a derision against
persons of her age than a compliment to her. Beside him,
his wife's pretty mouth tightened, but she said nothing. Her
eyes beseeched Pippa to understand. Pippa gave her a slight
nod.

'Mother—' Dev's voice intruded on the awkward conversation '—what are you doing to poor Pippen to make
the lad redder than the lobsters you ordered for dinner?'

Before the Duchess could reply, Dev draped his arm
around Pippa's shoulders and steered her away. They didn't
stop moving until the distance of the room and the thirty
guests in it stood between them and the Marquis of Witherspoon and his wife.

'Thank you,' Pippa said with heartfelt gratitude.

'Least I could do. Owe you my life.' A footman passed
by and Dev snared two flutes of champagne. Handing one
to Pippen, he said, 'Here's to getting through this evening.'

Grinning, Pippa added, 'And to finding my cousin.'

'That, too,' Dev said in a hollow voice.

Pippa looked at him, but he smiled at her, that lazy,
parting of lips that made her body do funny things. She
forgot everything else.

Dev raised his glass and so did she. He downed the liquid in two gulps and reached for another.

'Should you have so much?' she asked, sipping hers and relishing the tickle of bubbles in her mouth and down her throat.

He shrugged. ''Tis as good at numbing the senses as the horrible stuff you pour down me every night and tastes a sight better.'

She supposed he was right. In a whisper she asked, 'Are the Marchioness and Marquis of Witherspoon in love?'

'A love match? Doubt it.' He drank his second glass only slightly slower than the first. 'Don't know them well, but he treats her with a cold politeness that makes it unlikely.'

'She works at the hospital.'

'Does she? Interesting. I wouldn't have thought it of her. She's quite the thing in the *ton*. They don't run in my circles. More like the ones my older brother frequents—or she does anyway.'

Pippa shot a glance in the direction of the couple they discussed, only to see the Marchioness on her own with two younger men paying homage to her beauty. 'But she is French. I would have thought that would make her unacceptable.'

Dev replaced his empty glass on the tray of a passing footman and took a third. 'You think? Don't. Her being French only makes her exotic. Old 'Spoon married her when she was barely a child, back in 1804 or thereabouts. Her family was killed on the guillotine, and she was living with distant cousins when he visited Paris.'

'For not knowing them, you know a lot about them.' Pippa wasn't sure what made her sound so waspish. Dev's interest in other women was nothing to her. To prove it, she gulped the last of her champagne and boldly waved the footman over and took another.

He grinned, a rakish parting of lips. 'Everyone knows a little about her. As I said, she's one of the leaders of the *ton*. An intimate with Sally Jersey and that group.'

Even Pippa had heard about the Almack patronesses, of which Sally was one of the more vocal ones. 'She does run in high circles.'

'Exactly.' Just then the butler signalled that dinner was ready. Dev put his empty glass on a nearby table. 'Best find a lady to escort into the meal. Not that my mother is a stickler for such things, but some of the other women here are.'

On that word of warning, he moved to the Duchess and offered his arm, his limp less pronounced than it had been that morning. Pippa looked nervously around the room. Luck was with her. One of the gentlemen offered to escort two ladies in, one on each arm. It was not normally done, but no one commented, least of all Pippa. She slunk in last and found her seat on the Duchess's right.

Dinner was subdued and excellent. She thoroughly enjoyed the Duchess's conversation and banter.

Dev sat at the head of the table in lieu of his father. He drank the last of his red wine, which went with the meat course, and the butler poured a fresh glass of white wine to go with the fish course. His eyes sparkled golden in the candlelight. He flirted with the young woman on his right who responded with a giggle and a heightened colour in her cheeks.

Pippa looked away.

Alicia, Duchess of Rundell, raised one sooty brow in enquiry as she caught Pippa's attention. Pippa inclined her head and smiled. The last thing she wanted was the Duchess's acute interest on her. She feared that Dev's mother already saw more than was comfortable.

'Pippen,' Alicia said in an aside, 'the ladies will be leaving shortly. You may go with us—' she smiled '—in deference to your youth.'

Relief eased the discomfort that had been churning in Pippa's stomach. She had dreaded having to stay behind with the men drinking port and brandy and smoking cheroots. The sense of reprieve was short lived. If she went with the ladies there would be talk.

'Thank you, your...Alicia, but I will either stay with the rest of the gentlemen or go up to my room. I have an early day tomorrow.' She glanced at Dev. 'So does your son.'

'Of course. So silly of me to forget that the two of you are hieing off to Paris before the rest of us have even gone to bed.'

Pippa smiled as she was supposed to.

Taking a fork, the Duchess rapped on her empty crystal goblet. 'Everyone, let us forgo the pleasure of separate entertainment after dinner.' She sent a roguish grin around the table. 'I suggest that we go into the salon, roll back the carpet and dance. So much more fun, you know.'

Surprise, followed by interest and then delight, flitted across the face of each guest.

'Perfect,' Jane, Marchioness of Witherspoon, said softly in her French-accented voice. 'Only you, Alicia, would think of, and then do, so original a plan.'

Others concurred.

With a laugh, Dev stood and circled the table to offer his arm to his mother. 'May I have the first dance?'

She rose and accepted his escort. 'No other. Unless it were Pippen.'

Pippa stood so quickly her chair toppled over. 'Thank you, your Grace, but I concede your first duty is to Dev.'

She stood still and watched them exit, Dev expertly wielding his cane, and wondered why the Duchess had so suddenly changed her plans. It was almost as though she had reacted to Pippa's statement about going to her room.

A giggle from her left snapped her attention back to the other guests. The young woman, girl, actually, who had been seated by Dev was looking at her with expectant brown eyes. Pippa sighed mentally.

'Miss Perryweather, may I escort you into the salon?' She offered her arm, thankful she was tall for a female. Having to act the part of a man was hard enough, it would be mortifying if she had to look up at the ladies while doing so.

'Yes, you may, Mr LeClair,' the girl giggled.

Inside the parlor, Pippa seated her charge and excused herself. The last thing she wanted was to be constrained to ask the chit to dance. Her dancing master, after pulling out his hair at her reluctance, had barely managed to teach her to follow a gentleman's lead, let alone how to lead.

Spying the Duchess, Pippa made her way quickly to that lady. 'Your…Alicia. Ma'am. I would be glad to play the pianoforte. Surely you need someone to do so, and it would be a shame if someone who truly enjoys dancing had to miss out when I am but an indifferent practitioner of the art.'

Dev, who stood beside his mother, laughed out loud. 'You? Don't tell me part of your training was playing musical instruments.'

Pippa coloured but stood her ground, her chin raised. 'Me. I am not superb, but I am adequate. For a small gathering of this type, my skills should be up to the requirement.'

'Deverell.' The Duchess rapped his arm with her closed fan hard enough to make him draw in his breath. 'Stop teasing Pippen. The boy cannot be worse than you.' She turned a gentle smile on Pippa. 'Thank you for offering, and I will take you up on it. I was going to do it myself, but much prefer to dance.'

Pippa gave Dev a triumphant look before going to the pianoforte. Michaels put the second candle in its holder, then lit the wicks. He cast Pippa a look of pity.

'I hope you don't embarrass yourself, Master Pippen.'

'As I told her Grace, I am adequate. I don't play with passion, but neither do I hit a lot of wrong notes.'

Ignoring the butler's raised white brows, she flexed her fingers and began warming up. All of the music was for the waltz, a new dance that was only recently allowed in polite circles. She had occasionally played some of the pieces because they were so flowing and beautiful. As soon as she started the first piece in earnest, couples stood up.

Between dances, Pippa managed to glance around. Each time, Dev was soliciting a partner, and each time she could not prevent the twinge of envy that made her hit the keyboard a little harder than necessary.

When dancing, he held his partners the *de rigueur* twelve inches away, but Pippa knew that was close enough to feel one another's body heat and for the woman in his arms to smell his bergamot soap. Her imagination provided the scent, turning her insides to warm cream.

What would it be like to be held in Dev's arms? She hit a wrong key and chastised herself. She would never know.

He moved with grace to the music. Only once or twice did his right leg buckle when he turned his partner. As the night progressed he faltered more and more until finally she could stand it no longer.

Why he was being so stupid as to continue dancing when it pained him, she did not know. But she would certainly put a stop to it.

Pippa finished the last piece with a flourish. Before anyone could request another, she stood and bowed.

It was as though the Duchess understood perfectly. She clapped and said, 'Bravo, Pippen. A fine demonstration, but I declare I am monstrously tired.'

The guests, with mild looks of surprise on their faces, took the hint. Over the next thirty minutes they drifted to the door. Pippa suppressed her grin of appreciation. Deverell's mother knew exactly how to handle every situation.

When the last of the guests were gone, Pippa turned to Dev and let her irritation out. 'How could you be so stupid as to dance every one? 'Tis a wonder you did not fall flat on your face, taking your partner with you.'

Irritation creased his brows, but he only turned his back to her and walked away. Pippa planted her feet and put her fists on her hips and watched him. He limped. Badly.

The temptation to let him go beckoned her like hot chocolate on a cold morning. Discomfort might teach him not to exert himself beyond his capabilities, but it would not ease the reason that drove him to perform beyond his means.

She sighed.

A light hand took her shoulder and turned her to face the Duchess. 'Go with him, child. He has need of your skills. I will be up shortly.'

The Duchess's eyes were filled with such compassion that Pippa knew there was nothing she could do but help Dev. She would have done so anyway. This just dissipated her ire with him sooner than it might otherwise have done.

She caught Dev as he was halfway up the main staircase. He leaned heavily on the bannister with one hand and eased himself up the steps one at a time. She ran to him, finding herself slightly out of breath by the time she reached him.

'Here,' she said, taking his free arm and laying it across her shoulders, 'use me.'

He looked at her with chilly affront. 'I don't need some

still-wet-behind-the-ears pup to help me. Especially one who has just tried to scold me when he has no authority.'

Contrition blunted Pippa's initial retort. It never did any good to fight. 'I was worried about you. You are my patient, and you weren't taking care of yourself tonight.'

'I was doing very nicely and taking care of myself exactly as I wished.' He moved up one stair.

Pippa could feel the tenseness in his muscles and hear the slight, sharp intake of breath as he brought his bad leg up to join his left. Still he left his arm on her shoulder. She took that as a good sign.

'You were dancing more than you ought. Why, you are barely out of bed and should always use a cane.'

'I'm not a blasted invalid,' he snarled, taking two steps in rapid succession.

Pippa's heart twisted. This was so hard on him. More than ever, she was glad she had been able to save his leg.

'No, you are not,' she said calmly. 'But you are still healing. In time you will be able to dance.'

He slanted her a bitter look. 'But not as well as once I did.'

She met his heated stare. 'No, not as well. I am sorry for it. For your sake.'

Her compassion seemed to ease the emotions that rode him. His face lost some of the tightness around the mouth, and he even managed a weak smile.

'I know you are, Pippen. You did more than anyone could have expected. Without you, I would've lost the blasted thing.'

His hazel eyes held hers. Pippa felt as though she was falling into their ever-changing depths. One minute they were light brown, flecked with green. The next they shone like golden candles. She wanted to stay like this for eternity.

The heat of his body penetrated the layers of clothing between them, and the scent of bergamot filled her senses. Underlying everything was an awareness of him as a man that she had never felt for another. He might be leaning on her, but the strength of his shoulders could crush her, and the muscles of his chest were taut beneath the fine lawn of his shirt.

A dark growth of beard shadowed the strong line of his jaw. His breath was sweet like the champagne he had been drinking all evening. The urge to lean into him was great.

He shook his head and frowned down at her. 'Pippen, you are a strange lad. Strange. There are times when I wonder—'

'Children, this is not the time for a serious discussion. Dev is nearly off his feet.'

The Duchess's voice shocked them so that Pippa jumped away, and Dev had to clutch the bannister to keep from toppling. Pippa grabbed at him, and he once more wrapped his arm around her. With his mother clucking behind them, they mounted the rest of the stairs and made their slow progress to his bedchamber.

The door was opened by Horton, a footman who had taken the place of Dev's previous valet who was still recovering from his own war wounds. Pippa guided Dev to the bed where he collapsed. She and Horton got his boots off.

'Horton,' she said, turning away while Dev wrestled with his cravat, 'bring me hot water and fresh cloths.'

'Yes, Master Pippen.'

The servant left and Pippa turned to face her charge. He looked like a fallen angel. Brown shocks of hair tumbled across his wide brow and red delineated his high cheekbones. No wonder he was known as 'Devil'.

'Help me with these breeches,' Dev ordered, getting off the bed.

Pippa gulped. The last thing she wanted to do was help him undress. In the past weeks, she had seen all of Dev and been sorely pressed to resist temptation. Now that he was well and aware of everything around him, she knew it would be even harder to resist the sensations his body elicited in her.

From the doorway, the Duchess said, 'Why don't you wait for Horton, Deverell?'

Pippa shot her a questioning look. Dev's mother smiled benignly back.

Dev glanced from one to the other. ''Tis not as though Pippen hasn't seen everything I have to offer. You, however, could leave the room, Mother, and spare my blushes.'

The Duchess laughed. 'I saw you in diapers, my boy. Wait for Horton. Pippen is too tired to support your weight any more tonight.'

Dev gave Pippa one more searing study, then agreed. 'As you wish.' He sat back down on the bed and sank into the mounds of pillows. 'I shall be asleep before he returns with everything Pippen requires.'

His eyes were shut, and Pippa could hear the soft sound of his breathing when Horton returned. She told the servant to help Dev get undressed and under the sheet. Then she and the Duchess went into the hall to wait.

'Shall I come back in with you?' Alicia asked. 'Or will Horton be enough?'

It was all Pippa could do to keep her jaw from dropping. Somehow the Duchess suspected her secret. 'There is no need, Alicia. I have put hot compresses on Dev's leg before.'

His mother gave her a mischievous look. 'When he was awake and watching?'

Pippa sighed. 'Once. Mostly I did them when the leg was still healing and I needed to draw the pus out. Now the heat will ease some of the ache from over-exertion.'

'My son is very stubborn,' Alicia said softly. 'It is one of his strongest virtues, even though it sometimes drives him into the wrong situations.'

Pippa's lips twisted wryly. 'Such as tonight?'

'Exactly. He was proving to himself that he could still do everything. He loves to dance and was very good at it.'

'He is still more than passable, ma'am.'

'To you, perhaps. But he knows better.' She put one delicate hand on Pippa's arm. 'Give him time, child. He will come around.'

As Pippa opened her mouth to make some innocuous reply, the door opened and Horton bowed to them. 'Your Grace. Master Pippen. Lord Deverell is ready.'

Alicia's hand dropped from Pippa's arm, and she smiled at her. 'I am going to my bed. I want to be up in time to see the two of you off.' She leaned over and, before Pippa knew what she intended, kissed her on the cheek. 'Take care of him for me, child. He is my youngest and I nearly lost him.'

'Always, milady.' The words were out before Pippa realized she was going to say them.

Alicia touched a finger to Pippa's cheek. 'I know.'

With that, Dev's mother left. Pippa stared after her, listening to her own words repeat themselves in her head. Always. What was happening to her?

'Master Pippen?'

Horton's voice snapped her back. Stepping briskly into the room, she asked, 'Is the hot water by the bed?'

'Yes, sir.'

'Thank you.'

Pippa went to the side of the bed closest to Dev's leg

and lifted the sheet aside. The scars were nearly healed, the angry red easing into pale pink. She knew that with more time they would turn white and be barely noticeable. She wrung out one of the clothes and laid it across Dev's limb.

'Ah, that feels good.' Dev's eyes caught hers. 'You always know what to do.'

She smiled at him. 'I have had many years of practice with the people on my gran—on Earl LeClaire's land. The county surgeon thought I was too young—' and a female, she silently thought '—and would not have the determination to work hard, but I proved him wrong. The midwife often let me assist.'

Dev raised one eyebrow. 'She let a boy help in birthing?'

Pippa realized her mistake too late. 'She let me help some,' she fibbed. 'Not a lot. Let me see the compress. 'Tis probably cool by now.'

Dev smiled at her in a knowing way, but did not try to bring the conversation back to her training. She changed the cloth and paced to the fireplace in an attempt to put distance between them.

'Horton,' Dev said, 'you may go to bed now. Master Pippen will finish up here.'

Pippa swung around. She was going to be unchaperoned in his bedchamber. Her heart raced before she managed to tell herself it was not the first time. Only…only before he had been unconscious most of the time. Nor had the Duchess been around with her enigmatic comments that made Pippa think Dev's mother knew her secret. What would the Duchess say if she knew about this?

Pippa shook her head to clear the maggots out of it. The Duchess knew nothing. She was just distraught over Dev being hurt. That was all.

The door closed quietly behind the servant and they were alone in the room, their gazes locked. Pippa stood poker straight, hot and cold chasing each other down her back. She told herself she was overreacting. The naked man in the bed, with only a sheet covering his lower body, was Dev. She had seen all of Dev there was to see. She had even touched all of him. But that seemed like an eternity ago.

She licked dry lips.

'You have some of the most feminine mannerisms,' he said, his voice grating with irritation. 'Has no one ever told you to stop them?'

She stopped and glared at him. 'Such as?'

He looked at her through slitted eyes. 'Such as licking your lips. Women lick their lips, not men.'

She stalked over to him. 'I have seen men doing it.'

'Not much,' he stated baldly. 'You will have to stop that if I am to take you to London for some town bronze,' he said.

'Town bronze?' she echoed him.

'Exactly. When we are done finding your cousin, I want to take you to London and give you the entrée to the *ton*. 'Tis the least I can do.' He slanted her a roguish grin. 'How else do you think I am going to get you jackets made by Stultz, as I promised this morning?'

'I did not think anything of it. You were irritated over this dinner party and merely talking.' Nor could she go even if he were serious. When she found her twin, she was returning home. The last thing she needed was to continue this masquerade.

He frowned up at her. 'I said I was taking you to London. I don't go back on my word. You would do well to remember that, Pippen.'

Taking affront at his overbearing attitude, she stated, 'Neither do I.'

'No man of honour does,' Dev said. 'And you may too

often do things that remind me of a woman, but you are a man—or a boy,' he finished with a cheeky grin.

The breath Pippa had been unintentionally holding whooshed out. Imitating a man was not as easy as donning the clothes. She should be glad she hadn't given herself away, instead of this sense of disappointment. She was here to find her brother, not make Deverell St Simon notice her as a desirable woman. No matter how attractive she found the man.

'And stop standing over me like a parent over a recalcitrant child,' the subject of her thoughts said. 'Any minute now you are going to assume the position.'

'What?' One minute she was telling herself to stop wanting him and the next he was spouting still more gibberish.

His eyes glinted. Almost as though he were teasing her. 'Hands on hips. Feet planted apart.'

'Oh.'

He let out a long breath and it was as though all the energy he had used tonight came out with the air. 'Never mind, Pippen. Finish what you've started and then we need to rest.'

By this time Pippa's emotions were a riot of contradictions, with the only constant being her feelings for Deverell. It was more than past time for her to get some sleep and put some distance between herself and this man she found so appealing. For once, she did as he ordered without feeling any irritation at his imperiousness.

Dev continued to stare into the darkness long after Pippen was gone. His leg was a dull ache that no amount of Pippen's hot compresses, rubs or herbs could ease. Nor did the large amount of wine he had consumed help. Just as no amount of coddling would change the fact that he was a cripple—from now until the day he died.

He flung an arm over his face, wishing he could blot out the fact of his infirmity as easily as he could block out the flickering light of the single candle by his bed. But he could not.

Instead he thought about Pippen. If anything could make him put aside his bitterness over his wound, it was his sense of shame over his intended betrayal of the boy. Pippen had saved his life and trusted him with finding his missing cousin, while he, Deverell St Simon, a man who had always held honour above everything else, intended to betray that trust. In a just cause.

If only the person he would be hurting was not Pippen. He owed the youth more than he could ever repay. He had told the lad he would take him to London for town bronze.

A bitter bark of laughter shook him and made his leg flair. He ignored the pain. Pippen would no more go to London with him when this was done than the boy would torture a patient. Pippen would hate him, and rightly so.

But he had to find Viscount Staunton and bring him in for retribution. The man was a scoundrel of the worst sort. A peer who had betrayed his own country and the men who had made him what he was. Because of Staunton and men like him, Patrick was dead.

A sneer curled Dev's lip. Betraying Pippen's trust would be soul wrenching, but bringing a traitor to justice would recompense the deceit he must play. Avenging Patrick would be enough. He had a job to do, and he would do it.

## Chapter Six

Dev was in one of the foulest moods of his life when he sat down for a quick breakfast. He shovelled eggs, toast and ale into his mouth with a concentration he hoped would blot out the other members at the table. He found himself unable to meet Pippen's clear open green gaze.

Blast the boy! Wellington would snort in disgust if he were privy to Dev's doubts and regrets. The Iron Duke had a one-track mind: the preservation of Britain. Any traitor that stood to hurt the country was expendable in the great man's opinion. In Dev's, too. If only the traitor weren't Pippen's lost and loved cousin.

He took a gulp of ale and turned as polite a face as possible to his mother. 'Pardon me, Mother, but I didn't hear what you said.'

She laughed. 'You were always my child who day-dreamed. I remember when you were ten and wanted to run away and join the East India Company. You would go into the home woods and pretend you were in the jungles of India. You pretended to hunt tigers, played by the poor grooms.'

Dev grimaced. 'That was a long time ago, and I know the difference between reality and daydreams now.'

For a moment the Duchess's face clouded. Then she forced a smile and changed the subject. 'Dev, don't you think Pippen's eyes are the exact shade of the emeralds I have put aside for your future bride?'

Dev nearly choked on a mouthful of eggs. 'Mother. Where did you get that idea? Pippen's a boy. His eyes don't look like any jewels.'

The Duchess shook her head slightly, amusement curving one corner of her mouth. 'Observation. Only observation.'

Dev glanced at Pippen. The boy sat like a mute, his body still, mouth pinched and both cheeks splashed with colour.

'You've embarrassed him,' Dev said, beginning to see humour in the situation. At least the banter took him out of the darkness of his thoughts.

'Have I?' the Duchess asked, her brow wrinkling in concern. 'I did not mean to.'

Pippen gave a shaky laugh. 'No, not embarrass…exactly. 'Tis not every day that my eyes are compared to emeralds.'

'Shouldn't think so,' Dev said, taking a bite of toast. 'Most men don't like having any part of themselves compared to jewels.'

'But it is true, none the less,' the Duchess said. 'Your eyes are the exact shade of the emeralds.' She smiled at Dev. 'My father gave them to me when I married the Duke, and I am saving them for Dev. I gave the black pearls to Alastair when he married Liza.'

Dev slanted his mother a quizzical look. 'Why all this talk of marriage and necklaces? It isn't exactly the topic I would have thought we would be discussing this morning.'

'No, it is not,' Alicia said. 'But I thought of it. Let us change our discussion. Where will the two of you be staying your first night?'

'Don't know,' Dev said. 'Depends on how far we get

and if the weather holds. The last thing we need is rain if we are to make good time.'

'And we had best be getting started,' Pippen said in a small voice, almost as though the lad were afraid to speak for fear of what would be said next.

'Right,' Dev said, rising and throwing his napkin on to the table. 'I hope you made a good meal of it, Pip, because we are not stopping for a long while.'

For a second the boy's eyes flashed, but he spoke mildly enough. 'I made as good a showing as possible. And we should be stopping every few hours so you can get out and stretch your legs.'

'Get out?' Dev queried, one brow raised.

'Yes. You must walk around some. Sitting all day in a jolting coach will do your leg no good.'

'Coach?' Dev felt his temper starting up.

'You should ride in a carriage,' Pippa said matter of factly, as though there was no question of what would be done.

'I think not.' Without waiting for further comment, Dev pivoted on his good leg, used the cane to steady himself and strode off. His ramrod-straight back brooked no discussion.

Once outside, the sunlight and breeze eased some of the tension inside him and Dev came to a stop. He rotated his shoulders and told himself not to react so strongly. The boy was only trying to help. It was not Pippen's fault that the last thing Dev wanted to do was make this trip.

He sighed and ran his right hand through his hair. It seemed that lately he'd been doing a lot of things he didn't want to do.

'Milord,' the groom said, having come up without Dev being aware. 'The horses are saddled and the spare clothes

you and Master Pippen need are packed in the saddle bags.
Exceptin' yer coat.' He held out the garment.

'Thank you, Tom.'

Dev took the many-caped greatcoat of buff cloth and
wondered if he should wear it, or lay it across the saddle.
He decided to lay it before him when Pippen came out of
the front door. The boy wore only the brown coat he always
wore.

'Where is your heavier coat?' Dev demanded. 'We are
bound to run into nasty weather, and then you'll be glad
of the extra weight.'

The boy flushed. Again. Dev shook his head. There were
times he wondered what kind of upbringing the lad had
received.

'I don't have a coat.'

Turning aside, Pippen strode to the gelding that would
be his mount. He paused for a long moment before putting
his foot in the stirrup and mounting. The movement lacked
grace and were it not for the impeccable training of the
horse, Dev was sure Pippen would have missed his seat
and landed on his bottom in the road.

'Tom,' Dev said, 'have Horton fetch my black greatcoat.
Master Pippen will be glad of its warmth before this journey is over.'

The groom hurried to do his bidding.

Pippen glared at Dev, then his face softened. 'Thank you
for your thoughtfulness. I've no doubt it will come in
handy.'

''Tis the least I could do,' Dev said, turning to mount
his own horse.

He had not been on a horse since the battle, but old habits
die hard—if at all. The only awkwardness was getting his
injured leg to move as it should. For an instant, as he bal-
anced on his left leg he thought his right leg would not

swing over the animal's back. Then, as though his mind gave the injured limb strength, his leg arched over and his booted foot came to rest against the stirrup.

As he settled in his seat, he did his best to suppress the jolt of pain that wanted to twist his mouth. He must get used to the discomfort of mounting and riding a horse. He'd be damned if he intended to spend the rest of his days travelling in a coach.

To turn his thoughts from his throbbing leg, he watched Pippen on the second gelding. His seat was not solid and he twitched. The boy looked awkward as a youth caught looking at a pretty girl's ankle. If Dev didn't know better, he'd say Pippen had spent little time riding. But that was impossible. The lad lived in the country and was of good birth. He should be proficient on horseback.

Just as they prepared to urge their horses forward, the Duchess erupted from the front door. She rushed to Dev so that he had to lean down.

She grabbed his face and kissed him. 'Take care. I nearly lost you once, I could not bear to do so again.'

With a gloved finger, he gently flicked away a tear from his mother's face. 'I shall do my best. Take care of yourself and give my love to Father.'

'I shall,' she said, smiling wistfully up at him before turning to Pippen. 'Be careful, child. And watch over my headstrong son.'

Pippen nodded. Even with the several feet separating him from the youth, Dev could see moisture glistening in the boy's eyes. Damned if he wasn't as much of a watering pot as a girl.

Disgust twisted Dev's mouth as he urged his mount on. The sooner they started, the sooner they'd finish. He heard the clop of horseshoes on the cobbles behind him as Pippen followed.

* * *

Pippa frowned as she watched Dev enter the tavern. It was evening on their second day of travelling. They were on the outskirts of Paris, and Dev was in a foul mood as the result of too long spent in the saddle. But Dev had refused to listen to her when she'd told him to stop and rest at a smaller inn three hours ago.

Men! They were stubborn as mules and belligerent as bulls when their minds were set on something and it was denied them.

Last night had been just as bad. Dev had nearly fallen getting off the horse. If she hadn't had just as much trouble and very likely bigger saddle sores, she would have berated him for going so long before stopping. But never having ridden any way but side saddle, she had been too miserable to do more than see their horses were stabled, prepare each of them a draught to ease their pain and then stumble into the small bed in the tiny private room Dev had been able to procure for her.

Bringing her attention back to the present, Pippa sighed and told the ostler in her barely adequate French, 'See that you rub them down and feed them plenty of oats.'

The French youth nodded as he led the horses away. Pippa wished Dev were as easy to manage. She winced as she walked toward the door.

The tavern's public room was hot and crowded. Even though it was well into September, the weather was warm and the room didn't need the extra heat from the large hearth fire. The sting of smoke made her squint as she searched for Dev.

He stood near the bar, talking to a buxom serving wench. He had a smile on his lips and a look about his eyes that she had never seen before. A twinge of anxiety made Pippa stride toward him.

'Dev,' she said, coming up to his side and tugging at his sleeve.

'Not now, Pip,' he muttered, never taking his eyes off the wench. 'Do you work late tonight, Giselle?' he asked in French.

'Only till everyone has had their fill,' she answered in her native tongue.

The woman grinned at Dev, showing two crooked but white front teeth. Her black hair was caught up in a knot and her eyes were large and blue. There were poppies in her cheeks and plenty of curves under the clean white blouse and brown skirt she wore. She had not the look of a loose woman, which Pippa imagined added to her appeal. Philip would have done exactly as Dev was. The knowledge was no comfort.

'Dev,' Pippa said in an attempt to catch his attention, 'we need rooms. An inn this close to Paris will fill quickly.'

He frowned at her. 'Then procure them. You don't need me for that.' Before he finished speaking, his focus was back on the woman.

Fast losing a temper she had not realized was slipping, Pippa stated, 'I may be able to get the rooms, but I won't carry up your baggage.'

'Then get one of the servants,' Dev said in the autocratic manner he sometimes used. It was a sign of just how occupied he was with this seduction.

Pippa snorted, but realized that for the moment there was nothing more she could do. And why should she bother? Deverell was a grown man and entitled to amuse himself where he wanted. The serving woman certainly seemed interested. Giving herself a mental shake that extended to her shoulders and made the cape of her riding coat swing, Pippa went to find the owner.

\* \* \*

Less than an hour after paying for adjacent rooms, she heard the door to Dev's room open and shut. While waiting for him to come up, she had prepared a distillation of bark to ease the pain she knew he suffered. She picked up the drink and crossed the hall.

Her knock brought a muffled, 'Come in.'

Entering, she said, 'I've brought you something for the pa—'

Dev stood by the open window, his back to the door. He was clad only in breeches and stockings. The ridges of muscle in his back flowed with each stroke as he washed himself with a damp cloth. Knit breeches showed the narrow leanness of his hips and tight lines of his legs. The sight brought back memories of him lying in her bed with only a sheet to cover his nakedness. Suddenly it was difficult to breathe and the room was like an oven. Pippa licked dry lips.

Dev turned to her, the yellow light of the two candles that stood on each side of him bronzing the hair that dusted his chest. Pippa forced her gaze away, looking anywhere but at his exposed flesh.

'Oh, it is you.' Disappointment dulled the gleam in his eyes.

'Only me,' Pippa said, her sight snapping back to him as she stepped further into the room. Her hackles rose for no reason she would admit to. 'Did you expect your serving wench so soon? I heard her tell you it would be some time.'

'What is the matter with you?' he said, putting down the cloth and going to sprawl in the single chair.

'Nothing.' Pippa gave herself a mental scolding. 'I've brought you something to ease your discomfort—you would ride longer than you should have.'

'You nag like an old woman, Pippen.'

Pippa felt the blood drain from her face. Had she given

herself away by…by…? She refused to name the emotion
that had sent her tongue lashing.

Dev leaned over to pull on his Hessians and winced.
'What you need is a woman,' he added in the voice of a
man goaded beyond endurance.

'Your wench when you've finished with her?' Pippa
snapped. She slapped the glass on the small table beside
Dev and stepped away. The scent of bergamot wafted from
him. It would always remind her of him.

Dev's eyes narrowed. 'You've a mighty sharp tongue
tonight. Take my advice and do as I intend to do. You will
find it eases many troubles.'

'Hire a whore for the night?' Pippa sneered, hands on
hips. 'What does that prove?'

Dev's scowl deepened. 'That you are a man. Something
I'm beginning to wonder about where you are concerned.'

Throwing caution to the wind, Pippa stood her ground.
'And what if I don't have those urges? So? Does that make
me less of a person?'

'Be careful what you say and to whom. Those proclivi-
ties might be indulged by some, but the law's against
them.' Dev pulled on his remaining Hessian, the line between his brows deepening. 'Blast!' he muttered. 'Can't
even pull on a boot.'

He hurt. Contrition smote Pippa. She'd been haranguing
him when she should be taking care of him. 'Here,' she
said brusquely, 'drink this. 'Twill ease the pain. Then, instead of whoring, you should rest.'

'Back to that, are we?' Dev said, pulling on his linen
shirt. 'Well, I've had enough of your orders. Tonight I am
going to do what I please, and the devil take you if you try
to interfere.'

Pippa's sympathy for his discomfort washed away like a
river plunging down a mountain. 'No wonder they call you

Devil Deverell. You are more interested in your pleasure than your health.'

He grabbed her right arm in a bruising grip. 'Listen well, Pippen. I won't stand your nagging tonight. I am a man and I intend to live like one, not like some papping baby who must be coddled from dawn to dusk and then tucked into bed.'

With an expletive that Pippa had only heard in the stables, he flung her from him. Never had she seen him so angry or so careless of another. Before she could try to stop him, he strode out of the door, slamming the heavy oak panel behind him.

The fury drained from her in a rush, leaving her so weak she sank like a rock on to the chair Dev had vacated, and cradled her head in her two hands. Dev felt maimed, less than a man because he walked with a limp and couldn't ride a horse at the speed and for the duration he once could. She had mistakenly thought that by saving his lower leg, she had kept him from this. She had known he resented the limitations the weakened limb imposed on him, but she hadn't realized how truly deep his bitterness went. Until now.

By bedding the serving woman he would prove to himself—and to others—that he was still a man and could still do what men do. Understanding brought no comfort.

She didn't want him making love to another woman. She wanted to give him that comfort and to share that intimacy with him. Her hands dropped to her lap and began to shake as she stared into space, picturing what it would be like to sleep with Dev. Heaven. And hell because he did not care that way about her.

Pippa rose and went back to her room. She flung herself down on the bed, pillowed her head on her crossed arms and stared at the ceiling. Even knowing that he would not enjoy making love to the serving wench as much as he anticipated because his leg would pain him brought no ease. She wanted to be the woman he kissed and held.

Pippa's stomach twisted into coils, and her head started pounding. She squeezed her eyes closed, shutting out the sight of the dingy white ceiling. But she could not stop seeing Dev kissing the Frenchwoman. Pain made her breathing shallow and sleep impossible. She rolled to her side and stared into the dusk-shadowed room.

With a sigh, she sat up and rubbed her throbbing temples. She would drink the bark she'd prepared for Dev. Without it, she would never sleep. She might even take a little laudanum to help her calm down. There was nothing she could do to stop Deverell. She had to live with what he intended.

She told herself his actions didn't matter. He was a grown man and could do anything he chose. All she cared about was that he help her find Philip. Philip's disappearance had brought them together and finding her twin was all that mattered. And as soon as they found her brother, she and Dev would part, never to see each other again.

For when she found her brother, Pippen must disappear and Lady Pippa LeClaire would return home from her visit on the Continent and continue to help the local midwife. That was the life she wanted, the only life she'd wanted since childhood. Deverell St Simon made no difference to her future. None whatsoever.

She needed to sleep. She needed to forget this obsession with Dev's love life and with her own desire to be the woman he turned to. She needed to get the bark from Dev's room.

Walking on feet that insisted on dragging like leaden faggots, she went to his room where she had left the bark. She expected him to still be downstairs waiting for his lady, so she entered without knocking.

Locked together like twining snakes in a pool of golden candlelight, Dev and the wench kissed. His shirt was off and her blouse was around her waist, his hands kneading the fullness of her breasts. Their breathing was loud in the silence.

Pippa gasped and her chest contracted in sharp agony. She felt betrayed. It did not matter that she had known Deverell intended this. It did not matter that she was supposed to be a boy. Nothing mattered except the agony of seeing him doing things to another woman that—she took a great shuddering breath—she wanted him to do to her.

Dev's head snapped up and he roared, *'Out!'*

From the shelter of his shoulder, Giselle gaped, her hands inadequately covering her voluptuousness. *'Merci.'* She pushed away from him and clumsily pulled up her blouse.

'Damn you, Pippen,' Dev said, advancing on her when she did not immediately flee the room. He grabbed her shoulders and shook her like a storm shakes a tree. 'I told you to leave me alone.'

His fingers bit into her flesh. His eyes flashed dangerously, and his jaw formed a harsh angle. He was furious. And he had been drinking. His breath had the sweet scent of red wine.

She had never seen Dev drink to the point that a wild light lit his face. The drink would dull some of the physical discomfort he felt. Now, more than ever, she understood how much he needed to feel like a virile man.

'Take me,' she whispered, knowing as she spoke the fateful words that they were the only thing she could do. Making love to him herself was the only way to keep him from spending the night with the French servant. Making love to him was the only way she could show him that his leg meant nothing to her. His leg did not make him less of a man. 'Make love to me.'

His face darkened.

The bedroom door slammed. Pippa and Dev jumped, but neither looked away from the other.

Dev released her and moved away. He turned his back on her and ran his fingers through his dark hair, disarraying it and making it sweep across the nape of his bare neck in such a way that Pippa was hard pressed not to reach out and smooth it.

'Dev—'

'Get out!' He swung back to face her. 'Get out now. I don't know what I have done to make you think I'm a catamite. But I am not.'

She took a step toward him. The beginning of a smile lifted one corner of her mouth. He misunderstood her, which meant her disguise was safe. But she no longer cared. All she wanted now was to feel him kiss her as he had kissed the other woman. She was too far on this road to change her mind. Nor could she. If she failed to seduce him and prove to him that she desired him, then she would fail to heal him. He needed to make love to her. She wanted him to make love to her.

Dev backed up. 'You have accomplished what you set out to do. I won't be sleeping with Giselle tonight.' His lips twisted. 'But neither will I sleep with you.' He took a deep breath and his voice became calm. 'Go away, Pippen. And don't worry. I will keep your secret.'

Her smile widened. 'Dev,' she said softly, 'I have something to show you.'

He scowled and put out one hand as though to ward her off. 'I am not interested.'

'You will be,' she murmured, taking hold of her courage even as she began to undo her shirt. One by one, she slipped the wooden buttons through the holes until the muslin hung open to her waist where it tucked into her breeches. She shrugged out of it.

Dev's eyes widened.

Slowly she unwound the linen strip that held her breasts captive. Her attention never left the face of the man before her. She saw when comprehension lit his grey eyes into twin flames. The length of cloth fell to the floor.

'Out!' Dev growled. 'Get out before I thrash you. Or—' his voice lowered '—I take what you are flaunting.'

Pippa swallowed hard. He had never intimidated her before. This was not the time to allow him that advantage. For his own good, she had to convince him to love her. Because she…loved him.

The realization took her breath away. Seeing him locked with the serving wench had made her admit that what she felt for him was more than a healer for a patient.

Because she loved him, she had to heal him. Body and soul. Until he felt attractive to a woman, Devil Deverell would not feel whole. Like riding his horse for longer than was good, he needed to make love to a woman to be whole.

Feeling her face flame and the heat lower to her chest like a rash, Pippa sat in the chair and pulled off her brother's too large Hessians. She yanked off the extra pair of socks she wore. Next she unrolled her stockings. Standing again, she unbuttoned her breeches and shimmied out of them. She was down to her small clothes.

Dev stood immobile before her, his face unreadable. 'Why are you doing this?'

His voice was tautly controlled, but she sensed anger and frustration and something else. Something dark and sweet and powerful.

She licked dry lips and chose her words carefully. 'Because I want to. Because I have lived with you for more than three months.' Her hands began to shake when he remained frowning. 'For a month of that time, I cared for you. I learned your…' Another flush marched across her fair skin. 'I know your body intimately. I know how you are formed, and I…I think I know what brings you pleasure.'

He lifted one brown eyebrow in sardonic disbelief.

Pippa struck her unconscious pose, hands on hips, feet shoulder width apart. 'Well, I do. I know you like to be touched. You like having your hair smoothed from your forehead. You like sweets—'

'You know nothing of me,' he said across her words. 'You don't know what I think, and you certainly don't know what I enjoy in bed.' He took a deep shuddering breath. 'Now, get out.'

Pippa took a step toward him. Determination firmed her tread and kept her gaze on his face. Storms tossed in the hazel depths of his eyes and warned her that while he wanted to bed the Frenchwoman, he was not going to willingly do the same to her.

If she left him now, he would not heal. And the next night or the next inn they stayed at he would find another willing woman, another woman who wasn't her. Dev making love to someone else was an unbearable thought.

She moved until her breasts brushed lightly against his chest. 'No.'

Before he could say another word, she wrapped her arms around his neck, pulled his head down to hers and kissed him. It was an inexperienced meeting of lips, and instead of responding as he had to Giselle, he remained motionless, his arms at his side, his mouth sealed.

Pippa broke an inch away. 'Help me, Dev. Let me be your woman tonight. Let me ease your pain.'

He shoved her violently away and flung himself into the

only chair. 'I don't need or want your pity, Pippen. Or whoever you are,' he added sarcastically.

'Pippa,' she said softly.

Dev stared at the woman before him. Minutes ago she had been the youth Pippen. Granted, he had frequently thought the boy too feminine for his own good. He remembered the green-eyed angel he'd imagined while lying on the edge between death and life. That apparition had been Pippen…or Pippa.

He perused her body and felt his loins responding. Too much wine made his thinking less than sharp and made it much easier for his body to do things his mind said no to. His mouth twisted.

Damn, he'd had too much to drink. He had intended to dull the aching throb of his leg so that he could better enjoy and pleasure Giselle. Now the slight disorientation made him even more susceptible to the woman standing so openly before him.

She was tall for a woman, although average for a boy. The face he had thought too smooth and beardless for a man was bathed in the golden glow of the candles, luminous in its purity. His gaze lowered. Dev swallowed hard and knew he should look away from temptation.

Her breasts were smooth and full without being voluptuous. Her waist was slender as a willow, and her hips flared so that all he could think about was nestling his against them. A groan rose in his throat.

He wanted a woman tonight. Had wanted one for months. Tonight was the night he had determined to make love to prove he was still a man, that he could still enjoy being with a woman and giving her pleasure as he took his own.

As though sensing his weakness, Pippen…Pippa knelt at

his feet. The warm, musky scent of her permeated his being.

'Let me help with your boots. I know how it hurts you to take them off.' Suiting action to words, she pulled them off one by one.

Dev studied her. In all their weeks together she had never flirted or sent him looks that smouldered with awareness. Now in one night she was everything enticing. The deep green of her eyes held promises no woman had ever made, of more than a romp in bed, of knowledge and awareness of him as a person. The dark cleft between her breasts was a mystery he longed to explore. Even her short hair seemed exotic. The urge to tousle it made his hand move out and up until his fingers buried themselves in the thick, ebony strands.

Her eyes met his boldly, and she leaned into his caress until she nestled between his sprawled legs. She slid her torso up his chest as he unconsciously pulled her head to his. His need was so great it was like a vise around his chest. Great shuddering chills raced from their hot contact to all parts of his body.

'Do you know what you are doing?' he asked. 'Or are you seducing me by instinct?'

A short, nervous laugh was his answer. He knew her too well to really think she was experienced.

She trailed tentative kisses along the line of his clenched jaw. The urge to take what she so boldly offered swamped Dev. The two bottles of fine French wine he had consumed bade him to succumb.

With a groan as much of pain as passion, he cupped her face in his hands and met her mouth with his in a kiss of fierce desire. When she opened to him, it was as though he plunged over a precipice, his stomach cartwheeling and his head spinning.

Pippa didn't know if she was standing or kneeling. Dev's touch made her head spin and her toes curl.

His tongue slid into her mouth, sending sensations shooting through her that she had never experienced before. She wanted to consume him and be consumed in return. She wanted to have everything he could give her. She wanted to give everything back to him.

Her hands roamed restlessly along his shoulders. Her fingers slid down his chest to twine in the golden brown curls that studded his muscles.

His mouth moved against hers, sliding from side to side while his hands held her head steady for his penetration. She moaned.

He drew instantly back, his eyes glazed, his voice rough. 'Did I hurt you? I'm sorry. I've never been with a woman who's—'

'Shh,' she interrupted him, pulling his head back to hers, his mouth down to hers.

When she could barely breathe and her skin felt prickly with tension, he stood, drawing her up with him. Their bodies moulded to each other. She felt his hips cradle against her stomach as he fitted her even tighter to him. Inexperienced as she was, she recognized his hardness pressing against her.

A tiny thrill of exultation made her smile. He wanted her. Tonight he would be with her instead of another woman. It was all she wanted.

'Help me,' he murmured, releasing her mouth and her body to fumble with the buttons on his breeches.

With eager fingers, she helped ease the tight fitting clothing from him. He stood before her, proud and virile. She had seen him many times before as she nursed him, and she had known then that he would be devastating when he was healthy. But she had not realized just how much he would affect her.

Pippa's breath caught.

He opened his arms to her and she stepped into them. It was like coming home. A sigh slipped between her lips just before he sealed them with his.

They slid to the floor, their bodies never losing contact. Side by side, they lay exploring each other's secret pleasures. His teeth scraped across the rim of her ear, and it was more intense than any touch of a hand. When his palm cupped her breast, she thought she would expire.

'Talk to me,' he crooned. 'Tell me what you like.'

She had no words to express what he made her feel, only tiny gasps and soft moans. Her head tossed from side to side as he ravaged her with his mouth, teeth and tongue. He slid down her until he knelt in the V of her legs. His hands roved over every curve and indentation of her. She thought that surely she would explode.

'Please,' she begged, not knowing what she asked, but that she needed something only he could supply.

'Soon,' he whispered, his voice hoarse with passion. 'Soon. I can't wait much longer.'

Her back arched as he stroked down her ribs to her hips and along her flanks. When he took one of her breasts into his mouth, she bucked. So intense was her pleasure that she felt herself melt inside. A throbbing began in her loins.

'Do something. Please,' she moaned.

'Soon,' he promised.

She thrashed beneath his ministrations. Tiny sounds escaped her throat. Her fingers gripped his waist and pulled him closer. She wanted to feel him against her.

'Spread your legs,' he said, inching closer.

When she complied, he pressed against her, sending heat coursing through her limbs. She reached for him to guide him in. As her fingers closed over the hard length of him, he groaned.

'Pip...' he dragged out his nickname for her. He licked lips gone suddenly dry. 'Don't...' He gulped. 'Don't hold me that way. It's too...much.'

His words aroused her even more. 'What do I do instead,' she gasped as he nipped her shoulder.

'Wrap your legs around my waist,' he said, his voice barely audible.

She did as he said and felt him slide into her. It was the most exciting thing she had ever experienced. He filled her to bursting. Instinctively she surged up to take him completely.

A sharp pain stopped her in mid-thrust.

'Oh!' she gasped, drawing back.

His hands gripped her hips like vises and prevented her from easing away. 'No,' he murmured. 'This will only hurt for a second. I...' he took a deep breath '...promise.'

Before she knew what he was doing, he plunged into her. One quick thrust and he was completely sheathed in her. They lay that way for long moments. He rained tiny kisses along her eyes and down her jawline. His hands played along her torso, cupping and kneading her swollen breasts.

Her pain turned to pleasure, and she began to move against him. She began returning his kisses. Her hands gripped his hips and held him to her.

'What now?'

He chuckled, ending with a groan. 'Just what you're doing.'

They moved in rhythm as though they had spent all their lives making love. The gentle slap of skin on skin filled the room, mixing with the sounds of two people reaching the ultimate physical joy.

Tension mounted in Pippa until her moans crescendoed just as Dev thrust deeply and made her explode into a thousand tiny fragments. Her gasps mingled with his shout.

They lay entwined as the candle gutted and went out. The only light came from the moon shining through the window. The cooler evening air brushed across their sweat-slicked bodies.

Pippa stirred. Only now that the heat of passion was slacked did she begin to feel embarrassed by her boldness and the results. Dev's naked body pressed to hers in the most intimate of embraces.

'I...I need to go back to my room,' she murmured, feeling the heat of mortification warm her face and chest.

He nuzzled into her, his sweet wine-scented breath wafting across her neck. 'Not yet.'

He rose and pulled her up with him. They stood, torso to torso, hip to hip, thigh to thigh. 'Come to bed, Pip. Let me show you how wonderful lovemaking can be when there is no pain.'

She hesitated.

He bent and kissed her. It was a gentle, slow touching that evolved into something deep and primitive. His need reached out and caught her heart. She was lost.


Pippa lay awake long after Dev's soft snoring told her he slept. She still could not totally believe what she had done. All her life she had reached out to people in pain and tried to ease their suffering. But never had she put their needs so much before what was best for her.

It was because she loved Deverell St Simon.

She sighed and closed her eyes on the moon-drenched room. The scent of impending rain wafted through the open window. A horse whinnied in the stables. Her senses were acute. Too acute.

She could still feel Dev's lips on hers, his body in hers. The memory was shattering.

Love. Physical and emotional. She had given him everything she had to offer, and he had taken it. She would do it again.

# Chapter Seven

Dev surfaced slowly. A beam of early sunlight slashed across his face. For the first time in months he was relaxed. His leg was only a minor ache, not the usual incessant throb. He felt good. Damn good.

And warm.

Someone snuggled against his side, one leg thrown over his. He turned his head.

A woman's face nestled in the hollow of his shoulder. Her short, curly black hair clung to him. Her full red lips were slightly parted, and her warm breath caressed his chest.

Memory flooded back. Pippen. Or Pippa. Or whoever she really was. It hurt to think.

He had a raging headache. Two bottles of port had submerged his good sense, but not his ardour. Dev nearly groaned. The desire to kiss her awake was making his loins tighten in sharp response to her nearness.

Her breasts pressed against his ribs, and the hot apex of her legs caressed his thigh. Oh, yes. This was more temptation than he was used to resisting.

But who was this woman really, and why was she looking for Staunton? Was he really her cousin? All he knew for certain was that she was a healer and had saved his life. And she was of gentle birth. She might have done a risky and hoydenish thing by pretending to be a boy, but her manners and the way she carried herself spoke of Quality.

She moved. Her thigh slid down his, sending sparks coursing through him. Surely this was hell. He dared not touch her intimately again. He shouldn't have done so last night, but his judgement had been impaired. The sight of her white limbs glowing in the moonlight had shattered his resistance, just as her body had shattered his mind.

Without warning, her eyes opened. They widened. She gulped.

There was a softness about her that Dev had glimpsed before, but never focused on. Her mouth was full and red, swollen from his kisses. Her eyes were brilliant.

'Mother was right,' Dev said, all his questions disappearing in the wake of his response to her. 'The emeralds will be perfect on you.'

She blinked. The thick black lashes Dev had too often thought effeminate acted like elaborate fans, brushing her blushing cheeks.

'Emeralds?' Her voice was husky. What had been a light tenor for a young man was really a woman's beautiful alto.

Dev felt his body tightening. What a blind fool he had been.

'Yes. The emeralds I intend to give you when we are wed.'

'Wed?'

He resisted the urge to stroke the hair back from her face. 'Yes. Wed. After last night it is the only thing we can do.'

Her eyes narrowed and she pushed at his chest. 'After last night? You mean you feel obliged to marry me because of what we did.'

'Of course. A gentleman does not sleep with a respect-

able, single woman and then not marry her.' Dev scowled
at her, wondering why she was being difficult about this.
There was no other option.

She pushed harder. 'I don't wish to marry you.'

'But you will,' he said, remembering why they were in
Paris. She would hate him after they found Staunton. The
thought pushed all ideas of dalliance from him. 'Get up and
get dressed,' he said curtly. 'We have a few things to discuss.'

'Besides marriage?' she countered. But she sat up, her
back to him.

He couldn't help himself. The delicate curve of her back,
the sweep of her hips caught him. He traced a finger down
her spine to the cleft just above the swell of her *derrière*.

She drew in a sharp breath. She seemed to lean toward
him, and Dev sensed with a man's instinct for knowing
when a woman wanted him that he could slip his arm
around her waist and they would once more enjoy the pleasure they could give one another. The urge to have her was
a sharp agony that quickened his pulse.

He let her go. 'We have things to straighten out,' he said,
his voice a raw husk. 'Like who you really are.'

She didn't look at him as she pulled the sheet up and
wrapped it around her slim body. With a grace he had occasionally noticed when she dressed as a boy, she moved
to her discarded clothes.

'Please don't look,' she said, keeping her back to him.

Dev turned away. He might want nothing more than to
drink in the beauty of her, but he was a gentleman. Gentlemen didn't watch a woman dress when asked not to, just
as a gentleman didn't sleep with a virgin and then not marry
her.

'All right,' she said.

He rolled back around and sat up in the bed.

She gasped and her gaze dropped. He was fully aroused and did nothing to hide that fact. Dev watched the blush start at her cheeks and descend to her neck.

'I lost my modesty a long time ago,' he said, standing. He glanced at her shocked face. 'You have seen me naked, and you have seen me in this state.' A wicked grin laced his features. 'I seem to recall that you enjoyed it very much.'

She twisted around on a bare foot. 'That was last night.'

'True.' He found his breeches and pulled them up, careful not to hurt himself in the process. 'Now you owe me an explanation. Several.' As an afterthought, he added, 'I'm dressed.'

She turned around and her attention instantly went to his hips. He shrugged. 'It will take some time for that particular ailment to correct itself.'

She licked dry lips and her gaze met his. 'I suppose you want to know who I really am.'

'For starters.'

He sat in one of the room's two chairs and motioned for her to take the other. Instead, she paced.

'I am Philippa LeClaire. Philip LeClaire's twin. Earl LeClaire is my grandfather.'

Dev frowned. This was worse than he'd imagined. Once he betrayed her and turned Staunton in, she wouldn't have anything to do with him. No matter what they'd done last night.

'Now I understand your determination to find Staunton. But why did your grandfather let you come to Brussels alone and disguised as a boy? If you were found out, you'd be ruined.' He didn't add that she was already ruined by sleeping with him.

She paused and looked away. 'Grandfather doesn't know,' she said quietly.

'What?'.

She shrugged and had the grace to look as though she knew what she'd done was wrong. 'He thinks I came here with my aunt, Tabitha Montcleve, for a chaperon.'

Dev shook his head. 'And what is to keep him from finding out?'

For the first time since awakening, a tiny smile tugged at her lips. 'He and Aunt Tabitha hate each other. They never speak, so he'll never know she's still in London.'

'What a family,' Dev murmured. 'Where are your parents? Surely they would never knowingly allow you to do such a hoydenish thing as this.'

She paused and said softly, 'Dead. My mother died in childbirth. That's why I became a healer. To help other women. My father died later in a carriage accident.'

'I'm sorry.' Dev rose and went to her. She stepped away from him, but he followed. 'Come here, Pip.'

She watched him steadily and must have seen the sincerity he felt because she moved into his arms. He stroked her hair and held her gently.

She took a deep breath. 'I must find Philip. I'm so afraid that if I don't…Grandfather will die too. He has a bad heart and getting the letter about Philip nearly brought on another attack of apoplexy.'

Oh, God, Dev thought. This is getting worse and worse. He felt like a cad. 'We'll find your brother, if he's alive.'

'He is. I know it,' she said fervently. 'I would know if he were not.'

'That twin thing,' Dev said, half believing because of her belief.

'Yes. When we were younger, oh, maybe ten or twelve, he took one of the dogs for a romp. He missed dinner. Grandfather and Burns, our nanny, were worried that something awful had happened to him, but I knew he was all right. I sensed it. He came home thirty minutes later, his pants and shirt torn because he'd tripped over a log and ripped them, but otherwise fit as a fiddle.' She lifted her head from Dev's shoulder and met his eyes. 'I knew he would be. Just as I know he will be this time.'

Her eyes gleamed from unshed tears. Determination etched a sharp line between her brows and edged her jaw.

Admiration and a desire to protect and comfort her welled up in Dev. Without thought, he gently took her lips with his. It was a tender touch, meant to ease some of her pain. But his need for her soon turned it deeper.

Pippa reeled under the sensual devastation of his kiss. All her resolve to act as though their lovemaking had been a pothole in the road that could be ignored fled. She collapsed against him.

An eternity later, he released her. Pippa stumbled back. Her calf hit the edge of a chair, and she collapsed into it. Stunned, she stared at Dev who still stood.

'You are marrying me,' he stated. 'I told you I keep my promises.' A grin broke through his determination. 'And no woman who swoons when I kiss her is going to get away.'

She smiled back, all her earlier objections forgotten. She loved him. Surely he felt the same, or he couldn't make her feel so completely overwhelmed by emotion.

'Come here,' he ordered. 'I haven't finished with you.'

The sun was well overhead and the room hot when Dev woke again. He eased himself from the bed and dressed. He had to start looking for clues as to where Staunton had been and to whom he had talked. The first place to start was the stables. Ostlers and grooms knew everyone who came and went in an establishment like this.

But before leaving, Dev paused to kiss Pippa lightly on

the cheek. She slept through his caress, her face flushed and her body relaxed. She trusted him implicitly. More than ever he wished he didn't have to ruin that trust, but bringing to justice a man who had helped kill many British men was more important than one person's happiness. Even if that person was Pippa.

To put the image of Pippa's disillusionment from his mind, Dev walked briskly from the room.

A coin here and another there, soon had several of the ostlers talking to him. One, a slight youth with a gaping hole where his two front teeth should be, told Dev he'd seen a man who met Staunton's description.

In his lisping French, the boy said, 'But he was French as I am, not English.'

Dev kept quiet. It was possible that Staunton spoke French like a native. The skill would be indispensable to a spy.

'He often met with Jorge.' The youth nodded his head in the direction of the water trough. 'Over there when Jorge would stop by. The first time it seemed an accident. But on the fourth time, I thought they were trading something. Jorge is often curious—just as you, *monsieur*—and willing to pay a franc or two for information.'

'Where is Jorge from?' Dev handed out another coin for the direction.

'Dev,' Pippa said from directly behind him just as the ostler finished speaking.

Dev managed to keep from jerking around and wondered how many more lies he was going to have to tell her. She stood in the shadows, but he could tell she was in her boy's clothing and that she wasn't happy with him for leaving her behind. He thanked the ostler before turning.

'So, you're finally awake, sleepyhead.'

She frowned at him, her glance going from him to the ostler who was backing away. 'I worked harder than usual.'

'Ouch,' he murmured, taking her arm and steering her outside.

'Why did you sneak out?' she hissed at him, trying to draw her arm away.

He held her steady. 'Because you needed the rest.'

'That was kind of you,' she said with an ironic twist of lips. 'But why do I feel there was more to it than that?'

He couldn't meet her open gaze. 'Because there was. I don't want you involved in this search any more than you already are.'

She dug her heels in until they stopped. 'Why?'

His brows snapped together, and he pulled her forward in spite of her resistance. 'It could be dangerous. Just as talking where anyone can overhear us could be dangerous.'

Dev continued dragging her as he tried to decide how much to tell her. They were on the street in front of the inn, the traffic creating enough noise to drown out their voices when he allowed them to halt.

'Pippa, why do you think your brother was here in Paris when all of Wellington's troops were gathering at Brussels?'

Her face took on a pinched, worried look. 'I...I had tried not to think about it.' She took a deep breath. 'But it was unusual.'

'Very.'

'Was he doing something dishonest?' She gripped his arm and her fingers dug through the heavy cloth of his jacket. 'Did Wellington tell you something?'

Dev gazed down at her. The best thing would be to tell her the truth, up to a point. If she knew Staunton was considered a traitor then she would wonder why he was helping her find him. He couldn't tell her that. Guilt and remorse slammed into him. He owed her so much. He owed Patrick and others like him more. He looked away.

'He was…is a spy. He disappeared from here.'

Her jaw tightened. 'A spy. Why didn't Wellington tell me that?'

He forced himself to meet her angry gaze. 'Because he thought you naught but a boy.'

'But he told you. Is that why you came with me? Because Wellington told you to?'

So much truth in her words. Dev clamped down on the urge to tell her everything. 'No. I came because I had already promised to help you. You know that. The only reason Wellington told me was because he knew we were determined to come here, and he didn't want me—or you— in jeopardy because we didn't know the truth about your brother.'

'Why didn't you tell me sooner?'

He sighed and ran the fingers of the arm she wasn't holding like a vise through his hair. 'I was hoping to search for him without having you along. Stupid, I know, but I didn't want to worry you more. Spies live dangerous lives.'

The lines around her mouth softened. Seeing that she believed his tale of half-truths made Dev feel worse.

'Oh, Dev,' she said softly, 'I'm sorry I doubted you. Even for a second.'

Damn, but it was hard to keep meeting her gaze. 'Then will you trust me enough to let me search for him without you? Having you along would only distract me and make it more dangerous for both of us.'

She considered for a long time. Around them, pedestrians swirled like a river around a large boulder. Horses with their riders or drawing carriages clopped along the cobbled street. Hawkers yelled their wares.

At last she said, 'I know you'll do your best. I appreciate

your help and how difficult these last days have been on you. I…I don't want to make everything worse.' Her hand fell away from his arm. 'Do you have information?'

The last was so unexpected, that Dev started. 'Yes. The ostler gave me a man's name and direction.'

'Ah…' her eyebrows rose '…that is what you were doing. If it were anyone else, I would insist on going.' She stepped away, stepped back. Uncertainty was writ plain to see on her face and in her actions. 'But since 'tis you, I'll wait at the inn.'

'Thank you,' he said, humbled by her trust. A trust he didn't deserve.

'But…' she shook a finger at him '…if you aren't back in two hours, I shall go and bribe that same young man and then follow you.'

He caught her hand and brought that admonishing finger to his lips, completely forgetting where they were or how she was dressed. 'Understood.'

He watched her go back to the inn, making sure she was inside before heading off. He was piling up more and more acrimony. The more he lied to her, the more she would hate him when all was said and done.

A pain that had nothing to do with his leg filled him. He pushed it aside. This went beyond any one individual. He had to remember that.

Some time later, he returned to the inn. Jorge had given him a description of another man, a man who fit the particulars, as Wellington had told him, of the British spy who'd been murdered. Everything was pointing to Staunton. Jorge had also given him the name and direction of a third man. Tomorrow he would go there. But right now his two hours were up.

He found Pippa in the tap room, seated in a dark corner, nursing a mug of ale. He went to her.

She jumped up as soon as she saw him. 'What did you learn?'

'Shh.' He sat down across from her and ordered a beer. When it came he took a long drink and wiped the foam from his upper lip. 'I found out that anyone can be bribed, if the money is high enough.' He shook his head in disgust. 'The man denied knowing your brother, but when I gave him enough gold to weight down a strong man's hand, he told me he had seen a man of your brother's likeness. He also gave me another name. I plan to visit him as soon as I leave here.'

'Leave here?'

He set the mug down. 'Leave here, Pip. Your brother's trail is months old. The less time we waste here, the better. I doubt he's even here now, but maybe this next man will have a clue as to where he went.'

She agreed, but when she left the tap room her step wasn't as light as normal. He knew this was hard on her.

His next errand led him to one of Paris's biggest slums. Trash filled the gutters and an eye-watering stench filled the air. People dressed in rags walked through the muck or slept in it. Dev had seen poverty in London and had done what he could to help those he met. Here he hesitated to give anyone money, for fear that he would then become a target. It was bad enough that his good clothes set him apart.

Knocking on the door of the address given to him, Dev kept an eye over his shoulder and was thankful for the pistol in the pocket of his coat. When there was no answer, he used his cane to hammer on the door. Just as he decided to leave, the door cracked open.

A woman's raspy voice asked in French, 'What do you want? Ain't nothing here for a swell.'

Dev stuck his foot in the opening and with a glance over his shoulder, held out his hand. On the palm was a franc. 'I have some questions,' he said in French, 'and I will pay well for the answers.'

The door opened wider and he slipped inside, keeping his back to the solid wood. There was no telling who was with the woman.

The room was dark and dingy. The smell of sweat and onions was like a slap in the face. His nose wrinkled automatically.

'Told you this ain't no place for Quality,' the woman said defensively.

She was as thin and rusty looking as a worn nail. Her dress was patched and in need of cleaning. Her hair hung in lank shanks around her tired, lined face. He added another coin to the one in his palm and gave both to her.

'What's this for? I haven't told you anything yet.' But she took the money and it disappeared faster than Dev could follow.

'I'm looking for Pierre Mont. Do you know him?'

Fury replaced the greed that had just lit her muddy brown eyes. 'He's dead.'

Dev nearly groaned out loud. So close. 'When?'

'A month ago. Why?'

Dev drew out another coin. 'I think he knew someone I'm hunting for.'

She snatched the money. 'What do you want to know?'

'Can you tell me someone who knew Mont? Someone he might have told a secret to?'

Her thin mouth twisted bitterly. 'Me. He was my man.'

Hope unfurled again and Dev dug out another franc. 'How did he die?'

'Stabbed. Lived for days while the wound festered. I couldn't do nothing. No money.'

He had to look away from the grief she made no effort to hide. 'Do you know who killed him?'

She shook her head. He handed her another coin. She took it.

She licked her dry lips, and her claw-like hands curled. 'He was out of his mind at the end. Fever eatin' him up. He kept talking about some foreigner and Holland.'

'English?'

She shrugged, the cloth of her dress hanging loosely off her shoulders. 'Maybe. And Holland. Didn't seem like he meant the country, but maybe.' She shrugged again and held out her hand.

Dev gave her everything he had left. Without another word, she turned and left through a small door in the back of the room. Having no wish to stay any longer, Dev walked briskly away, using his cane for support.

It was darker outside than when he'd gone into the house. More ragamuffins were around, and there was a distinct air of danger. Dev picked up his pace and kept his right hand on the pistol in his pocket. It had two shots.

Maybe it was his speed or the look of cold awareness he had, but no one accosted him. Once or twice a man or woman edged his way, but when he stared them down they quickly retreated.

A little less than three hours after leaving Pippa for the second time that day, Dev re-entered the inn. He was exhausted. He needed food and rest, and then he would think on what the woman had told him. Holland, but not the country, and a foreigner, maybe British.

That night Pippa and Dev ate in the tavern. She hunkered down on the hard bench with her arms propped up on the scarred pine table top. Now, more than ever before, she found it hard to impersonate a boy. After Dev's loving and with his hazel eyes devouring her across the span of wood, she felt as though her body was shouting 'female' to any who looked. Even her mannerisms were reverting back to her feminine gestures. Twice today she'd caught herself tossing her head to get her non-existent hair off her face.

'Eat up,' Dev said, taking a swallow of his ale.

She noted that tonight he wasn't drinking to excess. 'I'm not very hungry,' she answered, pushing the overcooked mutton around her plate.

'Would *monsieur* care for more ale?' Giselle's husky French voice asked. She sidled closer and stopped inches from Dev, her right hand propped on one canted hip as she thrust out her ample bosom.

Pippa clamped her jaw on a brusque no. This was Dev's decision to make. Instead of looking at him and hoping to see uninterest in his eyes when he gazed at the Frenchwoman, Pippa watched a table of men toast one another. All her determination barely kept her from turning back to Dev and beseeching him with her eyes to get rid of Giselle.

'She's gone now,' Dev said quietly.

Pippa's gaze snapped back to him. 'Oh? I barely even realized she was here.'

'Liar,' he said softly. 'Let's go upstairs.'

He stood and pushed back his stool with his good leg. Still, he winced. Pippa forgot her jealousy in her concern for him.

She jumped up and circled the table to offer him her shoulder. 'You've had a long day and wouldn't use a carriage. Nor did you get much slee—' Her scolding stopped abruptly as she realized the implications of what she had said.

'No, I didn't,' he murmured. 'But I enjoyed every second of my labours and would again.'

Pleasure mixed with embarrassment as Pippa stumbled and caught herself up before dragging them both to the floor in this public room. He made her forget propriety.

'You shouldn't say such things where people can hear,' she muttered.

His arm tightened on her shoulder. 'You're the only one who can hear me, and you already know what I'm talking about. And…' he grinned down at her '…you started the conversation.'

She had. Instead of continuing down this path, she shut up. It was a rare experience for her to know someone else had beaten her to the last word.

Silently, they climbed the stairs to their rooms. At Dev's door, she released his waist.

'I'll return as soon as I fix you something for the pain. Then you'll be able to get a good night's sleep.'

His eyes flashed and he grinned. 'There are better ways of forgetting the discomfort.'

'Perhaps.' She looked up at him through the shade of her lashes. There was a hard-angled hunger about his face that made her breathless. 'But this will also help.'

Before he could refuse, she nipped into her room. Minutes later, she knocked on his door and entered without waiting for his reply.

He stood looking out the window. The sun was setting and blood-red rays splashed across his bare chest. She went to him and gave him the draught. He downed it in one gulp before setting the empty glass on the table.

'Thank you for your care,' he said, drawing her into the safe haven of his arms.

She went willingly and leaned her head against the hollow of his shoulder. Warmth and the musky scent that was his own enveloped Pippa. She felt comfortable and cared for. Perhaps with time he would love her. He already liked her. Unconsciously, she sighed.

'What is wrong?' he asked, tightening his hold on her.

'Nothing.' The last thing she was going to do was tell him her insecurities and longings where he was concerned.

He misunderstood. 'We'll find your brother, Pippa. I promise. I got a good clue today. You know that.'

She turned into him, sliding her hands up his chest and into his hair. 'Love me, Dev. Make me forget everything else.'

Hunger narrowed his eyes and sharpened his jaw. 'I want nothing more, Pip, but I can't.'

'What?' Hurt made her voice falter. 'You don't want to?'

He groaned. 'That's not it. I shouldn't have made love to you last night or earlier today. It isn't right. We aren't married yet.'

She dropped her hands and clasped her fingers together to keep from reaching for him again. 'I understand.' She moved away.

'Pippa,' he said, reaching for her, exasperation writ clearly on his face. 'That isn't it. I want to love you more than anything else, but...'

'But what?' The anguish in his face and the bright blaze in his eyes were beginning to penetrate her sense of rejection. He did want her. He might say differently, but his body was refusing to heed his command.

He shook his head. 'You're from a good family. I shouldn't have even touched you.'

'Do you regret it?' she asked softly, deciding to use any means to overcome his late scruples.

'No.' He turned from her.

She glared at his back. 'Then what difference does another time make? I'm no longer a virgin. Stopping now won't change that.'

'No, but maybe it will make me feel less a cad.'

'Then why were you flirting with me downstairs?' she demanded, wondering if the tightness in her chest caused by his rejection would ever go away.

Deep down she knew she should leave instead of continuing to throw herself at him, but she couldn't. Her desire for him was beyond his need for her as a woman. She wanted him to love her as she loved him. She wanted him to marry her for herself and not for his honour.

She moved to him and wrapped her arms around him. 'Please don't make me beg, Dev.'

He twisted around and caught her hands. 'I could never do that, Pippa.'

With a moan mixed of pleasure and surrender, he bent his head until his lips met hers. Their arms twined around each other and their mouths melded to one another.

Pippa wanted to be as close to him as possible. Dev wanted to forget everything but the feel of her pressed to him and around him.

# Chapter Eight

At Calais, they boarded a British ship bound for Dover. After long thought, Dev had concluded that the 'Holland' mentioned by the Frenchwoman had to be Lord Holland, possibly that lord's country estate since Parliament was briefly out of session. It was a shot in the dark, but they'd agreed to take it.

Now, with the ship rolling beneath their feet, they stood as close together as two men can. Pippa leaned against the rail and watched France disappear.

'I shall almost miss it,' Pippa said softly.

Dev turned a questioning look on her.

She smiled. ''Tis where you and I found each other. As horrible as it sounds, without the war I would have never met you.'

'I can't find it in me to be glad for a country that cost so many British lives.' Dev stared out at the open sea. Storm clouds hovered on the horizon. He turned back to Pippa. 'We would have met anyway. You would have come to London for a Season.'

'No, I would not have. I'm not a social butterfly, Dev. I love the country, and I enjoy my work.'

Dev surreptitiously took her hand under the cover of their

greatcoats. 'Then I must be glad for what happened, much
as it pains me to say so.'

'Oh, Dev,' she said tremulously.

A strong wind caught the sails and the ship veered to
one side. Pippa's feet slipped on the saltwater-coated deck.
Dev grabbed her arm and kept her from falling.

'I think we would be safer in our cabin.'

Pippa, her short hair speckled with spray, agreed. She
had no more than put one foot on the step leading down to
their cabin when the ship bucked. Both hands wrapped
around the stair rail, she groaned.

Dev, some steps below, looked up, a worried frown obvious even in the dim light from a wildly swinging lantern.
'Are you all right?'

'Barely,' Pippa muttered. Her stomach was beginning to
lurch with every roll of the ship. Just as it had done on her
crossing to Brussels. She had forgotten the agony until now.

Dev found their cubbyhole and held the door open for
her. Pippa stumbled over the threshold, one hand plastered
to her mouth.

'What the devil?' He reached for her, but she eluded him
and went straight for the slop bucket. He followed.

Pippa lost her dinner.

'Pip,' Dev said, 'why didn't you tell me you get sea-
sick?'

'Didn't matter,' she muttered, her face tinged green
around the edges. Her legs felt like they were about to
collapse under her.

'Lie down. Now,' he ordered when she hesitated.

She fell to the bunk, too weak to lift her feet. Dev did
the service for her after pulling off her boots. Sweat popped
out on her brow and he went to the water pitcher, unstop-
pered it and wet his handkerchief. Returning, he laid it
across her forehead.

'I…' she turned a ghastly shade of grey '…think I…'

He dropped the wet cloth and grabbed the bucket. She leaned over and promptly cast up what was left. For long minutes all she could do was heave drily. Dev rubbed her back and wiped her mouth.

'I'm so sorry,' she finally managed. 'I never meant to do this. I'm not normally so poor spirited.'

'Hush,' Dev said. 'Can you sit up enough for me to get this jacket off? It cannot help you to be hot.'

'I think so,' she murmured, straining to raise her shoulders up.

That done, she fell backward, too spent to do more than murmur thank you. Dev undid the top buttons of her shirt and tucked the rough cotton sheet around her waist. He poured a small amount of water and brought it to her.

'Can you manage this?' He tipped the glass to her lips.

Pippa managed a sip. 'Bring my bag of herbs. Please.'

He gave her a quizzical look, but fetched the item. She rummaged until pulling out a small vial that contained a light brown substance.

Seeing Dev watching her, Pippa said, 'Ginger. A little of this in the water will help settle my stomach.' The ship rocked and she grimaced. 'I should have thought of this sooner.'

She instructed him on the amount and then drank down the concoction. 'More water, please,' she croaked after the last of the medicine. 'The ginger burns.'

'Burns?' Dev handed her a little water.

'Yes,' she managed to say around sips. ''Tis like pepper, only it does not make you sneeze.'

Minutes later she fell into a light doze. Dev perched on the wooden side of the bunk and smoothed the damp tendrils of hair from her face. A smile tugged at his lips. Their positions were reversed, and he found that he liked caring for her.

His leg ached from the long ride they had made yesterday, coming from Paris. The only place to lie down was the bunk Pippa now slept in. With a wider smile, Dev gently moved her inward and lay down beside her. She snuggled close until her head rested in the crook of his shoulder. She always managed to find that spot, and Dev was coming to expect her near him.

Contentment relaxed his muscles as he fell asleep. Even his throbbing leg seemed less intense.

Later, they woke, flushed with the nearness of each other.

'How do you feel?' Dev asked, rubbing his hand up and down her arm.

'Much better.' Her gaze met his. 'Much better.'

'I am glad,' he murmured, leaning over and taking her mouth with his. 'Very glad.'

Luckily, he had locked the cabin's door when they first entered.

Hours later, they disembarked at Dover and headed for an inn where Dev was well known. At the door, he turned to her. 'Stay out here, Pip.'

She scowled at him. 'Why?'

'Because I don't want anyone seeing you who doesn't have to.'

'Why not? Are you ashamed of me? Do I look disreputable after my shipboard activities?'

He sighed. 'No, but the fewer people who see you as you currently are, the better.'

Understanding dawned. 'You are protecting me,' she said.

'Hush. The less said in public the better.'

Before she could tell him he was being overly cautious, he left and the door closed in her face. Pippa watched the hustle and bustle as time passed. She had just decided to go inside and search Dev out, when he hailed her from inside a coach that had just driven into the front yard.

She hurried to the vehicle and pulled open the door.

'Come on,' he said, 'we haven't all day. Our things are already loaded. Your herbs are in here.' He waved to the corner opposite him where her bag rested.

She clambered in. 'Why are we travelling this way? I thought you were too determined to prove yourself to sink this low.' She softened the words with a smile.

'I think I have proven myself enough for one day. I don't need to continue showing you I'm a man by riding a horse when there are better ways to use my energy,' he murmured wickedly, referring to their activity after wakening on the ship.

'Perhaps,' she agreed, sitting beside him, glad that her love for him had eased his feeling of inadequacy. 'But then again, that was a while ago.' She turned innocent green eyes on him, placing one hand lightly on his chest. 'I have never had the experience in a carriage, and I think it might be very interesting.'

He looked at her in amazement, but she could see his pupils dilating and feel his heart picking up speed beneath her palm. She knew her wish would come true.

It was a long, cold journey to Lord Holland's country house. Autumn was on its way and with it came shorter days and wetter travel. The sound of wheels on gravel was most welcome.

Exhaustion ate at Pippa. She knew that if she felt this badly, then Dev must be worse. His leg had to be hurting.

'Dev,' she murmured, sitting away from him and looking out the window, 'we're here. How are you feeling?'

He stretched before joining her at the window. 'As good as can be expected. Thank goodness you showed me the error of my ways.'

She turned a puzzled face to him. 'Me?'

'Yes,' he said tenderly, smoothing a curl from her forehead. 'You showed me there are other ways than killing myself on horseback to prove my wound is insignificant.'

Warmth suffused her. She caught his hand and brought the palm to her lips. 'If we weren't nearly at our destination, I would show you again.'

He kissed her lightly on the mouth. 'Or I would show you.' The carriage slowed to a halt. 'But not now. The last thing we need is for someone to see us.'

She nodded regretfully and released his hand. Turning the subject, she said, 'I hope my brother is here. I've been gone from home many months, and I know my grandfather. My letters might be written to soothe him, but I doubt they do. I need to find Philip.' Her voice fell to a barely audible whisper. 'For Grandfather and for myself.'

Dev heard the softly spoken words and his gut twisted. He turned abruptly away.

Soon he would have to ruin her regard for him. He could not help it. Staunton had done irreparable damage and, if left free, he would continue to do so. Napoleon might be on St Helena, but he had plenty of sympathizers who would be more than willing to see him free again.

The carriage stopped and Pippa flung open the door and leaped before the ostler could get the step down. Dev, unable to match her feat, exited sedately. To his amazement, his pride was not hurt.

They had barely taken ten steps before the front door

was opened and the butler ushered them inside. Their hosts met them shortly.

'Lord Holland,' Dev said, extending his hand and moving forward. 'Thank you and your lady for having us.' He made a bow to Lady Holland.

'Any time, Deverell. When your brother's letter arrived asking me to let you rusticate while your leg healed, I was glad to do what I can. How is Jonathan? I have not see him since Parliament adjourned.'

Dev smiled ruefully. 'I don't know, sir. I haven't seen him since his marriage.'

'Ah…yes.' Lord Holland gave Dev a knowing look before turning his attention to Pippa. 'And who is your companion? Another one of Wellington's heroes?'

'Most definitely,' Dev said, moving aside for Pippa. 'May I present Pippen LeClaire?'

Pippa made a bow to Lord Holland and then to his wife. That woman studied Pippa from head to toe.

'You look in need of a bath and food,' Lady Holland said in her abrupt way. 'We keep country hours here and dress for dinner.'

Pippa gulped. 'I am used to eating at five, milady. But—'

'But Pippen does not have formal dress, Lady Holland,' Dev said decisively. 'His clothing was lost in the turmoil of travelling from Brussels to here. Besides which, Pippen cared for many of Wellington's injured troops.'

Lady Holland gave him a shrewd look. 'So, you are telling me that, as a war hero, it is my duty to receive him at my table regardless of his dress?'

Dev said nothing, but met her eyes squarely.

'There is no need for this,' Pippa said hastily. 'I can eat off a tray in my room. Please—'

Once more she was interrupted. 'Young man,' Lady Holland said, 'I will do as I see fit in my own home. And I have decided that you will be an oddity. We meet for drinks fifteen minutes before. Do not be late.'

Dazed at the swiftness of the lady's change, Pippa stared at Lady Holland's disappearing back. Behind her the butler coughed.

'If you will follow me, milords, I will show you to the rooms prepared for you.'

Dev and Pippa thanked Lord Holland and followed the servant.

Pippa surreptitiously watched Dev as they climbed the stairs. He was already exhausted. She knew traversing two flights of stairs was not going to help his leg.

When she saw him wince and his left leg buckle just a little, she said softly, 'Here, lean on me.'

He did so without protest.

The butler deposited them at their doors, which were side by side. Pippa went into her room and immediately spied a door that she was sure would connect with Dev's. She rushed to it and rapped smartly. Seconds later, he opened it.

He grinned rakishly at her, his dimple begging to be touched. 'How convenient.'

She laughed up at him. 'Why would they give us connecting rooms?'

He shrugged. 'Probably because I told Jonathan to tell them you are taking care of me, and I need you close by.'

'Ah,' she said. 'How clever.'

'I thought so,' he murmured, entering her room and looking around. 'Quite cosy.'

She glanced around. A large four-poster hugged one wall. Thick carpet softened the waxed gloss of wood floors. Heavy blue damask curtains closed out the cold night.

'I shall be very comfortable. And how is your room?' she asked, edging by him.

His room was larger and more richly furnished, as befitted the younger son of a prominent duke. In addition to a bed, wardrobe, dresser and washing table, he had several large overstuffed wing chairs grouped around the fireplace.

A knock on his door made them both jump. 'Who is it?' Dev asked.

'Milord,' a deep male voice, muffled by the heavy oak of the door, said. 'I have brought you a light supper.'

Dev raised a brow at Pippa. She could stay or return to her room. She decided to return to her own room. She was more tired than hungry, and when her food was delivered she would politely decline. She should have done so downstairs, but had been too taken aback by Lady Holland to think straight.

Dev waited for the connecting door to close before bidding the servant enter. 'Set the tray on the table,' he said, thinking how nice it would be to stretch his leg out before the roaring fire. The heat would ease some of the ache.

The servant did as instructed, but not without casting a curious glance around the room. His eyes met Deverell's. For an instant, Dev felt as though he were being studied. Then the man's gaze fell away. Even after the servant left, Dev was left with the impression of a tall man with hair a shade darker than his own and vivid green eyes that reminded him of Pippa's. Strange.

Pushing the image away, Dev sank into one of the soft chairs and devoured his food. The warmth from the fire eased the discomfort in his leg, and he knew that if he didn't reach the bed soon, he would fall asleep where he sprawled.

Nor was this the time to go to Pippa. They must be careful if they were to keep her identity secret.

Dinner that evening was a lively affair. The prominent Whigs of the day were well represented, along with wits,

scientists and artists. Pippa was entranced by the conversations. The only thing marring her pleasure was a sense
of urgency about finding her brother. She found herself
watching everyone, listening for any word that might in-
dicate his nearness.

'Mr LeClaire,' Lord Holland said, 'tell us about your
healing. Dev says you were indispensable after Waterloo.'

Pippa flushed, realizing she was the synosure of all eyes.
'Why, milord, I believe Deverell does exaggerate.'

'Very pretty,' Lady Holland said. 'And yes, Devil Deverell often exaggerates, but somehow I don't think this
story has been.'

Pippa felt herself heat up even more. 'I only did what
anyone else would have done. I have some small knowledge of herbs and healing. I helped where the doctors and
surgeons needed me.'

Even as she spoke, Pippa felt a sense of unease. As
though someone studied her. She finished quickly and
turned her attention to the fish. Her good manners tried to
surface in a compliment to the chef, but she suppressed
them. The last thing she wanted to do was draw more attention to herself.

Still, the hairs on her nape rose. She cast surreptitious
glances around the room to no avail. The focus of the group
had now shifted, and Dev held centre stage.

After dinner, the group retired to the salon, for which
she was grateful. There were very few ladies. A fact that
hadn't surprised her. As a divorced woman who'd married
her lover, Lord Holland, Lady Holland was not considered
good *ton* and Society's sticklers did not frequent her home.
There were some women, and Pippa found that she would
have been more comfortable with them. They were intel-

ligent and discussed more than the current fashions and who was married to whom.

The night passed slowly, and Pippa made her excuses, knowing the rest of the guests would chat and play cards into the small hours. Making her way up the stairs, she hoped Dev would soon retire. She wanted to be in his arms.

Her wish was not long in coming true. She had barely taken off her coat and shirt and begun to unwind the cloth that bound her bosom when the connecting door opened. Dev stood in the doorway, his hair mussed and his evening dress replaced by a blue satin robe.

She smiled and he entered.

Without thought, she went to him. The kiss was long and deep, all her anxiety and need distilled into one intense meeting.

'Well,' he said softly, when they finally pulled apart enough for him to look at her, 'what brought that about?'

Desire and contentment curled in her deepest heart as she looked at his beloved countenance. 'I missed you.'

He smoothed the tangled curls from her face and kept his fingers enmeshed in their silken strands. 'Then miss me some more,' he murmured, gathering her even closer.

Much later, they lay on her bed, tangled in the sheets and each other. Passion slaked for a short while, Pippa stroked the wiry hairs of Dev's chest. Occasionally, she pulled one just to keep him from slipping into sleep.

'Minx,' he murmured, catching her fingers after the last tweak. 'Do you intend to keep me awake all night? For I warn you—' he moved quickly and pinned her to the bed with his body '—if you keep this distraction up, we shall have a repeat of what started all this.'

She giggled. 'I am more than happy to indulge your excesses.'

As his head bent to hers, and happiness welled up inside

her, Pippa began to think that maybe she should marry him. She loved him, and perhaps what he felt for her would become love. Then she forgot everything but the feel of him.

Several days passed much as the first. The company was lively and Pippa enjoyed herself immensely. Although she thought she would find pleasure anywhere Dev was. Still, she occasionally had the disquieting feeling that someone watched her, in spite of her never finding anyone looking at her who was not also ready to talk to her.

The third night of their stay, Pippa sat in the single chair her room boasted. She edged it closer to the fire and fought the melancholy that threatened to drown her. She'd had such high hopes when they disembarked from the ship at Dover. She had been convinced she would find Philip here.

A sigh escaped her. If only Dev would finish downstairs and come to bed. Tonight, more than ever, she needed his warmth and care.

She got up to prepare herself a tonic of chamomile, hoping it would relax her, and froze. The handle to her chamber door was moving. Someone was trying to enter. Someone who hadn't bothered to knock.

'Who is it?' she asked, irritated when her voice came out squeaky.

Instead of answering, the person pushed open the door and stepped into the room. A tall man, with light brown hair and dressed as a servant, confronted her. His green eyes burned into hers.

'*Philip!*' The recognition was sudden and sharp. Tears of joy blurred her vision. She catapulted herself on to his chest. 'Philip.'

'Easy, Pip. Easy,' he murmured, holding her close.

The solid muscle of him assured her he was real and well. She drew back enough to look at him.

He smiled down at her. 'I see you're still the reckless, determined to be anything but a girl, hoyden I know and love.' He hugged her. 'I am glad to see you are doing well, sister.'

'And I you,' she said, squeezing him again. 'We thought you were dead. They sent us a letter saying you'd been killed in battle.'

His full mouth, so much like hers, thinned. 'Who is "they"?'

'The Home Office.'

He released her without warning and turned back to lock the door. He then moved to the connecting one leading to Dev's chamber and did the same.

'We have much to discuss,' he said, angling back to her. 'First, why are you here, dressed as a man, and what are you doing sleeping with a man of Devil Deverell's reputation?'

Her mouth fell open, followed by confusion, quickly followed by irritation. 'What do you think I am doing here? Looking for you! As for Dev, what do you know about him that you feel free to judge him?'

He scowled, drawing his dark brown brows together. 'The last thing I need is for you to be arousing suspicion by looking for me. Secondly, I've been to London. I know the youngest son of the Duke of Rundell is considered wild, to say the least. Only a few months ago he chased some actress until his older brother had to intervene to keep him from marrying her.'

Stunned at the revelation about her lover, Pippa slumped on to the nearest thing. Thankfully the bed was high so that when her knees gave out she didn't have far to fall.

'He tried to marry someone a few months ago?'

'An actress.' Philip pulled the single chair near the bed. 'Now do you understand why I had to risk giving away my cover in order to stop this affair the two of you are having? He's no good for you.'

'How do you know all this?' she asked, wondering if the numbness she felt in her heart would eventually go away.

'I told you,' Philip said, impatience putting an edge to his voice. 'It was the *on dit* of London until Deverell went to Brussels. Then his brother married the woman and made the situation into a scandal.'

'Does he still love her?' she asked, her voice soft and vulnerable.

'How should I know?' Exasperation dug lines between Philip's brows. 'I doubt it since he is carrying on with you.' His voice turned cold. 'Something that has got to stop or I'll call the cad out myself and ensure that he is in no condition to continue.' Anger thinned his mouth. 'I shall call him out, anyway, after this is over. Someone must protect your honour.'

She stared at him, hearing his words but not comprehending them. If Dev had wanted to marry an actress, he must have been very much in love with her. Could that type of emotion disappear so soon? Or was he still pining after her, but wise enough to know she was now beyond his reach?

Even more importantly, what did he feel for herself? She had begun to hope he cared for her, that his offer of marriage was more than a way to make up for having bedded her. That hope crashed against the ache in her heart. Deverell was only trying to do the honourable thing.

'Snap out of it,' Philip said, rising from the chair and shaking her. 'He isn't worth it. I want you out of here immediately. I will take you to the stagecoach and put you on one home to Grandfather.'

It was an effort to make herself concentrate on what her twin said, but she knew she must. What was between her and Dev had nothing to do with the situation Philip was in.

She pushed his hand off her shoulder to stop the jostling he continued to give her. 'I cannot think with you shaking me up.'

He sat back down. 'I don't believe you have thought once since leaving home. What maggot got into your head?'

A tiny flare of anger sparked her temper. 'I might say the same about you. What do you mean by skulking about and letting us think you were killed? Do you know what that nearly did to Grandfather?'

He had the grace to look uncomfortable. 'I am sorry for it, but could not help it. I am…was…a—'

'Spy?' she provided with a twist of her mouth. 'That is what Dev thinks.'

'Does he? I wonder why?' A thoughtful look held Philip's handsome features.

'Because we tracked you here from Paris, where Wellington sent us to find you.'

His eyes narrowed. 'Why is Deverell St Simon with you? This isn't his style.'

The pain Pippa had been trying to ignore by concentrating on her twin's plight resurfaced with a vengeance. She held it tightly in rein. 'Because he thinks he owes me his life and wants to do whatever he can to help me.'

'So he sleeps with you? That is rich!'

'Stop it!' Pippa jumped off the bed and paced the short distance to the fireplace. She rounded on her twin. 'Stop denigrating Dev.'

'He will be lucky if I don't kill him. With that leg of his, it wouldn't be hard to beat him at swords or even pistols.'

Fury exploded in Pippa. 'How can you be so cruel?'

'How can he be so callous? He is using you, Pippa.'

Weariness descended on Pippa like a winter storm. Her shoulders slumped. 'I must talk to Dev about these things.'

Philip jumped up. 'You must get away from here and him. Go home and tell Grandfather I'm well and will return when I'm able.'

She glared at him. 'You go tell him yourself. Seeing you will do more for his health than any message I could take.'

His eyes narrowed. 'Then you come with me. And don't tell Deverell St Simon where you are going.'

'Leave without a word?' She blanched.

He crossed his arms over his chest. 'Yes.'

Pippa turned away from her twin's furious face. 'I couldn't do that, Philip. I trust him. What you have told me about the actress has done nothing to make me not trust him.'

'Has he told you he loves you? Is that why you slept with him? Because if that is so, then you are a fool.'

She sighed and still couldn't turn to face her brother. 'No, he has said nothing about love. But he wants to marry me because of what we have done.' She swung back around. 'That shows honour.'

Philip shook his head. 'Honour would have kept him from touching you in the first place.'

Heat mounted her cheeks. She could not tell even her brother, the person who had been closer to her than anyone else before Dev, that she had seduced Deverell.

'Have you ever been in love, Philip?'

Now it was his turn to look away from her. 'Once.'

'And did it make you do foolish things?' she asked softly, knowing that she would do anything for Dev.

He clenched his fists. 'Yes. Damn it.'

The handle on the door connecting her room to Dev's shook. Then heavy banging came loud and clear.

'Pip, are you in there? What is going on?'

Dev's voice penetrated the wood panel. Pippa shot a harried glance at her twin who put one finger to his lips.

'Let me tell him,' Pippa asked. 'He will help you.'

'I don't need his help. Or yours for that matter.'

'Is what you are doing that secret or…that dangerous?'

More than anything she wanted him to tell her no. She had just found him alive and despite their argument, she worried about him.

'What I do is my own business. I don't trust him.'

'I do,' she said softly.

'So you say.' Philip moved toward the door leading into the hallway.

'Please.' She tried one last time, wondering if she would tell Deverell without Philip's permission.

'I will think on it.'

Her patience snapped. For all she knew, Philip would leave the house and disappear as soon as he left her room. Then she might never find him again until he chose to be discovered. Or until he turned up dead, and even then she might never find out about it. They had been more than lucky to stumble onto someone who knew he was headed here.

She made her decision. 'You can stay here and meet Dev now, or I will tell him who you are, and we will go to Lord Holland and have the house and grounds turned inside out until you are found.'

Amazement quickly turned to fury in Philip. 'Whose flesh and blood are you?'

'Yours, Philip, but I cannot take the chance that you will disappear on me. Grandfather needs you. He nearly died when we got that letter. If I return without you, I don't know what will happen.'

'Pippa!' Dev's voice penetrated the door. 'What is going on? Let me in.'

Pippa kept her focus on Philip. 'What will it be?'

With ill grace, her twin nodded. Not taking her eyes off Philip, Pippa opened the connecting door. Dev, looking suspicious and worried, stepped through. He stopped cold when he saw the other man.

'You,' Dev said.

'What?' Pippa said. 'Have you seen each other before?'

Philip made a mocking bow. 'We meet again, Lord Deverell. Only this time I bear no tray of food for your comfort.'

'Who is this man?' Dev asked, moving to put a protective arm around Pippa. 'And why is he in your bedchamber?'

'The place you make your own?' Philip said sarcastically, taking a step closer.

Dev looked from one to the other. The hair was a different color, but the eyes were the same brilliant green, the lips full Cupid's bows. Even their stance bore a resemblance, the same hands on hips, feet shoulder width apart.

'Philip LeClaire, Viscount Staunton,' he said, positive he was correct.

'At your service,' Philip said with a sneer. 'Now let my sister go.'

Instead of releasing Pippa, who stood stiffly in his embrace, Dev studied the situation. Staunton wasn't a small man, which didn't surprise him, since Pippa was not a small woman. With his wound, he would be hard pressed to tackle him.

He grimaced to himself. Still one more time when his being less than whole made things difficult. Thankfully, he had slipped a pistol into his left pocket when Pippa's door had been locked. He withdrew it now.

'What are you doing?' Pippa asked, one hand raised in shock.

Dev, anticipating that she might intervene for her twin, reluctantly stepped from her. 'Move away from the door, Staunton,' he ordered.

Philip, his sneer turning to surprise, did as told. He cast a fulminating glance at his sister. 'And you trusted him,' he said bitterly. 'Remind me to tell you about the Frenchman I trusted.'

'What are you doing?' Pippa demanded again, her voice rising. Her hair seemed to stand on end, so agitated was she.

Not taking his eyes off Staunton, Dev moved closer to the spy. 'Sit in the chair.'

Rather than do as he was told, Staunton stopped with the chair between them. His gaze held Pippa's. Dev knew there was going to be trouble and cursed his infirmity.

'Don't make me hurt you,' he said through lips gone stiff.

'I don't understand,' Pippa said, her voice only marginally calmer. 'I thought you were trying to help me find my brother, Dev. Not capture him.'

The urge to run his fingers through his hair was strong. Denying it added to Dev's tension. 'Your brother is a spy who has betrayed his countrymen to death.'

'You are crazy,' Staunton said.

'You are wanted for treason,' Dev replied.

Shock froze Staunton's features. Pippa gasped. Dev took advantage of the situation and moved to the bell pull over the fireplace.

Seeing him, Pippa moaned in despair. 'You can't do this.

He isn't a traitor.' She turned desperate eyes on her brother. 'Tell him the truth.'

Instead, Staunton bolted for the door.

Hating what he was doing, but knowing he had no other choice, Dev fired. The ball went into the thick oak wood door not more than five feet ahead of Staunton, just as he had intended.

'The next one will hit you,' Dev said through clenched teeth.

Staunton turned, feet planted apart, face tense. He took the measure of his opponent and said, 'You would, too.'

Dev nodded. 'I lost too many friends at Waterloo to allow a man like you to escape.'

Outside the room commotion reigned. Footsteps pounded down the hall. Voices rose in surprise and panic. Minutes later the door burst open and two armed footmen stood framed in the threshold. Their shocked gazes took in the chaos of the room and the deadly confrontation.

'Take this man into custody,' Dev ordered before anyone could find their wits to speak.

As one they moved on Staunton who did nothing to resist them. 'You have won. For now.'

Immediately after, Lord and Lady Holland arrived. 'Frightful mess,' Lord Holland said. 'Was he trying to rob you?'

'No, sir,' Dev said, setting his pistol on the nearby mantel. 'I would like to explain the situation to you in private.'

'How diverting,' Lady Holland murmured. She moved to Pippa. 'Are you hurt, Pippen?'

Numbly, Pippa shook her head.

Staunton was bound and taken to the butler's pantry where the silver was kept, it being decided that that was the easiest room to guard. Dev promised his host an explanation first thing in the morning.

The room cleared quickly until only Dev and Pippa remained.

She turned stricken green eyes on him. 'I trusted you.'

# *Chapter Nine*

Dev reached for her, but she sidestepped him. 'Pippa, I'm more sorry than I can ever explain.'

'You are a devil,' she spat at him. 'You betrayed me and, more importantly, you betrayed my brother.'

'I did what I had to.'

'You did what you wanted to.' She took a step toward him. Her fist swung up and caught him squarely on the jaw.

'I deserved that,' he said quietly, wishing she would hit him again. The agony in her eyes made him feel even worse than he had anticipated.

She turned away and great racking sobs shook her body. 'I hate you,' she said, the words muffled by her hands. 'I hate you so much I could kill you.'

'I would do anything for you, Pippa. I owe you my life. But I cannot let your brother remain free.'

She rounded on him like a tornado. 'And to think I told Philip to trust you—as I trusted you. He didn't want to. He was cleverer than I.' Her mouth twisted. 'I loved you. I thought you could do nothing I would not admire. How stupid I was.'

Dev's stomach twisted. Love. It was a word, an emotion, he had avoided when he thought of her. He had been protective of his feelings after what had happened with Samantha. He had taken pleasure where he wanted without allowing himself to feel deeply. Oh, he had vowed to marry Pippa, but he hadn't let her into the part of him he had walled off when Samantha married Jon. He would be glad of that, if her pain didn't hurt him so much.

'Pippa, he revealed the identities of two British spies in Paris. Both men were killed.'

'I don't believe that. Philip would never do that.'

Dev shrugged, knowing there was no way he could convince her, but determined to do so. So he tried again.

'Then who would? We found a man who remembered Philip. Wellington told me another spy escaped, telling him that Philip was supposed to warn the remaining two and then make his way north to Brussels. The other two are dead and Philip never returned.'

Pippa scrubbed at her eyes. 'I don't know why those things happened. Why did you not ask Philip before having him bound and imprisoned?'

Dev groaned and ran his fingers through his hair. 'Because the two of you didn't give me a chance. If you remember, Philip didn't trust me. He was going to escape when I came into the room. I had no choice. I'll ask him tomorrow, but no matter what his answer, I must take him to London. I gave my word to Wellington.'

'Your word,' she spat at him. 'For what it is worth.'

Dev drew himself up straight, anger replacing the pain he felt for her. 'I have never broken my word, Pippa.'

She cast a contemptuous look over him. 'No, I don't suppose you have. You didn't promise to keep my brother safe, only to help me find him.'

'Enough.' Dev slammed his hand against a table. 'I have had enough of your recriminations.'

'Well, I have had more than enough of you!' She crossed her hands over her chest. 'Get out of my room.'

Instead of leaving, he studied her. Tear tracks ran down her cheeks, but her chin angled defiantly up.

'I'll leave if you promise not to do anything foolish, like trying to rescue your brother.'

She glared at him. 'I'll promise you nothing.'

Dev's eyes narrowed. 'I know you, Pippa. You are a hoyden who will stop at nothing to achieve what you want, and right now, you want your brother free.' He took a step toward her. 'Promise me.'

She sniffed disdainfully. 'I won't make a promise I might not keep.'

'Then I'll stay here.' He sat in the single chair and stretched his bad leg out. It was starting to throb.

Eyes wide, panic beginning to replace the previous anger, she said, 'You cannot stay here. I won't allow it. Get out.'

'Promise me.'

In one lightning move, she dashed to the mantel and grabbed the pistol. 'Get out. Now. Or I'll do to you what you threatened to do to my twin. I'll put a bullet in you.'

The hard line of her jaw. The tightness in her shoulders. The desolation in her eyes told Dev she would do so with relish, or thought she would.

'Then do so,' he said, leaning forward to massage his painful leg.

She took a great, hiccuping breath. Her eyes stared fixedly into his. She raised the pistol and aimed it at his heart.

Dev watched emotions flit across her features, but the only ones he could name were frustration and resignation. Slowly, her arm dropped.

'Once more, you have won,' she said in a tired voice. 'I

can no more shoot you than I could have let you lay in a Brussels gutter.'

She dropped the pistol to the floor. 'If you'll leave my room, I promise not to do anything tonight.' Her voice strengthened with a flash of her old determination. 'But don't think I won't do everything in my power to rescue my brother. Because I will.'

Slowly, awkwardly, his leg aching and making him clumsy, Dev rose, then bent to retrieve the pistol from the floor. He winced when his right knee threatened to buckle. He saw her gaze flit to his wound, but she made no move to help. For the first time since he'd awakened in her Brussels room, Pippa was failing to succour him. She was gone from him. A small coldness entered Dev's heart.

'I'll be in my room, Pippa. And I trust you to keep your word.'

Without waiting for her to comment, he left.

Pippa watched Dev limp from her room. The urge to go after him and rub his leg and give him a posset to ease the discomfort was strong, but overlying everything was her anger and sense of betrayal. Nothing in their time together could erase the emotional devastation his arrest of Philip had brought.

More weary than she could ever remember being, more exhausted emotionally than she had ever been—even caring for all the dying and wounded at Brussels—she stumbled to the bed and fell across it. It was just as well she had promised Deverell to do nothing tonight. She didn't think she could rise, even if her own life depended on it.

Tears of loss wet her cheeks. In the last days, she had let herself begin to think that Dev might be coming to care for her. She had begun to dream about marriage to him, to think it might be possible. All those dreams were now bitter ashes in her mouth. He cared nothing for her or he would

not have imprisoned her brother. His vow of marriage had
been empty and cruel. He had known all along that when
they found Philip he would betray them.

Pippa curled into a tight ball, unable to continue facing
the reality of what had just happened. Her head ached and
her stomach churned.

As soon as dawn pinked the sky, her promise to Dev
would be over. Tomorrow, before anyone but the servants
rose, she would rescue her twin. And to hell with Deverell
St Simon.

Pippa dozed fitfully. Her limbs were leaden and her eyes
swollen when she woke up. It was still too early for the
maid to start the fire so the room was cold. She rose awkwardly and lit a single candle. By its flickering glow she
gathered together the few belongings she would need, careful to take her bag of herbs.

Her promise to Dev was over.

Cautiously, she opened her chamber door only to be met
by the unsmiling visage of a footman. 'What are you doing
here?' she demanded.

He had the grace to look embarrassed. 'Lord Holland
told me to stay here and make sure you don't leave your
room unescorted, Master Pippen.'

Pippa's mouth thinned. They must have posted their
guard right after her fight with Dev. Even the knowledge
that the servant still thought her a youth did nothing to ease
the disquiet that filled her. Instead of fighting her gaoler
and creating a situation that would accomplish nothing except make the poor man feel more awkward than he already
did, she closed the door. She knew where this order of
incarceration really came from.

She stalked to the door between her and Dev's room and
yanked it open without knocking. She strode into the room

and stopped. She scanned the area. Everything was gone. The normal disorder she associated with Dev was missing.

She knew without even checking the wardrobe that his clothes were not there either. He was gone.

*And with him, her brother.*

She cursed her stupidity. He had probably left as soon as he exited her room last night. He had played with her like a well-worn deck of cards, and she had let him. But no more.

She rushed to the door leading from Dev's room to the hallway. With luck, she would be out the door and down the hall before the footman realized.

Luck was with her. The servant's back was turned to her and she managed to scurry down the hall and out of the house without anyone being the wiser. Reaching the stable without incident, she ordered the groom to saddle a horse so she could go for a ride. The poor man must not have been told about her imprisonment, for he did as she wished. She mounted quickly, and with one last glance at Lord Holland's house, galloped off.

Dev and her brother were probably travelling by carriage, and she could easily catch up with them. As soon as that thought came, she discarded it. She had underestimated Dev last night, she would not do so again. He probably had armed outriders to ensure that Philip didn't escape.

She would go to the nearest town and board the mail coach. She had plenty of money left from that she had withdrawn from the bank in Brussels, and she would be safer travelling with a group of people than riding alone. She would go to Aunt Tabitha in London. That was where Dev was taking Philip to be incarcerated in the Tower, for treason she knew her twin hadn't committed.

The carriage bounced with every rut in the road, and with every jolt, Dev's leg twinged. His head hurt and exhaustion ate at him like mice at ripe cheese. But he couldn't rest as long as Philip Staunton sat across from him, eyes open and body poised for any opportunity to escape.

Dev found that Staunton's steady gaze impressed him. It was a shame a man of the Viscount's quality had been corrupted. But how? The man certainly did not need money or land, and by betraying his country he risked losing everything he owned: title, land and wealth.

Staunton was an enigma he was not qualified to answer. His job had been to catch the man and turn him over for trial. If the Viscount didn't seem to fit his idea of a traitor, then it was because Staunton was good at what he did.

Dev also knew his feelings for Pippa were clouding his judgement of her brother. He pushed thoughts of Pippa away. The last thing he needed was to let his closeness to her make him unreliable. Staunton was too clever not to take advantage of every angle.

'Pippa says you are innocent.' Dev held his captive's gaze. 'I would like to believe her, but you must give me proof.'

Staunton's green eyes met Dev's without blinking. 'I have no proof. Only my word.'

Dev sighed in frustration. 'Your word is no longer good for anything. Two of our men were killed in Paris shortly after you disappeared. Wellington thinks you were responsible.'

Something like pain flickered across Staunton's face before his countenance once more became inscrutable. For long minutes he stared out the window at the passing trees and hedgerows. Finally he turned back to Dev with a strange mixture of determination and desperation on his features.

'I'll tell you what I know, but it proves nothing.'

Dev nodded. 'Perhaps between the two of us, we can find something that neither one alone would recognize.'

'Perhaps,' Staunton said, doubt heavy in his voice. 'I sent George ahead to Wellington with the latest information we had on Napoleon's march north. I stayed behind to contact the others…' He paused and the muscles in his face tensed. 'I told Peter and Alan to leave Paris immediately because I thought someone was aware of their real identities. I think they didn't get out in time. Then I went to join Napoleon's army as a French foot soldier, but before I could enlist I was attacked.'

Dev kept quiet in spite of the questions he longed to ask. Such as, where was Staunton wounded?

As though reading Dev's mind, the Viscount opened his shirt-front and pulled the material away from his right shoulder, showing a clean white scar. 'The knife went through from the back to the front. I was lucky.' His mouth twisted. 'My assailant missed the lung. Otherwise, the letter from the Home Office to my grandfather would have been correct.'

Another pothole sent Dev sliding to one side, and he cursed under his breath at the sharp pain. 'Does your shoulder still hurt?' he asked.

Staunton shrugged, then grimaced. 'Only when I do that. I use it to remind me of how precious life is and how someone betrayed me.'

'Why did you not go directly to Brussels when you were able?' Dev asked, thinking he saw the flaw in Staunton's attempted defence.

Staunton's eyes narrowed to emerald slits. 'Because someone obviously knew who I was and wanted me dead. The last thing I needed to do was come into the open, even to report to Wellington. Nor was there any information I could give the Duke that would have aided him. By the time I recovered from the attack, Waterloo was history.'

Bitterness had crept into the Viscount's voice. 'I have several suspects, but, again, no proof.'

'Who are they?' Dev demanded. 'Wellington can have them watched.'

Staunton stared at Dev. 'I'm not sure I can trust you. After all—' his voice dipped into an ominous growl '—Pippa thought she could trust you and where did it get her?'

Dev felt the blood drain from his face. 'I had a prior commitment. Wellington had already elicited my word that I would find you and bring you in for justice.'

'Justice!' A harsh croak of a laugh came from Staunton. 'The longer I am held in the Tower, the greater the likelihood that whoever is the real double agent or spy will escape.'

'Then tell me who you suspect, and I will follow them.' Dev's mouth twisted. ''Tis the least I can do.'

'I think not.'

The calm, softly spoken words lay between them like an insurmountable wall. Hazel eyes met green in a clash of wills.

Irritation welled up in Dev. 'Then who will you get to trail your suspects? You certainly cannot do it from behind prison walls.' When Staunton did not answer, understanding dawned on Dev. 'You cannot get Pippa to do it. She's a hoyden and would gladly do it for you, but that type of search is dangerous. You cannot justify using her that way.'

'And you can justify using her to slake your passion?' Staunton leaned forward until only inches separated them. 'How many times did you make love to her? What did you tell her to convince her to allow you to do so?'

There was no honourable answer to any of those questions so Dev said nothing.

'When I'm free,' Staunton continued, 'I will kill you for using her so.'

Fury boiled in Dev. 'I admit that what I did was wrong, but I intend to marry your sister.' He paused before pointedly adding, 'And what she and I did together does not threaten her life. What you intend to ask of her could get her killed. Look at what happened to you and the other two agents.'

For a second, Staunton looked doubtful, but that weakness was quickly replaced by implacability. 'We shall see. But whatever I decide, it won't be to trust you. Just as I shall tell Pippa she would be a fool to marry a man like you, one who used her to get to me. And she is no fool.'

The urge to throttle the Viscount rose strong and urgent in Dev. Somehow he resisted. The last thing he needed to do was add to the wall Staunton had built between them. Nor was it any of the Viscount's business what Dev intended to do with Pippa. He was her brother, but his grandfather Earl LeClaire was her guardian. When Staunton was safely behind bars, he would return to Lord Holland's house and get Pippa. From there, he would take her to her home and ask the Earl's permission to wed her. Pippa would fight him, but he was sure her grandfather would see the wisdom of such action.

In the meantime, he had to get Staunton to London. Fortunately, they should soon be met by one of Wellington's agents. Dev had sent a message to the Duke last night after he'd explained the situation to Lord Holland and asked for his host's cooperation. Lord Holland had also promised to keep Pippa safe. Dev hadn't told his host Pippa's real identity, only that the young man needed to be retained until he could return for him.

Somehow, bouncing down the road, Pippa's brother scowling at him and his leg hurting, Dev didn't feel completely confident that when he returned to Lord Holland's country estate things would be as he wished. But he had no other choices.

Five days later, Dev nervously flicked his riding crop against his booted leg, the uninjured one, as he paced Earl LeClaire's salon. The butler had said his master was touring the estate, but that was more than an hour ago. Patience had never been one of his virtues, and it was even harder for him knowing that Pippa might be here. When he'd returned to Lord Holland's estate, he'd been told that Master Pippen had managed to ride out the very morning after he had left with her brother.

Worry and anger had mixed in equal parts as Dev had pondered what to do. His first inclination had been to rush to London and watch the Tower. Pippa knew that was where her brother was headed, and Dev believed she would go there and try to free her twin. He also knew that in London she would be safe with her aunt Tabitha.

In the end he had decided to visit her grandfather. The Earl needed to know his grandson was alive, and Dev needed to ask him for Pippa's hand in marriage. But he hadn't expected to be left cooling his heels for so long once he arrived.

Dev's irritability was compounded by the fact that his right leg ached from riding the last two days straight with only enough rest to ensure he didn't fall out of the saddle from exhaustion. He was tempted to cross to the sideboard and pour himself a glass of whatever the Earl kept in the decanter. But good manners kept him from that transgression.

Just then, the door opened and without ceremony, a tall,

ruddy-complexioned man entered. His hair was thick and silver white, just brushing his well-worn brown corduroy jacket. Unlike Pippa, his eyes were a vivid blue. His strong jaw was outlined by muttonchop whiskers, and his full mouth would have been jovial if it weren't pinched in worry.

Dev found himself instantly comfortable with this man. 'Lord LeClaire,' he said, stepping forward, 'I'm Deverell St Simon. A friend of your granddaughter's.'

'Pippa?' The Earl came closer until Dev could see the deep lines that scored the edges of the older man's eyes and mouth. 'Is she alive? Where is she?'

The smile that had hovered on Dev's lips fled. 'She isn't here?'

'No!' the Earl roared, his face turning dangerously red. 'Nor have I heard from her since she landed at Dover.' His eyes narrowed. 'Were you with her, then? Did Tabitha introduce you?'

Dev knew he was headed for a rocky road, but how much did he reveal? From the Earl's colouring, he needed to be careful. 'Milord, perhaps you should sit down?'

'Not until you tell me where my granddaughter is.' The Earl's imposing height and ample, though not obese, girth stood firmly upright.

Dev had to follow the Earl's example, but his aching leg seemed like a waterlogged roll of paper, ready to bend at any moment. Still, he summoned the same determination that had seen him through battle and held firm.

'If she isn't here, I believe she is in London.' Dev paused, his mind racing. 'With her aunt Tabitha.'

The Earl visibly relaxed, the high colour of his face lessening but not entirely subsiding. He moved to the sideboard Dev had been eyeing earlier.

'Tabitha ain't my first choice, but she's better than nothing. And the two did go to Brussels together.' He poured a generous glass of liquor and asked, 'Care for a drink?'

'Please,' Dev said, hoping that whatever was in the decanter was strong.

The Earl handed him a glass as full as his own. Dev gulped down half, nearly choking as the liquid burned a trail down his throat. Whisky, the same stuff his brother Alastair liked so well. He had never been enamoured of the drink, but he needed its potency now. Within minutes, the ache in his leg seemed far away.

'Here now,' LeClaire bellowed. 'Sit down before you fall down. You're swaying like a birch in a heavy wind.'

'Just my leg. Been on it rather too long.' Still, he was grateful to take the chair indicated and even more glad of the warmth from the fire which was just feet away.

The Earl took a seat.

'Why did you think Pippa was here? And where did you meet her?' He peppered Dev with questions, his gruff voice still sounding strained. 'Do you know anything about my grandson?'

It seemed to Dev that telling the Earl about Staunton would be easier than threading his way through Pippa's adventures. He told LeClaire as briefly as possible about his grandson. Before he could launch into an abbreviated version of Pippa's story, the Earl surged up with a roar.

'Philip is no traitor. I will have Wellington's head for this impertinence, this insult to our family name. We fought for William the Conqueror. That upstart Wellington.'

The Earl paced the room, his heavy footfalls ringing whenever he stepped off the heavy carpet. Dev watched, realizing why Pippa was so worried about her grandfather's health. The Earl was like a volcano waiting to explode. His face was mottled, and his white hair stood on end.

Dev levered himself out of the chair and blocked the

Earl's path, forcing the older gentleman to stop or run him down. 'Milord, you should sit down and calm yourself. I understand you suffer from apoplexy and this excitement cannot be good for you.'

The Earl glared at Dev. 'I'll do what I damn well please, and no scoundrel who has helped imprison my grandson is going to tell me anything.'

Dev, knowing he wasn't going to win this confrontation, stepped aside. He should have known it would be a mistake to come here, but his honour had demanded it. Just as his honour demanded that he ask for Pippa's hand in marriage even though he knew the Earl would refuse.

The older man continued to stalk the room. Gradually his colour eased.

'Lord LeClaire,' Dev said, 'I have one more thing to tell you.'

Pippa's grandfather came to a halt, hands on hips, feet shoulder width apart. The stance was so much like Pippa that, for a second, Dev grinned, but no longer. The reminder was more unsettling than happy. That was Pippa's reaction when she had wanted him to do something. Right now, Dev knew it would be a long time before Pippa cared enough about him to want him to do anything but stay out of her life.

'Speak up and then get out,' the Earl said, obviously at the end of his tolerance.

Dev met the older man's gaze. 'I would like to marry Pippa.'

Incredulity arched the Earl's white, bushy brows. 'You have a lot of gumption for a scoundrel. First you tell me you have captured my only grandson and that you've sent him to the Tower to await trial for treason. Now you say you want to marry my granddaughter. Well, even if she'd have you—which I doubt after what you've done to her twin—I'd sooner see you in hell than have you in the family.'

Dev clamped down on a sharp retort about the honour of the Earl's family. Antagonizing the man more would do nothing for his suit. He intended to marry Pippa, even if he had to drag her screaming to the altar.

Without another word, Dev bowed and left.

## Chapter Ten

Two weeks later, Pippa stared at her image in the large mirror situated in the middle of her bedchamber in her aunt Tabitha's London house. She had arrived here a bedraggled ragamuffin, stiff and tired from travelling in stagecoaches. Between now and then, Tabitha had taken her in hand and made her into something Pippa had never imagined for herself. She was a beauty.

Where had her square jaw and high cheekbones gone? What had happened to the hard glitter of her eyes that her brother had so often told her was more like that of a bird of prey than a girl? Even the sharp angles of her figure which had allowed her to masquerade as a boy were gone. All disguised by style and illusion.

'I cannot believe that is me,' she said, her voice soft with awe. 'I've never looked this way.'

A light, tinkling laugh was followed by a movement behind Pippa. 'My dear, this was nothing. A little eye blacking, a smidgen of rouge, and the proper clothing.' Aunt Tabitha waved a small, well-shaped hand. 'Nothing. Everything was in place, just waiting for the right touch.'

Pippa turned, a smile of gratitude on her lips. 'Aunt Tabitha, you are a miracle worker. Without you I would have never known to do any of this. Just as I would have never been able to find my way into Society as quickly as you have guided me.'

Tabitha Montcleve, sister of Pippa's grandmother, laughed again and took her grandniece into a lavender scented embrace. 'Child, you underestimate yourself. I had nothing to do with this. You are the one who is wearing daring colours and being just a little *risqué*. Society loves gossip, and you are providing that in plenty. Now hurry or we'll be late for Maria Sefton's rout. And we must not miss it. She is one of the *ton*'s foremost hostesses.'

Aunt Tabitha stepped back while the maid draped a shawl over Pippa's bare shoulders. As always, Pippa was glad she had made the choice to come to Tabitha. She had told her aunt everything about her travels except that she had fallen in love with Deverell St Simon and become his lover. That was something she had to forget or she would go crazy. Nor would a lady, which Tabitha was, condone such behavior, and Pippa had found in the past weeks that her aunt's opinion mattered.

Arm in arm, they swept from the room and down the stairs. Tabitha's coach was already waiting for them, and it was a matter of minutes before they joined the line of people waiting to disembark from their carriages at Lady Sefton's ball.

Inside was a crush. People milled everywhere. The rich colours of dowagers in their purples and young ladies in demure white muslin swirled against the darker drama of the gentlemen in evening dress. Jewels of every description glittered in the blazing light of numerous chandeliers. In short, Lady Sefton's gathering was a huge success. The fact that this was the little Season, while Parliament was in session before the holidays, had not made a difference.

Pippa paused at one side while Tabitha went on to talk

with several friends. She scanned the room for anyone she might know and particularly for anyone who might possibly be one of the traitors she was determined to find for Philip.

'Lady Philippa, may I have this dance?'

Pippa started, not having noticed Mr Hopwell's approach. He was a tall, slim man dressed in the height of fashion. His brown hair was done in an immaculate Brutus, and his shirt points were high without being ridiculously so. He was also involved in the government.

'Of course,' she said, taking his proffered hand and going with him to form one of the couples. Out of the corner of her eye, she caught her great-aunt's satisfied smile. Pippa smiled back.

So far, she had managed to become one of the most sought-after young ladies in the little Season. This was ideal. The politicians and men active in government were in town, and these were exactly the people Pippa was most interested in meeting. When she had met with Philip on first arriving, her twin had told her the real spy must have connections that allowed him to mingle with the makers of England's foreign policy.

'How are you enjoying your visit?' Mr Hopwell's question forced Pippa's attention back to him and the present.

'Very well,' Pippa answered, following his lead. Thank goodness they were not waltzing. She had never been good at the dance.

Off to one side, the Marchioness of Witherspoon stood talking to a Cabinet member. She glanced at Pippa with a curious look on her perfectly moulded face. Pippa turned away.

Since coming to London, Pippa had seen the woman at several functions but had not met her. Nor did she want to. The last thing she needed was to have the Marchioness wonder where she had seen her before. That was how masquerades were undone.

The music stopped and Mr Hopwell escorted Pippa back to her aunt Tabitha, who stood up at their approach. Tabitha had come to London shortly after her younger sister married Earl LeClaire, and had soon married a well-connected gentleman. She had been a widow for the last twenty years. Barely coming to Pippa's chin, her aunt was still fashionable and lively. She was considered one of the premier hostesses in the *ton* and had frequently tried to get Pippa to come for a Season.

Aunt Tabitha smiled at Mr Hopwell and said, 'If you will excuse us.' After he bowed and left, she took Pippa's arm and drew her away. 'Child, I would like you to meet someone. I'm not on close terms with her Grace, but I have always found her to be most charming when we have met.'

Pippa raised one jet black brow. 'Her Grace? Which one, or are there that many?' she jested lightly.

Tabitha gave her a small smile of appreciation. 'There are more ''your Graces'' than ''your Grace''. It comes of having widows and dowagers. But come, her Grace requested that I bring you to one of the rooms set aside for informal meetings.'

Bitten by curiosity, Pippa followed. The demi-train on her cobalt blue evening dress swished with each step, its rich colour in direct contrast to the white muslins worn by most of the other young women present. For a moment, Pippa felt like an exotic animal out of its element, but that quickly passed. She had never been a shy young maiden, and was even less so now.

She and Tabitha slipped through a side door. By aristocratic standards, the room was small, but it was filled to the brim with trinkets and artwork. A thick burgundy rug cushioned the floor while matching curtains blocked out the winter cold. Flames licked up the chimney, providing warmth and light.

Standing a safe distance from the fire was a woman, her thick black hair caught up in a fashionable knot. A diamond-studded clip allowed several gleaming curls to tumble on to her long neck.

'Come, child…' the Duchess of Rundell held out her hand '…and let me get a closer look at you as you really are.'

Pippa faltered and would have turned tail and run if Aunt Tabitha hadn't gripped her arm. Forced to stand her ground, she sputtered, 'Your Grace.'

'Tut, tut, Pippen—or should I say, Lady Philippa. What happened to calling me Alicia?' The Duchess's lips curved into a mischievous grin.

Pippa took another step forward and felt her aunt release her arm. The quiet sound of the door closing told her Tabitha had gone.

'How did you know?' Pippa took another step forward.

With a tiny shake of her head, Alicia moved to Pippa and took her hands. 'How could I not? Even dressed as a boy, you had the slender curves and soft, smooth complexion of a young woman.' She gave Pippa a conspiratorial look. 'Not to mention the mannerisms of a woman. The time you rushed to comfort Dev after he found out about Patrick was more revealing than anything else.'

Pippa could do nothing but stare. And all this time she had thought her imitation of a man had been well done. 'Thank goodness not everyone is as perceptive as you, ma'am.'

'Particularly my son,' the Duchess said drily.

Pippa nodded, her gaze sliding away. She didn't want to bring Deverell into this conversation. In the past weeks, she had managed to put him from her mind. Or so she constantly told herself.

'Sit down, child. We have much to discuss.'

The Duchess released Pippa's hands and sat down in one of the two chairs pulled close to the fire. With a wary look, Pippa sat in the other.

'What do you call yourself?' Alicia asked. 'I cannot imagine your family calls you Lady Philippa or even Pippen.'

'Pippa, your Grace.'

'Alicia,' Dev's mother said firmly. 'Let us not start at the very beginning again.'

Pippa managed to smile in spite of her discomfort. 'Alicia. But I cannot call you that in public.'

The Duchess cocked her head to one side. 'No, I don't suppose you can since we aren't supposed to know each other. My, how you have changed.'

Pippa flushed. 'Aunt Tabitha took me in hand.'

'And a very nice job she has done. You are stunning. I understand that you are being called the Dark Aphrodite. Very appropriate.'

Pippa's blush deepened. ''Tis merely the trappings.'

Alicia's smile softened. 'The lip gloss, rouge and blacking only bring out your natural beauty. As does the bold colour of your gown. But if you were not already handsome, the extras would be overpowering. I knew, even in Brussels when you were dressed as a boy, that you would make a pretty girl. Dev will be very impressed.'

Pippa's discomfort at the compliments she wasn't used to receiving turned to cold anger. 'Lord Deverell is the last person I care to impress.'

'Ah, yes, the situation with your brother. I'm sorry, child. Dev was always my devil-may-care child, but when honour was and is concerned, there is no one else more strict than he.'

Pippa took a deep breath to try and calm herself. The last person she should denigrate Dev to was his mother. In an attempt to change the conversation, she asked, 'Why did you want to see me, and how did you know it was me?'

The Duchess looked away for a long moment, as though marshalling her forces, before turning her gaze back to Pippa. 'You are all the rage in Society, with your brother's situation and your own beauty. At first I didn't know for sure if you were the Pippen I remembered, but Deverell arrived in town recently and he told me everything, or what he considered important.'

Under the Duchess's kind, yet knowing look, Pippa found herself even more uncomfortable than she had initially been. Had Dev told his mother they'd been lovers? She doubted it, but his mother was very perceptive. She might easily have seen beyond the surface of Dev's tale. After all, she'd seen that Pippen had not been a boy.

'Dev wants to marry you, child. He thinks he must marry you and won't rest until he has accomplished it.'

Pippa stood abruptly, nearly knocking her chair over. 'Never.'

The Duchess smiled gently. 'Never is a long time, my dear.' In the same reasonable tone she continued, 'I remember you knocking over your chair in Brussels. I believe it was in my dining room when you'd been taken by surprise, just as now. But somehow, I cannot imagine that Dev's wishing to marry you is something you didn't already know.'

Pippa stood resolute against the older woman's patience and wondered if her mother, had she lived, would have been as diligent in caring for her children as the Duchess was. Knowing she would have liked greatly to have had a mother like this woman made it impossible for Pippa to stay angry at the Duchess's interference.

'You are right, ma'am. I knew Dev wanted to marry me, but that was before he betrayed me and sent my brother to the Tower.'

'It is Dev's honour. Can you find it in your heart to forgive him for what he has done and to accept him for what he is?'

The urge to do all of that was strong. No matter what she told herself in her sane moments, Pippa missed Dev. Missed him horribly. His little kindnesses. His loving. She even missed tending to his aches and pains. It was the way she imagined a wife would feel about her husband. No matter how much she reviled him now or how hurt she felt by his treachery, she could not totally cut him from her heart.

But she had to. She could never trust him again, and without trust there could be no commitment.

The Duchess's soft voice added, 'I would like you to think about what Dev is offering. I would like very much to have you in the family.'

Pippa gaped. She could not help herself. The Duchess was so forthright and honest, but she had never imagined Dev's mother would want her in the family. Nor would the Duchess if she knew everything. No mother would want her son marrying a woman so sunk in depravity that she slept with him when no vows of marriage or love had been exchanged. Yet, the thought of having the Duchess as a mother-in-law was enticing.

A light knock on the door was followed by it opening before the Duchess could say anything else.

'Mother,' Dev said, stepping into the room and closing the door behind him. 'Maria told me you were in here.'

His gaze passed over Pippa to his mother. A look of

shock crossed his features. He stopped in his tracks and his attention came back to Pippa.

'Pippa? Is that you?'

Pippa drew herself up. How dare he look so surprised. It wasn't as though he hadn't known she was a woman. The way he was reacting, one would think she had been a perfect dowd before.

'You have eyes,' she snapped. 'Who do you think I am?'

'I…you're…beautiful. That is, not that you weren't before, but…'

The Duchess's melodious chuckle filled the chilly silence. 'Close your mouth, Deverell, before you say something you can never recover from. Besides, you look like a carp caught out of water.'

'He looks like a Judas,' Pippa said softly, coldly, as she moved to the door.

Dev watched Pippa rush past him, resisting the urge to reach out and grab her. In seconds, the light scent of lilac was the only thing left to remind him that she had been here. She hadn't worn fragrance before, and he found he liked what she had chosen.

'Your timing is atrocious,' his mother said.

'My timing?' he asked, turning around to face her. 'What were you doing with Pippa in the first place?'

'Deverell,' the Duchess said, warning in her voice, 'I am your mother. Don't be demanding explanations of me.'

He ran the fingers of his right hand through his hair, messing the once-perfect Corinthian cut. 'I'm sorry, Mother. But why were you talking to her?'

'Because someone had to try and make her see reason, and it was patently obvious from what you have told me that you aren't going to be that person.' Exasperation tightened her mouth.

'What did you do?' Dev took a step toward her, beginning to fear what he knew she'd done.

'I told her she should marry you and let the past go.'

Dev groaned. 'That is the worst thing you could have done. Now her back is up and I shall be hard pressed to even get near enough to say hello, let alone talk to her.'

'Perhaps.' Alicia rose and drew her paisley shawl around her shoulders. 'We shall see. I'll call on her later this week.'

'Mother,' Dev said, at the end of his tolerance, 'you are a meddler. Please stay out of my affairs before they're beyond saving.'

The Duchess turned a hard stare on him. 'Have you told her you love her?'

Taken aback, Dev stepped away. 'No.'

'Then try. Love works miracles if you let it.'

Dev opened his mouth to answer, but nothing came out and his mother was gone before he could think of what to say. Tell Pippa he loved her? He liked her. He desired her. He owed her his life. But did he love her?

That was a question he couldn't answer.

Pippa didn't stop running from Dev until she was at the entrance to the large room where the dancing still went on. If anything, there were more people than when she had left to visit with the Duchess. What a disaster that had been.

What was Deverell doing here? And why had his appearance made her heart race like thunder clouds across a stormy sky? But she knew why.

No matter what he had done, no matter how awful his betrayal of her trust, no matter how hard she tried, she could not make herself stop loving him. Not yet.

'Lady Philippa LeClaire?'

Pippa jumped. She hadn't realized someone was beside

her. The Marchioness of Witherspoon stood not two feet away, a faint smile curving her full lips.

'Lady Witherspoon,' Pippa said, with only a small catch in her breath. What was the woman doing?

Lady Witherspoon shrugged her milk-white shoulders. 'I am being too forward, but that is not unusual. Although—' she cocked her head to one side '—you know my name, so perhaps I am not overly bold.'

Pippa kept the smile on her face. 'You are known as the ''Pocket Venus'' and your name is on the lips of all the gentlemen.'

'Ah.' She smiled. 'Something to be admired, no?'

Was there a hint of derision in her voice? Pippa could not be sure. 'Decidedly something that brings you to the attention of other women.'

'Yes, that is often so.' She waved a tiny, white hand in dismissal. 'But that is not why I have intruded. I wished to make myself known to you, and we have no friends in common so I had to do it myself.'

Pippa sighed in silent relief. The Marchioness didn't recognize her or she would know they had the Duchess of Rundell in common. 'I'm flattered, milady.'

'I wanted to tell you that I admire your courage. Your brother is in the Tower, yet you speak openly of his innocence. You must love him very much.'

What a strange thing to say to a complete stranger. Pippa looked at the Frenchwoman whose accent had become almost so thick as to obscure her words. Lady Witherspoon's large blue eyes were wide and worried, almost as though she worried as much about Philip as Pippa did. The idea brought an upward curve to Pippa's lips. Now she was being fanciful, another result of seeing Deverell St Simon. But still, the woman's actions were very uncommon. Yet, she found herself liking the Frenchwoman for her concern about a person whom she didn't know.

'You have a kind heart, Lady Witherspoon. Philip is my twin, and we have a twin's affinity.'

Mr Hopwell chose that moment to approach them. 'Ladies,' he said, bowing deeply, 'would you honor me by going into supper?'

Pippa considered declining, but he was familiar with many Cabinet members. Mr Hopwell was also very personable. Plus his grey eyes were filled with admiration, an emotion she decided would go a long way toward dispelling the irritation caused by Deverell's unexpected appearance.

Smiling brightly, Pippa said, 'I would be delighted, Mr Hopwell.'

Lady Witherspoon accepted the offer as well, and the three of them made their way to the supper room. Mr. Hopwell seated them and then hurried to the buffet table to fill plates with the offered delicacies.

'He is so charming,' Lady Witherspoon said.

'He can be,' Pippa answered without thinking, her mind having wandered back to Deverell. Why was he at this party?

'Can be?' Lady Witherspoon asked. 'I have never known him to be anything else.'

The puzzlement in the other woman's voice brought Pippa back to the supper room with a jolt. 'Oh, Mr Hopwell. Yes, he is very nice to be around. Always agreeable.'

'And a very good dancer.'

'That, too,' Pippa said, making herself smile.

The object of their discussion returned, giving each lady a plate piled high with lobster patties, oysters, and other delights. He waved to a footman and got champagne flutes.

'To the Exquisite Opposites,' he said, raising his glass.

'The Dark Aphrodite and the blonde Pocket Venus. May we always be blessed with your company.'

Still not used to the profuse compliments some of the men paid women in the *ton*, Pippa flushed. This was almost as bad as facing the Duchess of Rundell.

Lady Witherspoon laughed her tinkling laugh and changed the subject. 'Mr Hopwell, how is Parliament going? My husband does not attend regularly but, this being my adopted country and after what happened in my own not so very long ago—' she shuddered delicately '—I am always interested in the ways of government.'

Mr Hopwell smiled. 'I wouldn't dream of boring you ladies with such talk.'

'No, no,' Lady Witherspoon interjected, 'it would not be boring at all. Please.'

Pippa listening, wondered briefly why the Marchioness would care, but decided the woman meant exactly what she had said. She was interested. She was known as one of the most gracious women in the *ton*. Getting a man to talk about his interests was one of the surest ways of being thought charming.

As Mr Hopwell warmed to his topic, Pippa found her mind wandering back to her meeting with Dev and his mother. The memory made the skin between her shoulder blades tense. It was exactly how she had felt when Dev looked at her or touched her. Her gaze roamed the crowded room to come to rest on a man lounging in the doorway. Deverell.

Dev watched Pippa flirt with the Honourable Mark Hopwell over lobster patties and thought about calling the man out. But that would create a scandal and make people wonder what Pippa meant to him when he wasn't even supposed to know her. No, he might want to do bodily harm to Hopwell, but he wouldn't.

Still, it was damned hard to watch Pippa make eyes at the man and do nothing. What had happened to her?

'Lord Deverell St Simon?' a soft, feminine voice asked.

Dev turned sharply. A small, older woman looked up at him. Her silver hair was partially hidden by a plum-coloured silk turban, and her slender, almost frail figure was fashionably swathed in matching material. Her complexion was pale, perfect and lightly wrinkled. Laugh lines framed her full lips and accentuated her eyes. Her emerald green eyes, the same colour as Pippa's, sparkled up at him.

Dev returned her smile. 'Mrs Montcleve, my pleasure to meet you.'

She twinkled. 'I see that you are as astute as you are brave. But, please, call me Tabitha.'

'My pleasure, ma'am.' Dev made her a perfect leg, his grace only slightly marred by the stiffness of his right thigh. 'Would you care for something to drink?'

'A glass of champagne would not go amiss,' she replied, laying her hand lightly on his preferred arm.

Together they entered the supper room. Dev felt Pippa's gaze on them and smiled innocently at her. She, her grandfather and brother might think him lower than a grub, but if Aunt Tabitha was willing to talk to him then all was not lost.

He seated Mrs Montcleve and fetched her a plate before sitting across from her. 'Please excuse me for being so abrupt, ma'am, but since we have never been introduced I wonder why you have sought me out.'

She studied him for long moments. 'You are a very forth-right young man. I like that. Today's young people are too namby-pamby. In my day, we called a rake a rake and a trollop a trollop. I believe we shall do well together.'

Dev laughed outright, something he hadn't done in a long time. 'Tolerably. Are you a meddler like my mother?'

Without an ounce of contrition, she replied, 'Absolutely. Seeing young people make a muddle of their lives is the biggest waste I can imagine.' For a second she looked wistful, and her eyes took on a faraway look. 'I know what it is like to have that which you want most in life within your grasp and then to lose it. I don't want that to happen to my great-niece.'

'And why is your great-niece wasting her life?'

'Do not pretend ignorance. It doesn't become you.'

He bowed his head in acknowledgement of her hit. 'I have asked her to marry me, but she won't do so after what I had to do to her brother.'

'My great-nephew is innocent, Lord Deverell. I have no doubt that with time he will be proved honourable. Meanwhile, I expect you to woo Philippa until she sees the error of her ways. It would help immensely if you would tell her you believe Philip is not a traitor and help her prove that point.'

Dev met her gaze for long minutes, neither of them speaking. Pippa's aunt was more than he had anticipated and asked more of him than he was ready to give.

'Wellington thinks him guilty, and I cannot go against my commanding officer without more proof than Staunton was willing or able to give me.'

The older woman's foot tapped impatiently on the floor, matched by her rapidly tapping fingers. 'You are as stubborn as she. I'm not asking you to flout Wellington, only to help Pippa in her search for the real traitor.'

Before Dev could decide what to answer, a husky alto voice said, 'Aunt Tabitha, you are consorting with the enemy.'

Pippa stood not three feet away, her green eyes flashing like the finest emeralds when held up to sunlight. She looked ready to spit fire at him.

'Sit down, Philippa, before you cause a scene,' her aunt ordered.

'No, thank you. I would rather consort with a criminal. A traitor, to be exact.'

With that parting shot, she spun around and stalked off. Several heads turned to watch. Dev knew that by morning the latest *on dit* would be Lady Philippa LeClaire's snubbing of Lord Deverell St Simon. At least everyone would attribute it to his being responsible for her twin being imprisoned in the Tower. No one would know that everything was made worse because he had once been her lover.

'Foolish chit,' Aunt Tabitha said. 'But it is just as well that she is not here. I have much to say to you.'

Dev raised one brow. She rapped him with her closed fan. 'Ouch. My mother has that same nasty habit, ma'am.'

'And very likely for the same reason, young man. Now, listen well. From here on, you and I are allies. Pippa, foolish chit that she is, has been trying to discover who is the actual traitor. And Philip, selfish young man that he can be, has been encouraging her to do this dangerous act.'

Dev's hands clenched white. 'I knew this would happen. Staunton has much to answer for.'

Aunt Tabitha made a moue of disgust. 'Sometimes my great-nephew is beyond my comprehension. But he wants to get out of the Tower. What I need from you—' she impaled him with her green gaze '—is to protect Pippa. She won't listen to me when I advise caution—'

'And you think she will heed me, ma'am? I fear you are far out of it there.' Bitterness curled Dev's lip.

'Yes, I know, but you, at least, can follow her. I am too old to be out of my bed once I reach it.'

Dev leaned forward, anger beginning to form a hard knot in his gut. 'Is she sneaking out to run Staunton's errands?'

Tabitha glanced around to see that no one was close

enough to hear her whispered words. 'She is doing worse than that, I fear. I have reason to believe she intends to break into the homes of some of England's foremost peers.'

'What?' Dev hissed, barely keeping himself from shouting his outrage. 'That is beyond even what I would expect of her.'

Tabitha's tapping fingers escalated their pace. 'Exactly what I thought. I believe it is at Philip's urging.'

'That bas—scoundrel. Pardon me, ma'am. I know he is family, but what he is making Pippa do is inexcusable.'

She frowned at him. 'Do you think I don't realize that? That is why I have come to you. Regardless of what Pippa says, you care for her and you owe her a great deal. I am asking you to protect her from herself and her brother.'

'On my honour.'

A mischievous grin broke through Tabitha's irritation. 'I count on it, for we know where your honour has left you.'

Dev bowed his head in mock answer. 'I would do nothing differently where Staunton is concerned. Now, how are we going to work on this, ma'am?'

'I shall keep you informed through these tête-à-têtes. Tonight I came up to you because I want Pippa to see that I accept you and intend to speak with you. In the future, she will be upset with me, but not surprised to see me talking to you. If I have information you need and I haven't seen you, I will have it delivered. Most likely it will be by a street urchin so that no one in my employ can let slip to Pippa what I am doing.'

Dev's admiration for the spirited lady grew. He grinned. 'I see that Pippa and Staunton come by their adventurousness and, can I say it, deviousness honourably.'

She chuckled. 'The right side of the blanket is the way we would have put it in my day.'

He smiled at her, some of his earlier tension easing. With

this formidable lady's help, he would be able to keep track of Pippa. No matter what the hoyden did, he would be there. He would also get the chance to further his suit.

He raised his flute of champagne in a toast. 'To our partnership, ma'am. May we accomplish what we set out to do.'

Tabitha raised her glass. 'To your future wedding and the release of my great-nephew.'

Both drank down the liquid in one long gulp.

## Chapter Eleven

**D**everell lounged in the chair set well to the back of the Duke of Rundell's box at Drury Lane. From here he could see while not being seen. Just a few months before, he had come here to watch Samantha perform on the stage. It seemed a lifetime ago. He hadn't wanted to come tonight, but Tabitha's note had said she and Pippa would be here.

Below and to his right was Mrs Montcleve's box. Tabitha and Pippa sat there, the older woman waving to acquaintances. Edmund Kean was on the stage and, as usual, his acting was superb, but most of the members of the *ton* were here to socialize. He was intrigued to notice that Pippa tried to watch the play.

Dressed in a cold white muslin gown with vivid green ribbons, she stood out like a sparkling diamond. A simple, single strand choker of emeralds circled her long neck and solitary emerald drops fell from her ears. The colour of her dress might be that of a chit in her first season, but the rest of her ensemble was not.

Dev's gaze ran hungrily over her. The *décolletage* was a little too low for a young girl. The smooth whiteness of her breasts crested above green ribbon. She looked more like a dashing widow or young matron. His blood ran hot, and he remembered warm nights in Paris and long, passionate nights at Lord Holland's country estate.

She was his.

'Engrossed in contemplation of the Dark Aphrodite, the *ton*'s latest darling?' Jonathan St Simon, Marquess of Langston asked, entering the box and taking a seat.

Pulled with a jolt from the avenue down which his thoughts were headed, Dev gave his older brother a wry grin. 'It is becoming a boring habit of mine, I must admit.'

'Almost as boring as your mooncalf pursuit of Samantha was nearly a year ago.' To keep any sting from the words, Jon clapped Dev on the shoulder and drew him into a brief hug. 'We have missed you. Sam was wondering just yesterday why you haven't called.'

It was on the tip of Dev's tongue to say a gracious social lie, but he caught himself. This was his brother, married to the woman he had once thought himself irrevocably in love with. 'I didn't think you would want me to after what happened.'

Jon shook his head. 'Dev, how can you be so stupid? You made your peace with me long ago. I distinctly remember you visiting me before the wedding to give me your congratulations and impress upon me your acceptance of the fact that Sam and I were marrying. Anything else is forgotten.'

Relief spread through Dev like a warm draught of ale. The barrier he had felt between him and Jon seemed to melt away, and some of the old sense of teasing camaraderie came back.

'Since you stole away the first woman I fancied myself in love with, maybe you can help me with this hoyden.'

Entering into the spirit, Jon said, 'You mean Lady Philippa LeClaire, twin of the traitor you put in the Tower? I don't think there is much anyone can do to help you on that front.'

'I'm very much afraid you are right, Jon.'

'Don't be so glum. Break her brother out of jail and you will be a hero in her eyes. Short of that, you can storm her walls. Go visit them in their box. Confront her in a place so public that she will have to endure your company or leave. Make her do something besides avoid you.'

Dev gave his brother a thoughtful look. 'You think so?'

Jon grinned. 'It has been my experience in Parliament that very few will stand up to a blatant confrontation. They might talk behind your back, but not to your face.'

'It might be worth a shot,' Dev murmured, squaring his shoulders as though preparing to go into battle. 'The worst she can do is give me the cut direct.'

'Spoken like a true war hero,' Jon said, giving him a slight shove. 'And come to dinner tomorrow.'

'Absolutely,' Dev said, his mind already on the problem of Pippa.

He exited the box and made his way down several levels. Aunt Tabitha saw him before Pippa.

'Ah, Lord Deverell,' Tabitha said, a dimple peeking out from her right cheek. 'Come in and take a seat.' With her fan, she indicated a chair near Pippa. 'I hear you are possibly to receive a title for your bravery at Hougoumont.'

Dev's stomach twisted. Every time someone brought up that farmstead where Patrick died, he found himself fighting anger and grief.

'There is talk,' he said, knowing the edge in his voice made him sound harsh. 'But no one has offered me a title, and I don't think I would take one. Too many people— people I cared greatly for—died defending Hougoumont. I have no desire to gain from their sacrifices.'

Pippa, who had been studiously ignoring him, glanced at

him toward the end, and he thought that for a moment compassion showed in her eyes. But she turned away before he could be sure.

Aunt Tabitha made a moue of sadness. 'Yes, I can understand your feelings. Is that why you wear the black arm band?'

Dev nodded curtly. This conversation was not going as he'd planned. Bowing abruptly, he cut across anything else Pippa's aunt might want to say and said, 'Lady Philippa, would you go riding in Rotten Row with me tomorrow?'

'I think not,' Pippa said clearly.

Several matrons in the nearby box stopped talking. A gentleman who had been approaching halted. Aunt Tabitha gasped.

'Pippa,' she said, 'that is unpardonable. Please apologize to Lord Deverell.'

Pippa raised her chin higher. 'I will not.'

'Do you wish to set all the tongues wagging?' he asked softly, doing nothing to keep the hard edge out of his voice.

'They are wagging already. Everyone knows you are the man who had my twin put in the Tower.' She stared defiantly at him, her eyes flashing like emeralds.

'And they will wag even more if you refuse me so loudly and so blatantly.'

'Then let them.'

She tossed her head and turned to speak to a gentleman who had sidled up during the confrontation. The anger that had started with the mention of Hougoumont mounted. Dev saw red.

'Lady Philippa,' he said loudly and clearly, 'I will call for you at four tomorrow.'

Without giving her another chance to cut him, Dev pivoted on his heel and left. Irritation boiled in him, but he held it in check. The last thing he wanted to do was give the old biddies more to gossip about. As it was, this latest incident would be the *on dit* in every drawing room tomorrow.

Hours later under cover of dark, Pippa made her way toward the Tower. She had crept out of Tabitha's house after they returned from Drury Lane. Seeing Dev again, she had found herself weakening toward him in spite of the way she had treated him. The decision to visit Philip had been impulsive. She hoped that seeing her brother in the Tower would strengthen her resolve to resist Deverell St Simon.

The sound of scratching, as though boots scraped along cobblestones, made Pippa freeze. She glanced nervously behind her, but the fog off the Thames was so thick she could not see more than three feet. Still, no darker shadow moved within the opalescence of the swirling mist.

Leaning with her back to the brick wall, she took a deep breath and wished for the first time that she had brought a footman with her. Chill crept through the thick wool of her cape like prying fingers. A shiver skimmed down her back. But no further sound came to increase her unease.

She shook her head to clear it of the phantoms that seemed to plague her with each step she took. It wasn't as though she had not come this way many times before. She'd lost count of the visits she had made to her brother. The only difference was the time. Usually she came during the day. But that was the only thing that wasn't usual.

It was her earlier confrontation with Deverell. That was what made her skin prick and her heart race. If the truth be acknowledged, his proximity had brought back memories. Memories she wanted to bury forever.

Even now, with the creeping fog shrouding her sight, she could smell the citrus tang of bergamot and remember the first night she had encountered it. She had shaved him, the feel of his skin rough with beard under her fingertips, the urge to lean down and kiss him nearly overwhelming.

Pippa breathed deeply, inhaling the scent of moisture and…bergamot.

A hand snaked out of the night and grabbed her shoulder. She twisted, knowing who her waylayer had to be, yet not wanting to be caught. His grip held.

'Will you be forever mauling me?' she hissed.

'Will you be forever provoking me?' he countered, stepping close enough that she could see him and smell the bergamot even better. His teeth flashed in a rakish grin that did nothing to belie the hardness in his hazel eyes.

'How did you know I was here?'

One last time, she squirmed, trying to escape his fingers. His grip held firm. With a sigh of exasperation, she stilled.

'I have my sources. Ones I don't intend to reveal to you.'

She sniffed. 'Well, now that you have found me, release me.'

'I believe I have heard that order before. And as before, I'll do so when I see fit.' He edged closer, until the heat from his body seemed to engulf her. 'Where is your footman, Pippa?'

She lifted her chin. 'I can take care of myself. I did so for many long days in Brussels. And, I might add, I cared for others at the same time.'

He shook her, only enough to make her know he meant business. 'In Brussels you were dressed like a boy. And if you are going to prowl the seamier side of London, then you had best don your breeches again. A woman alone is fair game for any scoundrel.'

'Such as yourself?'

'Were I such, you would be beneath me now, not bandying words with me.'

Heat suffused her face, erasing the cold nip of the damp night breeze. 'A gentleman would not speak so to me.'

His laugh was a harsh sound that seemed to echo on the still air. 'And were you a lady, I wouldn't have to chase you the length and breadth of England. You would already be married to me.'

'How dare you!'

He glared at her, the grin of moments earlier gone as though it had never been. 'If I dared, I would do more than follow you to protect you. I would cart you off to Greta Green and be done with this intolerable situation.'

'I would leave you at the first chance.' She leaned into him, forgetting his hold on her shoulder, forgetting everything except her anger and her hurt. 'How many times must I tell you that I will never marry the man who betrayed my brother? I swear, talking to you is like talking to a simpleton. Only worse.'

Before she knew what he was about, his second hand came up and grabbed her other shoulder, pulling her to him. His face moved down swiftly, like a striking hawk, and his lips crushed hers. Emotions erupted in her. Anger warred with desire, swelling the torrent of response that surged in her.

She rose on tiptoe to meet his kiss, her mouth pressed to his. When his tongue demanded entrance, she gave it willingly. Her hands tangled in his hair and held him tightly.

As quickly as he had yanked her to him, he pushed her away. His breath came in quick gulps. 'And you deny any feeling for me? I could have you now. This instant. And you would revel in our joining.' His hands fell away and he turned his back to her. 'Damn it, Pippa.'

She stared at him, her senses still reeling, her lips still tingling. Always, he had always been able to make every-

thing else disappear. She took a step away, afraid of what
she might do if she didn't put some distance between them.
No matter what he had done, she still wanted him. She still
loved him.

She knuckled her mouth to keep from emitting the sob
of pain that threatened to escape. Drawing herself up
straight, she forced her voice to coldness. 'Now that you
have proven your power over my body, will you let me
go? Will you go away?'

He turned back to her, his mouth twisted, his eyes dark.
'No.'

A shock of pleasure and pain skittered through her, making her fingers shake in the folds of her heavy wool cape.
'Philip won't be pleased to see you.'

He shrugged, the dark outline of his greatcoat standing
out against the white of the fog. 'He would do well to talk
to me. His sending you to find this *traitor* he claims not to
be is enough to make me want to throttle him myself. From
now on, I'm going everywhere with you.'

'You are not,' she stated, indignation replacing the uncertainty of seconds before. 'You don't believe Philip is
innocent, I would never trust you to find the real culprit.'

'Don't be more foolish than you have already been,' he
said bluntly. 'Whether your brother is guilty or not, someone has tried to kill him. That same person may very well
try to do the same to you.'

His words sank in like leaden weights. She had been so
concerned about Philip that she hadn't thought of this. She
gulped, but straightened her spine. 'Whether that is possible
or not doesn't matter. Someone must do the searching for
Philip, since you have put him behind bars and he cannot
do it for himself. I'm that person.'

'We will see about that,' Dev stated, taking her arm and

propelling her toward the Tower. 'Let us get on with this visit. The night is far from young.'

Reaching the Tower gate, Pippa stated clearly, 'I am Lady Philippa LeClaire, come to visit Viscount Staunton.' The guard, as though used to peremptory visits by noblewomen in the small hours of the morning, moved aside. 'I know my way,' she said, dismissing his escort before it was offered.

Dev nodded at the man as he followed Pippa.

She paused at a heavy door and knocked softly. When, after several long minutes, there was no answer, she rapped harder. The noise echoed in the stone hallway.

'Your brother is a heavy sleeper,' Dev murmured. 'Nor do I blame him for ignoring so untimely a summons.'

'He will come,' Pippa said shortly. 'He has to be inside.'

Dev said nothing, but leaned against the cold stone of the wall, his right leg eased out so his weight rested on his good leg. She knew his wound ached from the cold fog. This prolonged standing would not help. Pippa felt a twinge of concern, but stamped down on it. He no longer merited her help or interest.

When more time passed, she began to worry. Surely nothing had happened. Philip's trial was not for several weeks. What was wrong?

As she wondered, a guard passed by. She stopped him and demanded, 'Has something happened to Viscount Staunton? He has kept us waiting, which is unlike him.'

The guard glanced from her to Deverell and all but snickered. 'His lordship has another visitor, milady.' His eyes were knowing. 'A woman.'

Pippa's eyebrows shot up. She gave the guard a repressing glare. 'I see. Thank you.'

She turned away, dismissing him. She didn't understand. Philip had said nothing about a woman.

Nonplussed, Pippa stood motionless while her brain whirled. There was only one reason she could think of that Philip would have a female visitor at this time of night. A blush rose up her neck and into her cheeks.

'Exactly,' Dev said drily. 'Now will you go home? I'm sure the last thing your brother wants is to see you.'

Even with so blatant a situation, it was well nigh impossible for Pippa to walk away. She needed to see Philip, to see him imprisoned and all because of the man who stood too close beside her.

She bit at her lower lip, a habit she had thought herself grown out of. She had stopped the abuse years ago. Until now. She stopped.

'Come on,' Dev said kindly, one hand under her elbow in an attempt to steer her away.

She dug in her heels. 'I will knock one last time. 'Tis not as though I don't know what is happening.'

She cast him a fulminating glance before shaking off his hand and banging again on the door. She lifted her fist to repeat the beating when the door cracked open.

'For heaven's sake,' Philip growled, standing in the small space that was only large enough for his body.

Pippa tried to peer around him, but could not. 'Philip, let me in.'

Philip's gaze went beyond her, and his brows snapped together. 'Why is *he* with you? I thought you had finished with this bounder.'

Fury hardened Dev's jaw. 'Let us in, Staunton. It is late and we already know you are entertaining a guest, so it is no matter whether we see the mystery lady or not.'

Philip's eyes bored into Pippa's. She looked away first, unable to stand the awareness in his gaze that told her he knew she understood exactly what he had been doing with the lady because she had done the exact thing with Deverell. She realized what she felt was close to shame, an emotion she had once thought she would never experience in relation to Deverell. Now it was more because she had loved him and been fooled into thinking he was someone he wasn't.

'Please, Philip,' she said softly, forcing herself to meet his look. ''Tis late and I...I want to see you. I will even turn my back so your companion can leave without being seen.'

He turned and said something to his guest which Pippa couldn't hear. The words sounded like French, but while she had the English upper-class girl's smattering of that language she was far from proficient. A female voice answered.

Behind her, Dev whispered, 'She told him it is all right for us to enter. She knows us.'

Pippa's eyes rounded in surprise.

Philip scowled. 'I see you are fluent in French, Lord Deverell. Somehow, I would not have thought it.'

The direct insult darkened Dev's hazel eyes to brown. 'Now that we have settled that you don't know everything, Staunton, are you going to let us in or waste the time your sister has spent coming here?'

Pippa heard more than dislike in the exchanged insults, she heard challenge and realized that if Philip weren't incarcerated the two men would be at each other's throats.

With obvious reluctance, Philip stepped away and allowed Pippa and Dev to enter. The room was spacious and comfortably appointed with furniture and wall hangings that Pippa had directed to be delivered from her grandfather's closed town house. Several scattered rugs cut the chill rising from the stone flooring. A large four-poster oak bed stood in one corner. Beside it reposed a matching wardrobe and wash stand. In the opposite corner a large fireplace, filled with flames, provided enough warmth to make her cape unnecessary. There was no window.

Sitting, back ramrod straight, in one of the two well-upholstered chairs drawn close to the fire, was the Marchioness of Witherspoon. Pippa's mouth dropped.

'*Chérie*, please do not look so…so startled.' The Marchioness's lightly accented voice was filled with chagrin. 'I did not want you to know, but neither did I want Philip to turn you away after all the trouble you went to coming here tonight. He wanted me to go earlier, but I convinced him to let me stay.' She shrugged her delicate white shoulders expressively. 'You see, Witherspoon is at Brighton for several days.'

'How convenient,' Dev drawled. He gave them his best, guaranteed-to-charm smile. 'For both of you.'

Philip took a step toward him. 'I will call you out for that slur.'

Dev eyed him coldly, one eyebrow arched. 'And you dare to condemn me?'

Philip drew back as though slapped, but said nothing. He whirled around and confronted Pippa. 'What do you want?'

The baldness of his question hurt, but Pippa put it aside. He was her brother, her twin. 'Only to see you. To visit, to talk over some of the things I have heard. I haven't been here in nearly a week.' She trailed off lamely. When Philip made no reply or asked her to sit, she said, 'Perhaps I should come back.'

'No,' Philip said curtly, his hand chopping through the air. 'Jane knows everything. She too has been gleaning gossip to help.'

'Everything?' Pippa asked, incredulous.

Philip paced the room, his hands stuffed in the pockets of his buff pantaloons. 'Everything. That I am a spy. That you were this man's lover. Everything.'

Disillusionment stopped the angry words in Pippa's throat. How could he have told this woman about her and Deverell? It was bad enough that he had trusted the Marchioness with his secrets, but to tell her about something that had nothing to do with him, to trust her with knowledge that could ruin Pippa in the eyes of the world was more than she could bear.

As though reading Pippa's mind, the Marchioness rose and crossed to her. Taking Pippa's cold hands, she said gently, 'Do not judge Philip harshly, please. He had no choice. I recognized you and asked him what was going on. You see…' she cast a look at the Viscount '…I am very good at remembering faces and yours is so beautiful that when I saw you here I realized you were the woman in the Brussels bank.'

Not even the compliment could ease the hurt still gripping Pippa. No matter what the provocation, she hadn't expected her twin to reveal such damaging information about her. Never Philip. Did everyone betray others without a thought for how the one whose trust had been shattered would feel?

'*Chérie*, I am sorry you had to find out like this.' She cast a reproving glance at the Viscount who had stopped his pacing to watch them. 'But I, of all people, understand what it is like to love a man. For I would do anything—anything—for your brother.'

And now to have someone say this. It was bad enough that she knew how much she had loved—no, still loved—Deverell, but that the Marchioness should say so in front of him… Pippa looked from the Marchioness to her brother, who showed no sign of understanding what he had done. She would not look at Dev.

'I think 'tis time I left,' Pippa said through stiff lips, pulling her fingers from the other woman's clasp.

'*Non,*' Lady Witherspoon said, stepping closer and laying a delicate white hand on Pippa's arm.

'Don't be a goose,' Staunton said, moving to his lover and putting a protective arm around her. 'Jane is distraught and your leaving will only make it worse.'

Pippa looked at her twin. All his concern was for the woman in his arms.

'Enough of this,' Dev said. He took Pippa by the arm and drew her away from the couple. 'You obviously don't need us here. Whatever Pippa has to tell you can wait.' He raised one brow sardonically. ''Tis not as though you will be leaving in the next day or so.'

If looks could kill, Staunton's would have felled Dev. 'Thanks to you.'

Dev made a curt nod. 'We have been down this path before, Staunton, and in front of the women is no time to do so again.'

Realizing that the men's animosity was mounting to dangerous levels, Pippa edged between them. She forced herself to smile at the Marchioness and go on tiptoe to kiss her brother's cheek, a habit from many years and one she did again without much trouble. He might have revealed her deepest secret to another person, but he was still her brother.

'Dev is right. My news will wait.' She cast Dev a look meant to keep him in place as she moved past him to the door. 'I'll come back.'

'And I will be with her,' Dev stated, following her. He opened the door and, with a palm to her back, gently pushed her through.

Irritation spurted in Pippa. 'I am perfectly capable of leaving.'

'I know,' he said, 'but you were taking your sweet time about it. 'Tis late and we have some way to go.'

'We don't have anywhere to go,' she faced him defiantly.

He shook his head. 'I know you are angry with me, Pippa, and I know your brother has hurt you. You want to be alone. Believe me, I understand that. But I won't let you go home on your own at this time of night.'

He gripped her shoulder and steered her through the halls and out of the Tower door. The night had become colder and the fog heavier. Right on the Thames as they were, the splash of water on the shore seemed loud in Pippa's ears. Suddenly she was glad of Dev's company.

They made their way through the streets without a word. It was a long walk.

'Why did you not take a horse?' he asked when they finally reached Tabitha's house. 'It would have been easier on both of us.'

Pippa winced, realizing his leg must be causing him horrendous pain. 'I was coming alone, and I didn't want anyone in Aunt Tabitha's employ to know I was gone. Taking a horse would have alerted a groom who then would have insisted on accompanying me.'

'So your aunt doesn't know what you are about.'

'No, and I want to keep it that way. It would only worry her more.' Pippa sighed. 'Thank you for bringing me home. Now I need to get inside.'

Dev nodded and escorted her to the back door where she inserted a key in the lock. 'I see you are prepared.'

She gave him a wan smile. 'As much as I can be. Good-night.'

She left him standing there with the fitful light of a half moon playing along the planes of his face. There were lines of worry around his mouth.

He might have turned her brother in, but he was determined to care for her. In spite of knowing she should not let it matter, his concern warmed her. Tonight's revelations about her brother and the Marchioness made her wonder if Dev cared more than her brother.

She swiped at moisture forming in her eyes. She was being maudlin. Philip loved her. He was her twin.

She reached her room, went inside and closed the door. With a sigh, she sank into a chair and let her head loll back. She was so tired and so confused.

## *Chapter Twelve*

Dev handed the reins of his horse to his groom. 'Jimmy, keep him moving.' He grinned, knowing the boy would not do anything else.

'Yes, milord,' Jimmy said, indignation writ hugely across his narrow face.

With a determined step, Dev went to Tabitha Montcleve's front door. He didn't expect Pippa to go riding in the park as he had arranged, but he was determined to make her tell him no to his face—again. He rapped smartly on the knocker.

An aged butler answered immediately.

'Good day,' Dev said, taking off his hat and handing it and his riding gloves to the servant. 'I'm here to take Lady Philippa riding.'

The butler took the items, scepticism raising his white brows slightly. 'I shall see if her ladyship is available. Please have a seat in the drawing room.'

He showed Dev the way to a light, airy room furnished in the current rage of Greek Revival. The settee had lion-paw feet and a lyre-shaped back, as did the grouping of chairs around the fireplace. A rosewood table reposed beneath the long window that looked out on to the street.

Dev sat gingerly in one of the chairs. His mother was always decorating, but she usually stayed with more substantial furniture. His father had made it plain he would not risk his neck by sitting in a flimsy chair.

'Oh, here you are,' a trilling female voice said.

Dev rose and turned to bow to Tabitha. 'Are you Pippa's representative, come to tell me she's indisposed, or more bluntly that she won't be seen with me?'

Tabitha laughed. 'I have come to tell you she is going riding in the park. I assumed that meant with you.'

'Whatever could have brought this about?'

Instead of answering, Tabitha moved to a sideboard and poured out a generous portion of wine. 'Will you have some?'

'Certainly.' Dev crossed to her and took the proffered glass.

'I never drink sherry or ratafia,' she said. 'Too namby-pamby.'

Dev grinned as he sampled the strong port. 'I should think not. You are too strong-willed to drink something so weak.'

She laughed again. 'I can see why you are called "Devil Deverell". The name suits you. Too bad my stubborn niece can't be brought around.' She took a sip. 'Ah, that is just right. However, I believe Pippa is wavering.'

She moved to take a seat. Dev followed.

'How so, ma'am?'

'Why, she is going riding with you, is she not? That is a definite improvement.' She raised a hand for silence, got up and went to put her ear to the door. Coming back, she lowered her voice. 'We are alone for now, so tell me what happened last night. Something has softened her toward you.'

'She has told you nothing?'

'How could she? She thinks she is sneaking out without my being any the wiser. If I didn't know you would be with her, I should have to stop her. That would create a pickle. She would resent me instead of, I hope, growing to care for me.' Tabitha set her glass down and stared out the window. 'When her mother died, I tried to get Julian—LeClaire—to let me come and help raise her. He refused. Ever since, I have asked her to spend time with me in London. This is the first time she has done so. I have enjoyed it.'

'I think she has too, ma'am.'

Tabitha returned her attention to him and smiled. 'But you didn't come here to listen to the meandering thoughts of an old woman. I don't know what is keeping that girl, but while we have the privacy, you must tell me what happened last night.'

Dev set his glass down on a nearby table. He had known at the time that her brother's imparting of her past to Lady Witherspoon had upset Pippa. He hadn't realized how much. If she was going riding with him, then she must have been deeply hurt and now be turning to him.

He looked gravely at Tabitha. 'I believe I know, but I don't feel it is my place to tell you. Please try to understand. I'm sorry.'

Tabitha seemed about to say something, then stopped. She took another sip of wine. 'You have honour and a sense of privacy. I hope my stubborn niece brings you into our family soon.'

The door opened and the butler entered. 'My lord,' he paused, his gaze going to Mrs Montcleve. 'Madam, I did not know you were here or I would have had refreshments sent in.'

Tabitha snorted. 'Don't bother, Watkins. Lord Deverell and I have been drinking this lovely port.'

'Yes, madam.'

'Now get back to the reason you entered,' she prompted him, rising to pour herself and Dev another glass.

'Yes, madam. Your lordship, Lady Philippa sends her regrets, but she has a prior commitment.'

'What?' Dev and Tabitha said in unison.

The butler drew himself up straighter and met each one's gaze. 'That is what she said, madam. My lord.'

'I'll be…'

Dev happened to look out the window as Pippa ran across the pavement and climbed into a pretty pale blue phaeton. The Marchioness of Witherspoon held the reins and with a smart flick of the leathers set the carriage in motion. No tiger accompanied them.

Tabitha came up alongside him and saw the rear of the carriage disappear briskly. 'Now when did this happen?'

'I believe,' the butler intoned, 'a message came this morning for her ladyship. It bore the arms of the Marchioness.'

'Thank you, Watkins. That will be all for now.'

The butler bowed himself out.

Tabitha tapped a finger against her mouth. 'I didn't realize they knew each other.'

Dev, watching the phaeton turn the corner in the direction of Hyde Park, said, 'They had supper together with Mr Hopwell at Maria Sefton's ball.'

'I remember now. Well, young man, you had best be after them. There is no sense in letting Pippa think she can snub you like this with impunity.'

'The least I can do is put a spoke in the wheel of whatever they are plotting by being close at hand.'

'Plotting?'

Dev grinned at her. 'Did I say that? I'm sure it was a slip of the tongue.' The last thing he wanted to do was reveal to Tabitha what had happened the night before. That was for Pippa to do.

'Hum, so you say. But never mind. Be on your way.'

Dev made an awkward leg, thought briefly of how he had used to be renown for his grace, and left. Now was not the time to bemoan his wound. Pippa was up to something, and he wasn't going to be far behind.

Pippa settled herself in the elegantly upholstered carriage. The squabs were blue velvet to match the paint. 'Very nice,' she murmured by way of opening the conversation.

'Thank you,' Lady Witherspoon said. 'I am glad you came. I was afraid that you would not, after last night. Because of what your brother said, and my relationship to him.' She turned large blue eyes on Pippa before looking back at the crowded street. 'I wanted to speak privately with you and felt this was as close as we could get.'

Pippa sensed the other woman's nervousness and immediately felt the need to ease it. 'I was pleased you asked. It seemed…how do I put this delicately?' An embarrassed smile lifted one corner of her mouth.

'Ah, you are trying to be polite about what Philip and I mean to one another. There is no need. I feel you and I are like sisters. We can speak plainly.' She flicked her whip over the lead horse's head before casting a worried glance at Pippa. 'I hope that is all right.'

Pippa's hands tightened in the folds of her skirts. She truly didn't know how she felt about the situation. 'Of course that is fine. It was obvious that Philip loves you very much.'

'And I him.' She turned the phaeton between the gates that led to Hyde Park. 'For a long time. But there is Witherspoon. He would never divorce me. Nor would that be good for Philip. His reputation.'

Pippa nearly laughed aloud from sheer anxiety. 'Philip's reputation. He has none. Even if he is found innocent, it will always be remembered that once he was thought a traitor.'

'True.'

They slowed their pace and fell behind a line of other carriages, all of which were touring the park. Men and women stopped their vehicles and spoke across empty space to one another or carried on conversations with people walking. Everyone who was anyone was out.

Pippa forced herself to smile at the occupant of a nearby cabriolet whom she had met at a rout. Lady Witherspoon stopped to speak briefly with Mr Hopwell.

Pippa uncurled her fingers and tried to relax her shoulders. Rather than dwell on Philip's circumstances, she should be enjoying this outing and getting to know her companion better.

'When did you meet Lord Witherspoon?'

'I was barely sixteen, in 1804. Napoleon was at peace with England for a brief time and many Englishmen came to Paris. My *maman* introduced us and arranged the marriage. It was a very good union for me.' She sighed. 'Of course, I did not know I would meet Philip.'

'Do we ever know things like that?' Pippa asked, thinking about Deverell.

They were still now, waiting for the carriages in front of them to move. Lady Witherspoon laid a gloved hand on Pippa's. 'No. That is the hardest part about living.'

Pippa clutched the other woman's fingers in sympathy. 'Have you and Philip thought of running away? Now that Napoleon is defeated you could go to the Continent.'

The Marchioness gave a trill of laughter. 'You are very

*risqué.* Philip said you were no prim-and-proper miss, something I did not think after hearing about your adventures.'

Pippa blushed. What she had suggested should have been the furthest thing from her mind. But she wanted her brother to be happy.

A high-perch phaeton paused beside them and the woman in it waved. 'Lady Witherspoon, so nice to see you.'

The Marchioness looked over and a genuine smile lit her elfin features. 'Lady Stone. It has been so long. But you look magnificent. Motherhood agrees with you.'

The other woman was a statuesque redhead and a beauty. In her arms was a small bundle. Beside her sat a strikingly handsome man with black hair frosted by silver at the temples. His grey eyes were studying Pippa.

'My lord,' Pippa said coolly, nodding her head.

Lady Witherspoon coughed nervously. 'Pippa, may I present Lord Alastair St Simon and his wife Lady Stone?'

Pippa felt the colour drain from her face. The tension in her shoulders which she had managed to ease returned with a vengeance. 'Pleased to meet you, my lord and lady.' She was glad her voice didn't show her discomfort.

'So you are the young woman who is giving Deverell the time of his life,' Lord Alastair said, his voice deep and slow.

''Tis about time someone caused Deverell some heartache. Now he will definitely forget about Samantha,' Lady Stone said matter-of-factly. She shifted the sleeping baby to her other arm. 'You must come to dinner, my dear. I promise not to invite Deverell.'

Pippa didn't know what to think. She expected them to revile her, not ask her to their home.

'Leave off,' Dev's voice said from close by, moving between the two carriages. 'Pippa has enough to contend with snubbing me. She doesn't need the two of you complicating the matter by being nice to her.'

'Deverell, you scoundrel,' Lord Alastair said, reaching out a hand to shake the one Dev extended. 'Jon said he saw you at the theatre.'

'Just last night. But he neglected to tell me you are a papa.' Dev grinned wickedly. 'But then he was probably too embarrassed. You go from the fashion setter of the *ton* to being so unfashionable as to take the air with your wife and baby.'

Alastair cuffed Dev on the shoulder. 'I am setting the latest rage. Are we not, my dear?' he asked his wife.

She kissed him on the cheek. 'And that will certainly have all the toadies wondering how they are going to emulate you when most of them do not even care to be in the company of their spouses.'

Dev grinned so hugely at their antics that Pippa could see there was genuine love between him and his brother. 'Only you could set such a standard,' he said with a droll rolling of his eyes.

The baby chose that moment to waken. Blue eyes looked at the world in wonderment before screwing up into tears. A loud wail left no doubt that the pride of his parents' life was unhappy where he was.

Lady Stone tsked and gave the child her finger to suck. 'We had best get to a more private place, Alastair. Your heir has certain expectations; if they are not met, he will be even more vocal in his displeasure.'

Her husband laughed and directed the coachman to move on. 'See that you come to visit,' he called over his shoulder. 'Both of you. Singly or together.'

'Marriage has been good for my brother,' Dev said, giving Pippa a meaningful stare. 'He is more relaxed.'

She met his gaze haughtily. 'He obviously has a wife who loves him.' She turned to Lady Witherspoon and asked, 'Can we move on, please? The company has lost its sparkle.'

The Marchioness looked ruefully at Dev before urging her horses on. 'That was very rude,' she said in a low voice.

Her nose in the air, Pippa said, 'I don't care. What he did to Philip is unforgivable. It makes it unnecessary for me to treat him with civility.'

'*Chérie*, he is a good and honourable man who only did what his conscience bade him. Although…what he did to you was very much wrong.'

Pippa went to Dev's defence without thinking. 'What we did was my fault.'

'I see,' Lady Witherspoon said. 'You are in love with him.'

'Not any more,' Pippa stated.

'Philip says he wants to marry you.'

'Philip talks too much.' Pippa turned her back ever so slightly to the other woman. Feeling instant remorse for her intended snub, she shifted back around. 'I'm sorry. 'Tis just that where Deverell St Simon is concerned I am not rational.'

'I understand. I feel that way about your brother.'

The impulsiveness Pippa so dreaded in herself surfaced. 'Then will you help me find the real traitor? Together we can do more searching and clear Philip's name.'

Lady Witherspoon took a sharp breath. 'I do not know. It would be very dangerous.' Her small chin firmed. 'But, yes, I will help.' She added a cautionary, 'But we might not succeed.'

'Yes, we will. I won't let us fail.'

For once, Pippa knew in her heart that her tendency to rush into things had not steered her wrong. The Marchioness loved Philip. No matter that she had hesitated. Pippa knew the other woman would do everything in her power to help. Just as she had always known that Philip was alive, regardless of what the Home Office had believed.

Dev lounged against a solid Grecian pillar, one of several scattered around Mrs Fitzpatrick's ballroom. Three chandeliers dripped with candles, providing enough light to make every lady in the room glow. Potted palms and orange trees clustered in groupings behind which small groups of people chatted and gossiped. It was a crush.

Dev's mouth twisted sardonically. The hostess was probably beaming over her success.

'We seem to be meeting everywhere but at a family gathering,' a deep, drawling voice said.

Dev turned with a grin. 'Alastair. Didn't know you were an acquaintance of Mrs Fitzpatrick's.'

'Barely. Enough to always get an invitation.'

Dev snorted. 'Everyone in the *ton* invites you in the hope that you will grace them with your presence and they will ever after find themselves in the golden circle.'

Alastair hit him on the shoulder. 'Enough of your toadeating. I'm here because I know your nemesis's aunt is one of our hostess's cronies. I thought you would show up tonight in hopes of pressing your suit still again.'

Glumness soured Dev's smile. 'My suit, as you so optimistically call it, is merely a need on my part to protect Pippa from herself and her scoundrel of a brother.'

'Don't be so down in the mouth. Chase her. Ask her to dance. Do it here, in a place so public that to refuse you will be tantamount to slapping you in the face. Very few women, or men for that matter, have the stomach to create so public a display.'

Dev gave his brother a thoughtful look. 'You think so?'

Alastair clapped him on the back. 'I kidnapped Liza and made her marry me. What I'm telling you to do is nothing.'

Dev gaped at him. 'You did? You never told anyone.'

'It wasn't something I was proud of. Just something I had to do.'

Dev looked at his brother with new respect. 'I might have to do as you suggest. You certainly don't regret your actions.'

'Never,' Alastair murmured.

Dev squared his shoulders as though preparing to go into battle. 'The worst she could do is give me the cut direct.'

'Spoken like a true war hero,' Alastair said. 'Now I must find Liza. And don't forget Mother's little gathering tomorrow.'

'I shan't,' Dev said, his mind already on the problem of Pippa.

He pushed away from the Grecian pillar he had been leaning against and began to thread his way through the press of Mrs. Fitzpatrick's guests. It was another crush, even in this off season. Some people played cards in another room, many chatted in small groups and quite a number of the younger ones danced.

If he recognized the strains, the orchestra was about to start a waltz, for it was one of the tunes Pippa had played so long ago in Brussels. She had been so protective of him that night, getting up from the pianoforte and ending the evening without a by-your-leave. She had courage.

She would marry him, if he had to follow in Alastair's footsteps and kidnap her. He strode purposefully toward her. Tabitha saw him first and smiled.

He returned the older woman's greeting before turning to Pippa. 'May I have the honour of this dance?'

Pippa turned a haughty face to him. 'I don't believe you have any honour to begin with. My answer is no.'

He gritted his teeth. 'Dance with me or I will drag you on to the floor. Then all of Society will wonder what is really between us.' He held out his hand.

'Pippa—' Tabitha entered into the battle '—do as he says, for he is right. At this moment they all think your refusal is because of Philip. If Lord Deverell does as he threatens, they will begin to wonder if there is more between you than your brother.'

Reluctantly, slowly, she put the bare tips of her fingers in his palm. 'If I must.'

Titters and whispers accompanied them. Let the *ton* have a field day with this, Dev thought, he no longer cared. Pippa's insults had gone beyond what he was willing to endure from her.

The music began in earnest. Couples around them started moving. Pippa stood stiffly when Dev put his left arm around her waist.

'You are making another scene by refusing to dance while everyone around us does so.' A muscle in his jaw twitched.

Reluctantly she began to move but it was like holding a wooden doll in his arms. The glare she sent him would have felled a less determined man. Dev gave back as good as he got.

'I don't waltz well,' she said through lips as stiff as her body.

'Nor do I.' His bad leg buckled so that the twirl was less than perfect.

Instantly, every feeling Pippa had ever felt for Deverell St Simon surged back. The urge to take away his pain and to hold him softened the harsh line of her mouth. Even though he held her lightly, the heat from his body seemed to engulf her senses. She wanted nothing more than to melt into him, as she always had.

They moved smoothly, successfully completing another twirl. She smiled up at him, forgetting everything but the feel of his arms around her.

'Very good,' she murmured.

'As good as can be expected,' he replied, his mouth twisted up but showing no real bitterness. 'As you so often assured me, my wound has healed well. I will never do everything I once did or do it as well, but I shan't let that stop me from doing what I want. Including waltzing with you.'

'I never thought you would.' And she hadn't. Even from the start, before she'd even known him, she had sensed he was stubborn and would do exactly as he pleased. 'I'm glad I didn't amputate your leg.'

'Not nearly so glad as I am.'

The music soared and he pulled her tight against him, both of them unconcerned with propriety. They dipped and swirled, their steps perfectly matched. Only when the music stopped did they come back to reality.

Pippa stumbled but his arm around her waist steadied her. Her eyes met his. Passion and awareness filled his gaze. If only they were meeting for the first time, she thought. If only Philip weren't between them.

Her breath caught. 'I need to return to Aunt Tabitha.'

'Pippa…'

'No.' She cut him off before he could say the words she saw in his eyes. 'There is too much between us.'

'Philip,' he said, his voice scathing.

She realized he regretted losing her more than the loss of his physical grace. The knowledge was a bittersweet pain in her chest. Before he could say another word, she slipped from his grasp and hurried to her aunt.

Dev didn't follow.

## Chapter Thirteen

Dev felt like a thief, lurking in the deepest shadows with Aunt Tabitha's note crumpled in the pocket of his greatcoat. It was just past midnight, but the streets were still busy, and many buildings glowed with lamplight. Soot hung heavy in the air and the muffled sounds of horses' hooves and wheels echoed in the narrow alleys.

He had followed Pippa here from Tabitha's town house, where he had watched her sneak out of the back door. On the way she had stopped to pick up the Marchioness of Witherspoon.

At this moment, Pippa was barely a hundred feet in front of him, on her way to break into the house of an English peer. If she was caught, she'd go to Newgate. Unless she got shot first.

Sweat broke out on Dev's upper lip. He had to stop her.

Lady Witherspoon's slighter figure stuck close to Pippa's side. The two had been inseparable since the night in the Tower, so this combination didn't surprise him. He was sure neither one had made provisions in case they were discovered—or even thought they would be found out.

He muffled a snort of disgust.

The sound of their footsteps stopped. He pressed into the

indentation of a doorway. In the dark-encrusted night, he saw them huddle together, their voices rising but still indistinguishable. After long minutes, Pippa moved away.

'Blast,' Dev muttered. Pippa was going to break into the house on her own. Not that doing so with Lady Witherspoon along made it any more safe or acceptable, but at least the other woman could stand guard.

First he had to deal with the Marchioness. Moving swiftly, he was on her before she realized anything.

'Hush,' he ordered, clamping one gloved hand over her mouth and the other around her waist. ''Tis Deverell St Simon. I'm not going to hurt you.' To himself, he added, *yet*.

She said something into his palm.

'I'll release you if you promise not to scream or run away. Otherwise, I shall gag and bind you.'

She nodded.

Slowly Dev took his hand from her mouth. When she stayed quiet, he released her waist and stepped away.

'*Merci,*' she whispered. 'But you gave me a fright.'

'Imagine how you would feel if I were a footpad,' he said sardonically.

'I should be in dire peril.'

Her tone was solemn, but Dev thought he detected a glint of amusement in her blue eyes. It angered him. 'You and Pippa are dealing in things you cannot handle. Where is she?'

Her chin lifted stubbornly. 'We are perfectly capable, *monsieur*. We both have pistols.' She drew a small silver-embossed gun from her reticule and pointed it at his chest.

Dev's anger rose. In one lightning motion, he gripped her wrist and twisted. The weapon fell to the ground with a clatter that seemed to echo loudly in the still air. He stooped and grabbed it, ignoring the protest of his leg.

Standing, he goaded her, 'You were saying?'

She sighed. 'You are the second person to catch me off guard. Perhaps it would be better to have you on our side. Although Philip will not like it.'

'To hell with Staunton. Now, which house did Pippa go to?'

She mentioned the name of a very prominent Cabinet minister. 'She went through the garden. There are French doors that can be opened into the library.'

'You seem very familiar with the place,' Dev said, impressed in spite of himself. He hadn't expected them to be quite so knowledgeable about this particular gentleman's abode. 'I'm going after her.' He took a step forward, then turned back to Lady Witherspoon. 'I'll return your pistol if you give me your word that you'll return home now.'

She studied his face in the pale light from the stars. 'What about Pippa?'

'Better that I catch her and give her a thrashing than the owner of the house she's burgling. I'll turn her over my knee, but I won't imprison her or shoot her.'

The Marchioness nodded her head and held out her hand for the pistol. 'You have my word. This time.'

Dev gave her the weapon and strode off. There was no time to lose. As Lady Witherspoon had said, the garden led to open French doors. Peering in, he saw a single candle flame with Pippa, dressed as a boy, in the small puddle of light. She was bent over a desk, her fingers riffling through a sheaf of papers.

Dev swallowed an oath and moved over the threshold. She looked up. Startlement widened her eyes and formed an O with her lips. He was on her before she could move.

One arm went around her waist, one hand on her mouth. The light scent of lilacs engulfed him, infuriating him more.

She squirmed in his hold. Her voice was muted by his gloved palm. When he didn't release her, she bit him.

'Damn,' he hissed, keeping his hand on her mouth. He put his lips to her ear and said, 'Don't do that again or I shall be forced to hit you. The last thing we need is for someone to hear us.'

She glared at him, her eyes sparkling in the scant light coming through the open doors. Her body where it pressed close to his was rigid.

'If I release you,' he whispered, his breath wafting over her cheek, 'you cannot say a word.'

She stared defiantly at him, neither nodding or shaking her head. He was tempted to haul her out the doors and be done with this, but he knew how important this was to her. It didn't matter that her mission was foolish and dangerous.

He took a chance. Dropping his hands he took a small step away.

'I'm not stupid,' she hissed. 'His lordship is away, and this is the servant's night off.'

Dev rolled his eyes and moved back in on her, resisting the temptation to touch her again. 'There is always someone in a house like this. Always.'

She didn't budge. 'I'm willing to take that risk.'

The urge to forcibly take her away was strong. Instead he said, 'You finish looking while I stand guard.'

She looked at him for a long moment, then nodded curtly. Dev moved to the door. He kept an eye on her while listening. Long minutes passed. Every second he expected to hear a voice or footfall. Pippa continued to scrounge through the papers, even going so far as to pry open the desk drawers.

Dev hoped to hell they didn't get caught. She was more bold than he had anticipated.

From what seemed a long distance, he heard the front-door knocker. In a flash, he was by Pippa.

'Quiet,' he ordered, dousing the flame with a finger and thumb.

He gripped her wrist and yanked her out the doors. They sped through the garden and on to the street. He refused to stop until they were several streets away and he deemed them safe. In their haste, they hadn't bothered to disguise the fact that someone had been prying. The drawer Pippa had been rummaging through was open, as were the French doors.

'Keep moving,' Dev said, continuing to walk even though he had allowed them to stop running. His leg hurt like Hades and his temper was barely in check. 'I shall throttle your brother with my bare hands. After I have given you a thrashing.' I should have never let you continue, he added to himself.

She dug her heels in and confronted him. 'You have no control over me. I did what I had to…and I will do it again.'

'The devil you will,' he growled, grabbing her shoulders and shaking her. 'You could have been killed. Thrown in Newgate at the very least.'

'Stop treating me like a child,' she demanded, trying futilely to loosen his grip on her.

'Then stop acting like one.'

She reached up to slap him, but his arm blocked her aim. Frustration and fury ate at him. He cursed and, with a sharp yank, pulled her to him. His lips slashed down on hers, claiming her with a thoroughness that spoke of familiarity and uncontrollable hunger.

'I could have lost you,' he muttered, anchoring the fingers of one hand in her short curls. He pulled her head back to better plunder her mouth with his.

Pippa sank into his embrace, her fury at him submerged by rising passion. His scent surrounded her as he drew her even closer, until she could feel the hard need of his arousal. The kiss deepened, his tongue teasing hers in imitation of more contact.

Her toes curled in her boots. Tingles shot from her lips to centre in her stomach.

'I have missed you so,' he said, breaking away enough to run his lips against her cheek.

His mouth came back to hers. The kiss gentled. Instead of demanding entrance, his tongue moved softly against her bottom lip, asking admittance. The sensations intensified until Pippa wanted to burrow her fingers inside his shirt and twine them around the thick brown hair she knew covered his chest. When one of his hands dropped to cup her breast, she arched into his caress.

How she had missed him. The feel of him pressed to her. The scent of him. Even her worry for him had become a part of who she was. Heaven help her, but she loved him beyond reason.

She moved into his caress. 'Dev, I...' The confession died in her throat as he kissed her breathless.

'You will marry me,' he murmured. 'I have a special licence.'

His words were like an electric shock to Pippa. She jerked in his arms and brought her clenched fists up to push against his chest. What was she doing?

Pippa could not believe she had let herself react so wantonly to Dev's embrace. She had acted like a harlot, eager for her lover's fondling.

'Let me go,' she ordered, pushing harder. 'I'll never marry you.'

He held her tighter, pulling her inexorably toward him. Determination etched lines around his mouth. 'What if you bear my child? It is not inconceivable. What do you intend to do then?'

She gasped. ''Tis none of your business. If it happens. Nor would I tell you.'

'How dare you,' he raged, his face inches from her.

'Hey, guv,' a raucous cockney voice said. 'This ain't the place for carryings on like that. 'Gainst the King's law.'

With an oath, Dev released her. Both of them had forgotten she was dressed as a boy.

Pippa knew her face was bleached of colour and her lips were swollen from his possession. This is what came of loving a man beyond reason, she thought bitterly. But she did not have to continue to let him dominate her.

A carriage rattled by, its lantern casting light over them. A sedan chair went by, the two men hauling it casting curious glances their way. In the heat of their emotions, they had forgotten they were on a well-travelled street. The effect they had on one another was sobering.

''Tis late, Dev,' Pippa said, turning away from him. She felt drained of all emotion. Exhaustion ate at her. 'I want to go home.'

He took a step toward her, then stopped. 'I'll escort you.'

Irritation briefly flared in her. This wasn't worth another confrontation. 'As you wish,' she said, her voice without inflection.

It was a long walk back to Aunt Tabitha's house, and Pippa felt every inch of it. What made everything worse was that she hadn't found out anything by breaking into the Cabinet member's house. All she had done was endanger herself and end up in a fight with Deverell.

Now that the urgency of the situation and their emotions was past, she realized that he had managed to appear just in time. 'How did you know what we were doing?'

'I have my sources,' he said.

When he didn't add anything, she gritted her teeth. She wasn't going to get into another confrontation with him. She always seemed to lose. She picked up her pace.

Up ahead was the corner to Aunt Tabitha's. Pippa turned it and halted. The house was ablaze with light. A travelling chaise with four prancing matched bays blocked the front door. Servants in livery milled around.

'Grandfather,' she breathed, recognizing the purple coats the coachmen and outriders wore.

'We have got to get you away before someone recognizes you,' Dev said, taking her arm and pulling her back into the shadows. 'The last thing the Earl needs is to see you dressed like this and to find out what you have been doing.'

'He would have another attack,' Pippa said softly, worry puckering her brow. 'I must creep in the back way and get up to my room and change.'

'I'll create a diversion.' Dev moved off before she could thank him.

Unwanted admiration rose in her as he strode purposely up to one of the grooms. Even at the distance, she heard him say, 'Someone has been attacked. Just around the corner.' He pointed in the opposite direction from where Pippa stood. 'I chased off the scoundrel, but cannot lift the wounded man on my own. I need help.'

With an autocratic wave of his hand for the servants to follow, Dev headed off. She saw him limp as though his leg had reached its limit. Compassion swamped her. He was in pain, yet he helped her. If only…

This wasn't the time to ponder what ifs. Moving quickly and surreptitiously, Pippa skirted down the street, keeping to the shadows of nearby houses. At Tabitha's, she edged along the side and into the garden in the back. Hopefully, everyone would be engaged in her grandfather's arrival.

She made it to her rooms without incidence and changed. Smoothing her hair back into some semblance of order, she took a deep breath and went to meet her grandfather.

Even from the top of the stairs, she could hear her grandfather's deep voice booming and the light response of her aunt. They were fighting. Over her.

'Are you telling me Pippa isn't here?' the Earl roared. 'I should have known better than to trust a scatterbrain to watch over her.'

'Now, Julian,' Tabitha said, her right foot tapping, 'do not think you can barge into my home and throw insults at me. I will have you escorted to the door if you don't mind your manners better.'

The butler, an older gentleman who had been in Tabitha's employ for forty years, kept a bland face, although Pippa saw his hands clench spasmodically. Sympathy for him made her descend the stairs quickly.

'Grandfather,' she said, pausing to catch her breath before flinging her arms around him, 'what brings you to London? I'm very glad to see you, but the trip cannot have been good for your health.'

He held her at arm's length and examined her. 'You look well enough, but where were you that Tabitha couldn't find you?'

Pippa smiled at him while her brain whirled. 'I was…in the garden. Taking a walk. I had much to think about and the dark and quiet help.'

He released her, but there was a slight wrinkle between his brows, and she knew he wasn't entirely convinced of her story. But he didn't enquire further.

'Well, go pack your bags, girl. I'm opening my town house and you are moving in with me.'

'Tonight?'

'Tonight,' he said in a tone that brooked no discussion.

Tabitha shook her head. 'You always were highhanded, Julian. I see you have not changed.'

'Nor have you, madam. You always spoke your mind, regardless of the consequences.'

Tabitha gave him an almost wistful look. 'Not always, Julian.'

Pippa watched the byplay between them and wondered why she felt as though they had once known each other well. Ever since she could remember, her grandfather had disparaged Tabitha, just as her great-aunt had done to the Earl. She had always thought they tolerated each other because of her grandmother. Now she was not so sure.

'Well,' the Earl said, 'don't just stand there, Pippa. Go and get a portmanteau for the night. A footman will come round tomorrow to pick up the rest of your things.'

'Yes, sir.' Pippa went to her aunt and hugged her. 'I shall still run tame here. If you allow it.'

Tabitha held her tight. 'I would be hurt if you didn't, child.' She smoothed back a curl. 'I'll miss not having you about. But…' she shot the Earl a look '…you must stay with your grandfather now that he is in town.'

'I'll miss you, too.'

Pippa turned and ran up the stairs. Tabitha had been like the grandmother she had never known. Her care and wisdom about men and life had made Pippa feel loved and secure in a way that living only with men had never done. Tabitha had understood her needs and her worries.

She would be back.

Pippa woke late the next morning. A maid had brought her hot chocolate earlier, but the still-full cup sat on the night table, cold. She rolled to her side and gazed out the window. Grey sky and scudding clouds filled the glass panes. Soon rain would fall.

The weather was as sullen as her mood.

She crawled out of bed and went to stand in front of a large mirror. Her fine lawn nightdress billowed around her feet. Frowning, she gathered the material into one hand at the small of her back so that her figure was revealed. She turned from side to side.

No change.

With a sigh, she released the fabric and went to slump in one of the feminine chairs. She gazed around the room, studying it in an attempt to keep herself from thinking. Pink and gold were the dominant colours. Satin and velvet the major materials. Everything was delicate and flowing, even the rosewood furniture.

A log popped, the sound loud in the still quiet of the room. Pippa covered her face with her hands.

What was she going to do? Until now, she had avoided the issue, but Dev's urgency last night and his mention that she might carry his child had made it impossible for her to delude herself any longer. Deverell's baby might well greet the world in eight months. She had always been regular—until this month. She was three weeks late.

She shot up and paced the room, energy surging through her. Part of her had known. The nearly imperceptible swelling of her breasts, the sense of euphoria, both had told her. Her training as a healer and midwife hadn't failed her. She had refused to admit it, even to herself.

Where there should be joy, she had only worry. All her life she had wanted children to love and raise. But not like this. Not when the father was a man she wouldn't marry because she could not trust him. And yet...

She loved Deverell. She always had, and in her heart, she knew she always would.

She sank to the floor, a thick pink-and-gold carpet easing her landing. The tears came.

A long time later, a noise outside her door pulled Pippa from her misery. She rose and went to the wash stand. She washed her face, knowing the cold water might feel good but it would do little for the swelling around her eyes.

But her decision was made. Deverell need never know. When she had cleared her brother's name, she would return to the country and her grandfather's estate. She would continue to work with the local midwife and do what she could on her own to help the sick. When her child came, she would have him and raise him with all the love she had to give. It didn't matter that she would never marry. Until Deverell, she had never wanted to put her life and future into a man's hands.

Grandfather would be upset, but he would come to love the child. Just as he would never throw her out.

The only sadness that remained was knowing her child would be a bastard. It would never know its father or have the honour of its father's name. Pippa's chest tightened painfully, and she fought off the tears that once more threatened to fall. She would make it up to her baby. No child would be more loved, more coddled, more cared for than her child. She and her grandfather would be enough.

No one would dare slight the great-grandchild of Earl LeClaire and, if anyone tried, she would see they regretted the action. She would protect her child.

She stood tall, pushing the sorrow away. She would make everything come out right. No matter what the cost.

A knock on the door jolted her.

'Pippa?' Her grandfather's voice came through the heavy wood. 'Are you all right?'

She smiled wistfully. All her life he had come to her door if she was late for breakfast. To him, anyone who missed the first meal of the day had to be sick.

'I'm fine, Grandfather,' she said, pulling on her robe. She

crossed to the door and opened it so he could see for himself.

'Well, you look kind of peaked, but there is plenty of colour in your cheeks.' He reached out and tweaked her nose, a habit from her toddler years. 'Get dressed and come eat something. You will feel much better with some eggs and kippers in your stomach.'

She grinned. 'Yes, sir.'

She closed the door behind him and leaned back against the solid surface. Food was the last thing on her mind. Fortunately she was not plagued with morning sickness, she just wasn't hungry. But she was eating for two now.

Later, dressed in a muslin morning gown, she sat across from her grandfather. 'Sir, I'm not ready to eat the house down,' she protested as the Earl directed a footman to fill her plate with a little of everything from the sideboard.

'You won't be eating me into the poor house, girl. Why, you are all skin and bones. What was Tabitha thinking to let you run yourself down like this?' He snorted and took a long swallow of ale. 'Probably dragged you to all the goings-on without regard for proper food and sleep. That is just like her.'

Pippa nibbled at a piece of toast. 'Grandfather, why do you dislike Aunt Tabitha so much? She is one of the sweetest and kindest people I have ever met, yet you never miss an opportunity to say something unkind about her.'

The Earl's complexion grew ruddier. He made a mission out of cutting a piece of ham. 'I have nothing against Tabitha. I just don't approve of many of the things she does.' He put the meat into his mouth and chewed.

Pippa thanked the footman for refilling her cup with hot chocolate. 'Is that why you never wanted me to have a London Season with her?'

He glared at her. 'Now don't start blaming me for your never coming to town. You never wanted to.'

'True.' She ate the last of her eggs. 'But neither did you want me to.'

He grunted and pushed his chair from the table. 'This is a pointless discussion. Finish your food, then get some rest.'

Startled by his sudden action, she jumped up. 'Where are you going? I thought we would spend the day together.'

His face gentled. 'Maybe the afternoon, puss. Right now I'm going to visit your scapegrace of a brother. I want to know everything he can tell me that might help his cause. I have hired the best lawyers.'

She should have known, Pippa thought as she watched his large form leave the room. She only hoped that seeing his grandson and heir locked up in the Tower wouldn't bring on an attack of apoplexy. It would be best if she went with him.

She threw her napkin on the table and hurried to her room to don a pelisse and gloves. She would be waiting in the foyer when Grandfather came down.


From his post at the corner of the street, Dev watched Pippa and the Earl get into a carriage bearing the LeClaire coat of arms. Relief flooded Dev. If she was with her grandfather, she wouldn't get into any mischief. He could go home and dry out.

Twisting around on his good leg, he headed in the direction of his town home, given to him by his mother when he came of age. The Duchess had been enormously wealthy in her own right when she married the Duke of Rundell, and she had kept that wealth in trust for those of her children who would not inherit the dukedom.

The rain had become a steady mist that obscured vision

and the streets were slick. Dev stayed far away from the well-travelled cobblestones.

In three days Viscount Staunton's trial was to begin. Dev had been notified by Wellington that his testimony would be required. The summons had arrived this morning before he left to come keep an eye on Pippa. It hadn't improved his mood.

What more would Pippa do in an effort to clear her brother's name now that the time was so short? He shuddered to even consider it.

# Chapter Fourteen

Dev glanced at his cards, then scanned the room. It was cards and dinner in the home of a prominent Cabinet member, and everyone who was anyone was present, including Pippa and Lady Witherspoon. Tabitha's note had indicated the Earl would be present as well, but so far Dev hadn't seen him. Tabitha waved at him from another table. He smiled back and made her a modified bow from the waist.

'Courting the Dark Aphrodite by being sweet to her aunt?' his whist partner asked. 'Put a wager in White's betting book yesterday that you'd lose.' The young man, his shirt points too high and his hair too pomaded, snickered. 'Everyone knows she'll have nothing to do with you since you put her brother in the Tower. Can't say I blame her.'

Dev's eyes narrowed dangerously. 'No one asked you, Cathcart. Now play or get out of my sight before I lose my temper and call you out.'

All colour drained from the youth's already pale face. 'Don't get testy, Devil. Everyone knows you did what was right. You being a war hero and everything. You still wear that black arm band, though it's been five months.'

Dev saw red. He edged his chair back and began to rise, intent on slapping the fool across the cheek.

'Ignore the puppy,' the man on Deverell's right advised, cutting short Dev's action. 'No one ever said Cathcart had brains. Pity you had to draw him for a partner. Pity our hostess made us draw in the first place.'

Dev's tension defused. Leave it to Ravensford, a crony of his brother Jon's, to put everything into the right perspective. There was no sense in letting an idiot like Cathcart make him do something stupid.

Dev led the two of spades. 'Be glad I don't call you out, Cathcart. Everyone knows you can't fence, and you're more likely to shoot yourself than your opponent in a duel.'

The youth turned brick red, but kept his mouth shut. Dev considered it a minor miracle. Now, if only Pippa were as easy to deal with.

Two rubbers later, and two monkeys lighter of money, Dev pushed away from the table. 'I've had enough for the moment, gentlemen. If you'll excuse me.'

He wandered the room. In one corner Earl LeClaire and Tabitha Montcleve talked, or argued, if the white bar of brows across the Earl's face was any indication. Tabitha's right foot tapped away, a sure sign of her agitation.

Pippa was nowhere in sight. In the opposite corner, behind a potted orange tree, was the hint of a white skirt. She'd worn a simple white muslin evening gown. At first, he'd been surprised, then he'd decided that she wore it to make herself less conspicuous. He didn't like to consider the only reason he could think of that might make her do so. This wasn't the place to go looking for incriminating evidence, there were too many people around.

He made his way in that direction, only to stop at the sound of a male voice. Angling around, Dev saw that the man was Mark Hopwell. Pippa's right hand lay lightly on

Hopwell's forearm. Her face was alight with laughter at something he'd said.

Dev's gut twisted.

They made a distinguished couple. Her black hair and ivory skin were an arresting contrast to his light brown hair and swarthy complexion. With a start, Dev realized Hopwell had the same colouring he did. That could be him with Pippa, if he hadn't done his duty. The picture was too painful.

He turned away.

He walked aimlessly until he found a deserted bench off by itself, a trio of palms shielding it from the rest of the room. Sinking down, he stretched out his bad leg. The scars were white now instead of angry red. He'd even begun to think the wound didn't look too bad, not that it mattered. No one saw his leg except he and his valet. Pippa had said it would heal like this, but he had never believed her. Never trusted her word. His lack of faith didn't matter now, for she was with another man and wouldn't have him.

When had caring for her begun to hurt so much? When had he started wanting her so much it was an ache in his chest that never went away? He shook his head.

He'd always liked her, even when she'd masqueraded as a boy. He had respected her healing skills and been grateful for them more times than he could remember. Then, when she'd revealed herself to him, he had desired her. Desired her as he had never desired another woman. And there was the sense of camaraderie, of being able to do and say anything to her and knowing she still liked him. Not even Sam had generated the same feelings. Nothing near.

He had worshipped Sam, he now realized. She'd been an idealized, unreachable goal, not a flesh-and-blood woman to heat his blood and share his burdens. He'd wanted to help and protect Sam, but he hadn't wanted to ravish her and then hold her close and tell her he would keep the world from hurting her. Sam had not been Pippa.

Dev groaned and tunneled his fingers through his hair.

Had this feeling started when he saw Pippa in her new guise, her fine-boned beauty accentuated and brought into prominence by things he could never possibly understand? His mother said the bold colours Pippa wore became her. It was more than that. Dev didn't know what, he just knew there was something there that had grown over the past weeks of watching her and longing for her.

He wanted her, and he was damned if he would let Hopwell steal her away without a fight. He pushed up from the settee, determination stiffening his neck. If the two of them were still together, he would interrupt them. He was a soldier, and he would fight for Pippa.

Dev strode in the direction they had been, only to see no one there. A quick look around showed Hopwell talking to someone else and Pippa nowhere to be seen.

Dev's blood ran cold.

He should have known better than to let her out of his sight. He had come here tonight, knowing there was every possibility Pippa would try to sneak into the host's library and rummage through his papers. That was why he'd come here in the first place—to stop her.

Well, he could find his host's library as easily as Pippa could. With a quick look around to see that no one was paying attention to his actions, he slipped into the hallway.

A passing footman bowed to him before continuing into the card room. Dev knew he would have to be careful. The last thing he needed was for someone to catch him opening the doors of his host's house. It wasn't done.

The picture he conjured up tickled his sense of humour but not for long. There was no plausible excuse if he were caught, just as there was none if Pippa were found out.

He went down one hall and turned the corner. It was darker here and no one walked around. Still, a sliver of light shone from under one of the doors. He would take a chance.

He glanced both ways to make sure no one was around and opened the door. He slid inside and closed the door.

Sure enough, Pippa was bent over the desk, the glow of one candle spreading across the papers she read. The pale white of her gown looked ghostly. Lady Witherspoon, in a darker gown, stood nearby, riffling through a sheaf of papers.

'You should shield that light, it shows under the door,' he said.

Pippa jerked and her arm knocked over the candlestick. Gasping, she dived for it. Dev was beside her in an instant. She grabbed the candle and he stamped on the rug, putting out the tiny flickers of flame that had started. The Marchioness stepped back, taking a piece of paper and secreting it in the folds of her dress.

Dev caught Lady Witherspoon's action from the corner of his eye. She met his gaze before nodding her head in acknowledgement and slipping out the door he had just entered.

Pippa put the candle on the desk and rounded on him, drawing his attention to her. 'How dare you scare me like that!'

How typical, he thought. 'Better me than someone else. Just what harebrained thing do you think you're doing? Someone could come in here at any minute. And with your accomplice gone, there would be only you. What then?'

'Jane's gone?' She looked around.

'Like a rabbit down its hole,' he said sardonically. 'She, at least, has sense enough to get out.'

She huffed. 'I don't need Jane. I would think of something.'

'Like you did with me? A fire would certainly keep anyone from questioning you right away.'

She glared at him. 'You've had your laugh, now get out. I don't want you here.'

Exasperation roughed his voice. 'I came to save you from your foolish actions. If you won't think of yourself, think how your grandfather would feel if someone found you here.'

Her chin lifted. 'He would understand. He wants to clear Philip as badly as I do.'

'It isn't bloody likely that he wants to do it at the expense of his granddaughter's reputation.' He picked up one of the papers she'd been reading and glanced down it. 'Besides, there is nothing here. These are personal correspondence and not a word applies to anything the government is doing.'

Exasperation tinged her voice. 'That is only one sheet.'

'And you plan on going through all the letters? You don't have time. And what if you're caught? What explanation do you have? This is nearly as bad as breaking and entering. Nearly.'

Her hands clenched. 'I've got to do this. Time is short.'

Compassion softened his eyes. 'I know. Your brother goes to trial in two days. But getting caught rummaging through a Cabinet member's desk won't help. In fact, it will hurt. They will think you're spying for Staunton.'

'They won't. I will tell them the truth...if I must.'

He shook his head, wondering how much more stubborn she would be. 'We are wasting time. If you're determined to do this, I'll stay by the door and listen for anyone.'

She stilled, her fingers splayed on the desk. 'You would help me?'

A crooked grin showed his white teeth in the yellow glow of the candle. 'Not willingly.'

She gave him a curt nod.

Pippa watched Dev move to the door, her forehead wrinkled in perplexity. His honour was so strict, she wondered how he could bend it enough to allow himself to aid and abet her action. Yet, two nights ago he had helped her creep unseen into Aunt Tabitha's house. If he had revealed her presence, her aunt and her grandfather would have had her watched, which would have made her excursions difficult if not impossible.

She made herself look away from him. There was no sense in pondering what made Deverell St Simon act the way he did. She had very little time and a lot of papers to rummage through. Impatiently, she pushed a curl behind her ear and continued searching.

Voices muttered out in the hall, the sound reaching Pippa's ears just as Deverell grabbed her. His eyes bored into hers.

'Don't give us away,' he muttered.

'What are you—?'

His mouth cut her off. The kiss was hard and practical, no melding of lips and tongues. It had a purpose, and Pippa realized that purpose was to convince anyone who came in the door that they were having a lovers' tryst. The idea boded ill for the future.

The door opened. 'What in bloody blazes is going on?' her grandfather's voice boomed.

Pippa and Deverell jumped apart. Pippa looked at her grandfather's beet-red face and prayed he wouldn't have an attack. She rushed to him, noting that Aunt Tabitha was with him.

'Now, Julian,' Tabitha said in a voice that brooked no

argument, 'lower your voice and give the children a chance to explain.'

The Earl advanced into the room, heading straight for Deverell. 'I won't have my granddaughter consorting with this scoundrel. I told him before that she won't marry him and, by God, I'll thrash the meaning into him if I must.'

Pippa grabbed his arm and tried to make him stop going forward. 'Grandfather, there is nothing between us.'

He scowled down at her. 'What kind of simpleton do you take me for?'

She fell back, head dropped. 'Pardon, sir. You are right.'

'Stop this nonsense,' Tabitha said, her brisk voice cutting through the tension. Her gaze went from the scatter of papers on the desk to Dev. 'Clean this mess up the way you found it, Pippa. Dev, light some candles. Julian, go and close the door. 'Tis past time we had a little discussion.'

Pippa stilled. Wide-eyed, she looked at Tabitha, who looked right back without flinching. 'You know.'

'Yes, child, I do. I'm the one who has told Deverell when and where you will be.'

The breath caught in Pippa's throat. Another act of betrayal. She gazed at Dev, but couldn't stand the pity in his hazel eyes. Dropping her head, she returned everything on the desk to its original position as best she could remember.

The Earl closed the door, and Dev lit the branch of candelabra on the mantel. When all was done, Tabitha ordered everyone to sit down in the small grouping of chairs by the unlit fireplace.

Now that she was no longer in danger of being caught snooping, Pippa noticed how cold the room was. Her light muslin gown did nothing to keep her skin from turning to gooseflesh. Nor did the anger in her grandfather's face or the sympathy in her aunt's.

In a few brief words, Tabitha told the Earl what she

knew. Pippa realized her aunt knew everything except what had passed intimately between her and Dev. Her sense of betrayal strengthened.

The Earl's face was purple in the yellow light of the candles. His fists lay on the arms of his chair. 'I should have known better than to put her in your care.'

Tabitha's face turned to ash. 'How dare you! If you had raised her to be a lady instead of another boy, she would have never thought to do the things she has done.' Her chest rose and fell. 'But it is over and done. The child is a caring person who is worried about her brother. If there is anyone to blame for this imbroglio, it is Staunton. He encouraged and relied on Pippa to spy for him.'

'You should have stopped her,' LeClaire said.

'And how should I have done that? Chained her in bed at night?'

'You should have sent her home.'

'And had her worry herself sick over Staunton? I think not.' Tabitha took a deep breath. 'I did the best I could. I got Deverell to watch her and he has done well. As I knew he would.'

'Kissing her and compromising her reputation are doing well?' One of the Earl's brows rose. 'In my day, the chit would have been ruined. She would be today if anyone but us had come through that door.'

Pippa could stand no more of her grandfather's disparaging of Dev. 'Better that I be ruined than that I be caught as a thief.'

Dev broke in. 'I intend to marry Pippa. Anyone who dared impugn her name would answer to me.'

'All well and good,' the Earl said, 'but it would not change the facts, only make people speak behind her back.'

'They would have done that anyway,' Tabitha inserted.

'As it is, very few will speak badly of the future daughter-in-law of the Duke of Rundell.'

Pippa jumped up, sending her chair backwards. 'This is me you are discussing, and I am not going to marry Deverell. No matter what. He put Philip in the Tower. He betra…'

Pippa trailed off. Deverell wasn't the only one to break her trust. Her beloved brother had done so by telling the Marchioness of Witherspoon about her activities. And now her aunt Tabitha had done so by enlisting Deverell's aid and telling him and her grandfather everything. Her temples throbbed, and her jaw ached from clenching it shut.

Dev stood. 'Madam, my lord, I think it would be better to discuss this later. Pippa is tired and needs some rest.'

Before anyone could comment, he crossed to Pippa and took her arm. Not waiting to see what the other two did, he guided her out of the room and into a secluded corner in the hallway.

'Stay here, love. I'll get your cape and call for my carriage.'

Pippa pushed away from the wall she had momentarily slumped against. 'No. I'm fine, and I must return to the party or Jane will be beyond herself with concern.'

'I—'

'No.' She put a finger to his lips. 'I owe Jane peace of mind.'

Dev shook his head, but took her arm and escorted her into the card room. Pippa entered with a slight smile playing around her lips and her head high. She hoped anyone who looked her way would attribute her lack of colour to the heat in the room.

The Marchioness waved a languid hand at them before turning back to Mr Hopwell. Mr Hopwell looked inclined to leave her company for Pippa's, but Dev put a proprietorial hand on Pippa's arm. She glared up at him.

In an undertone, she said, 'I may have defended you to Grandfather, but that doesn't give you the right to touch me so openly.'

He grinned wickedly. 'And what may I do in private?'

Pippa's nerves, which she had been holding in check with severe strain, snapped. 'That is not humorous.' She shook him off and moved away.

Fortunately, the Earl and Tabitha appeared. The Earl's colour was still heightened, but it was no longer a splotched purple. Pippa hurried to them. She would not make eye contact with Tabitha or her grandfather, but asked to be allowed to leave.

'I will go with you,' the Earl said in a voice that said any argument would be futile.

'Pippa,' Aunt Tabitha said, 'I'm sorry. Please come for tea tomorrow and let me try to explain.'

The lump in Pippa's throat threatened to explode. 'Perhaps.' At the pain in Tabitha's eyes, she said, 'Yes.' Impulsively, she hugged her aunt briefly, uncaring of curious looks. 'I love you.'

'Oh, child,' Tabitha said, moisture blurring her vision, 'you are the grandchild I never had. Take care.' She turned to the Earl and admonished, 'And you leave her alone tonight, Julian. The last thing she needs are your recriminations. She has been through too much.'

For a fleeting moment the Earl looked chastened before his jaw clenched belligerently. 'I shall do as I like, madam. Just as I have for these last twenty years.'

'Old goat,' Tabitha said softly, but there was a softness about her expression.

Momentarily brought out of her own self-absorption,

Pippa studied them. What had happened between them? But she knew neither would ever tell her.

She sat silently in the swaying carriage as they made their way home. The Earl said nothing, but Pippa could feel her grandfather's censure across the chill dark space of the coach. It increased her own sense of malaise.

The outside lanterns of the coach cast a glimmering light through the windows, making the inside murky one moment and sharply defined the next. It was like Pippa's thoughts. One instant she could understand why Philip and Aunt Tabitha had told others about her secrets. The next second, she was angry and hurt that they had done so. Her world was no longer black and white, but filled with many shades of grey.

And what about Dev? He had turned Philip in, yet he had stood by her. He hadn't liked what she was doing, but he'd been determined to protect her.

She sighed heavily. Her head hurt and her mind was a jumble of conflicting thoughts.

The carriage halted, and she and her grandfather got out. In the foyer, the Earl handed his hat, cane and gloves to the butler before turning to Pippa.

'I have minded my tongue the entire journey, but I have something to say to you. Come to the library.'

Pippa dreaded the scolding she knew was coming, but followed him with her head held high. She had only done what she had felt necessary.

'Have a seat.' He directed Pippa to one of the sturdy leather wing chairs.

She did as told. The fire was banked and the Earl had only lit two candles. The room was shrouded and cold.

'Pippa, I know you feel responsible for Philip.' He paced the room once. 'But what you did was foolhardy. I can hardly believe that even someone of Tabitha's questionable sense would allow you to do so. However, it is done. But from this second on, I forbid you to continue.'

She struggled with her rebellious streak. 'There are now only two days left, sir.'

'Exactly. And if you have not found anything yet, I doubt that you will.'

She bit her bottom lip to keep from arguing. Some small part of her knew he was right, but a larger part would not give up hope. 'The traitor has to be found, Grandfather.'

He sank into the largest chair, exhaustion turning down the corners of his mouth. 'I know how you feel, Pippa, but there is nothing more that can be done. I will go to speak with Wellington tomorrow. I have an appointment with the Prince Regent for Monday morning before the trial starts. I will try to get immunity for Philip or, at worst, ask that he be let free to go to the Continent.'

Pippa's head sank. 'This isn't what I had hoped for.'

'Neither had I.'

The weariness in his voice pulled Pippa from her own sorrow. Standing, she said, 'Come, Grandfather. 'Tis past both our bedtimes.'

He rose heavily. 'Go on up. I will stay here a while.'

She saw his gaze wander to the decanter of port on the desk. 'You know that isn't good for you. I'll fix you some chamomile tea.'

He made a face. 'That stuff is bitter. The wine will be much smoother going down and accomplish the same end.'

'It will also give you a raging headache in the morning and irritate your gout. Better that I put plenty of honey in the tea.'

After several more arguments, he gave in with an ill grace. Pippa smiled as she watched him climb the stairs.

She knew there was no port in his bedchamber because she had directed the maid to remove it.

Feeling marginally better, she headed for the kitchen to brew the tea. While she was at it, she would mix a small pot of cream for the tweenie's burned forearm. The child had brushed against a burning ember while lighting the fire in Pippa's room. Working with her herbs always eased the strain and made Pippa feel better.

# Chapter Fifteen

After church the next day, Pippa changed into a pomona green dress. A fetching straw bonnet with matching green ribbons framed her face. Several ebony curls peeked coquettishly out. Gloves and a spencer finished the outfit. Nothing could hide the dark circles under her eyes. Properly attired, she set out to call on Aunt Tabitha.

She wasn't comfortable with the impending visit. Even after tossing restlessly for most of the night, she hadn't come to terms with the knowledge that two of the people she had trusted the most had given away her secrets. Yet, somehow, she knew she would forgive her aunt, just as she had managed to forgive her brother. If nothing else, she would spend the rest of her life trying to forget their lapses.

Watkins, Aunt Tabitha's butler, opened the door. Pippa gave him her hat. 'How is your shoulder?' she asked, knowing he had injured it the week before while carrying one of the heavier silver serving dishes to be cleaned.

He unbent enough to smile at her. 'Thank you for enquiring, my lady. The salve you gave me has helped. I barely feel the ache.'

'Wonderful. I was hoping it would work.' She gave him

a conspiratorial grin. ''Tis what we use when a horse sprains a fetlock.'

Watkins looked momentarily taken aback before chuckling. 'Quite the thing.' A footman passed by, glancing their way to see what the laughter was about. Watkins stiffened up. 'Madam is waiting for you in the drawing room. She had Cook prepare your favourite sandwiches.'

'Please thank Cook. I can taste the cucumber already and the sweet butter.' Anxious to get her talk with her aunt over, Pippa moved rapidly. Belatedly, she realized she had outpaced Watkins who would be flustered if she didn't allow him to introduce her. She waited at the door for him.

With a flourish, he opened the door and announced her. Pippa smiled and moved past him.

Pale autumn sunlight flooded the room. Aunt Tabitha sat on a settee with crocodile legs. The table in front of her was heavily laden with a silver tea service and at least a dozen delicacies. Pippa's mouth watered in a very unladylike fashion.

'Child, come and sit down. I am famished and have barely been able to make myself wait for you.'

Pippa's apprehension eased at her aunt's informality. She took the seat offered and patiently waited for her tea, laced with plenty of sugar, and a plate stacked with cucumber sandwiches.

Not until they had both eaten enough to fuel an army did Tabitha clear her throat. 'Pippa, about last night—'

'No,' Pippa interrupted. 'Let us forget everything.'

Tabitha smiled sadly. 'That is only postponing the inevitable. In a week, a year, you will remember that I gave away your secrets and conspired with a man you claim to hate.' She set her empty plate down and clasped her hands in her lap. 'I would rather we discussed this now. I do not want you hating me some time in the future.'

Discomfort made the tucked and ruched neckline of Pippa's gown seem tight. 'As you wish.'

'Sometimes we have to do things that other people think betrays them because that is the only choice we can make and live with ourselves. Sometimes it is the best decision. But every time we do so, we risk losing a friend or lover.' Tabitha paused to gaze out the window as though looking at something that wasn't there. 'It is always hard.'

Tabitha's attention came back to Pippa. 'When I was younger, I was in love with a man I knew I would love all my life.' A wistful smile curved her Cupid's bow mouth. 'I was very young. But another woman, someone very dear to me, loved him too. I thought he would be happy with her and grow to love her so, in the end, I let him go. I chose to be sad so that she could be happy.'

'Aunt Tabitha, I'm so sorry,' Pippa said, leaning forward and taking one of the older woman's hands.

Tabitha patted Pippa. 'Do not be. I have lived a full life and found happiness. That was just an example to you. The man felt I betrayed him when I refused to marry him. But, you see, I did not feel I had any other choice. That is how I felt about your spying for Philip. I knew you would do it, with or without my help and knowledge. And I knew it was dangerous, no matter what you might have thought. The only person that I could be sure would look after you was Deverell St Simon, so I went to him.'

'That is how he always knew where I was going,' Pippa said with a martial light in her eye.

'Well, he always knew when you were leaving the house so he could follow you.'

'I would have been fine without him.'

'Perhaps. I could not take that chance. Nor did I feel I could tell you not to hunt for the real traitor. I know how you feel about Philip and, like you, I know he is innocent.'

'But why tell Grandfather?'

'That is harder to explain.' Tabitha released Pippa's hand and stood. She paced to the mantel and took down a dress sword. 'This belonged to my husband. Like your Deverell, he was an army man. He died in battle.' She paused and cleared her throat. 'This sword represented the military to him and what he knew he had to do. His duty. His honour. I felt honour-bound to let Julian know what had really happened.'

Pippa bit her lip to keep from saying how stupid she thought that was.

As though sensing her niece's reaction, Tabitha said, 'I know it would have been just as easy to keep him in the dark. I did not feel comfortable with that. He entrusted you to my care. And you must admit, the scene we walked into last night needed explaining.'

Pippa rose and took the sword. Holding it in both hands, she gazed at the shiny silver hilt and gold-and-red braid. 'A handsome weapon.'

'Very.' Tabitha took it and replaced it. 'Please try to understand, Pippa. I did not do anything last night or in the past weeks with the intention of hurting you. I did what I thought at the time was best for you. Sometimes that is not easy. Nor is it always the best way. It just is.'

Pippa looked away from her aunt's silent request for forgiveness. 'Just as Dev did what he felt honour-bound to do when we found Philip. But how can I forget that and marry him?'

Tears began to form in Pippa's eyes until they overflowed. The room was a blur.

'Oh, child,' Tabitha said kindly, drawing her into an embrace. 'Life is never easy. Sometimes we have to let the past go in order to continue living. Will you let Dev's strong sense of honour and duty keep the two of you apart?'

'I don't know. I just don't know.'

Pippa found comfort in her arms. It was like confiding in the mother she had never had. The two sat down and Tabitha continued to hold Pippa until her tears were past. When she raised her head from Tabitha's shoulder, the older woman smoothed back a stray lock of hair.

'Only you can mend the rift between you two. There is nothing Dev can do that he has not already done.'

Pippa hiccuped. 'I know, but I must think about whether I can let go of my anger and resentment.'

At the Duke of Rundell's town house, Dev waited patiently for his father to finish reviewing the account books. The room was large and dark. Bookshelves covered every wall, and where they ended walnut panelling continued to the ceiling. Brown crushed velvet curtains were pulled against the oncoming storm. Flames caroused in the massive fireplace. Unfortunately the room was so large the warmth didn't penetrate to the chair where Dev sat.

The Duke was a tall, slim, elegant man, his height hidden by the desk he sat behind. His hair was blonde with frosting at the temples, and his eyes were deep set and chocolate brown. The hands holding the papers were long, refined and very white.

'Now,' said the Duke, looking up at Dev. 'What brings you here in the middle of the afternoon? Usually you are at your club or some less reputable haunt.'

Dev resisted the urge to cringe. His father was a strict disciplinarian and known for his acerbic wit. 'Sir, I have a favour to ask.'

The Duke's thin lips curled. 'I should have known it was a service you wished rendered. Or your allowance has run dry.'

Dev's hackles rose. 'My allowance is intact, sir. I have

Grandmother's legacy, if you'll remember. I invest what you give me.'

'*Touché,*' the Duke murmured. 'What can I do for you?'

Dev never liked asking a favour of his father and this one was immense. But he had no other choice. His father was the only person he knew with enough influence to possibly change Viscount Staunton's fate. For Pippa, he had to ask.

'I know this will be difficult. You may refuse me, and I would be the last to blame you, sir. But…' Dev took a deep breath. 'Can you intervene in the case of Viscount Staunton? I would appreciate it more than I can ever repay.'

The Duke steepled his fingers. 'In what way do you want me to meddle? Have the traitor released or have him hung sooner?'

Dev couldn't trust himself to respond without anger so he said nothing. Moments dragged by.

'I assume you want him hung since you still wear your black arm band, and you sport a wound earned in a battle that might not have been fought if Napoleon hadn't escaped Elba.'

Acid dripped from the Duke's words, and Dev knew he had set himself an impossible task. But he tried anyway.

'Staunton deserves to die, sir. There is no doubt of that— if he is truly a traitor. His sister doesn't think he is.'

'If you believe her, why did you capture her brother in the first place?'

Nothing was ever easy when dealing with his father. 'Because I believed him to be guilty. All the evidence, what little we could gather, pointed to him. But now I'm not so sure.'

'Why?'

No longer able to sit still, Dev rose and paced. The drag of his bad leg was nearly impossible to see, but he could feel it. It reminded him of Hougoumont, and for the umpteenth time he wondered why he was doing this. And came back to the same answer—Pippa.

'He has had his sister break into the home of a Cabinet member and then gain entrance to the library of another during a card party.' He came to a halt in front of his father and leaned forward with his fists on the desk. 'They grew up together. Pippa says they have the emotional bond so many twins share. He wouldn't put her in jeopardy as he has done unless he truly is innocent.'

'A good argument.' The Duke reached across the wood and leather expanse of his desk to a large cut-glass decanter. He poured two glasses and handed one to Dev. 'Drink this down. It will ease some of your anxiety. Then perhaps you will sit again, and we can continue to discuss this without the tension you are currently generating.'

Dev felt heat move up from his perfectly tied cravat to suffuse his jaw and cheeks. His father had a knack for making him feel like a bumbling child. He took the drink and downed it in one swallow.

Whisky. It burned a hole down his throat to explode in his gut. He sat abruptly.

'I should have warned you,' the Duke said. 'But I thought it would do the trick. More?' He lifted the decanter.

Dev nodded. This one he would drink slower. 'Did Alastair get his preference for the drink from you, or vice versa?'

'We discovered it together. One of the things fathers and sons do.' He raised one blond eyebrow in a sardonic gesture.

The door opened and her Grace, the Duchess of Rundell, rushed across the room. Her husband raised both eyebrows at this behaviour.

'My dear, I am not going anywhere.'

She didn't stop until she reached him. He swivelled around and she sat in his lap. 'If I didn't know you were teasing me, I would be hurt at your tone of voice,' she said, her own tone both loving and reproving.

Dev watched them, marvelling at the love they had finally found for one another. He wasn't always comfortable with his father, but he loved him and was glad for the both of them.

'Perhaps I should leave,' Dev said, seeing that the two were momentarily absorbed in one another.

'No,' his mother said, getting off her husband's lap and pulling a small chair close.

Dev bowed his head in acknowledgement and stayed put.

'What brings you in here so precipitately, Alicia?' the Duke asked.

She dimpled at him. 'I'm come to beg for Dev's cause.'

The Duke rolled his eyes. 'I should have known.' His lapse of dignity was brief before his gaze pinned Dev to his chair. 'You fight unfairly. You should have told me from the outset that you have your mother's support.'

Dev's hands clenched the arms of his chair. 'Your reprimand is unfair, Father. I didn't tell Mother anything of my plan.'

'Rundell!' the Duchess expostulated. 'How very narrow of you. Dev told me nothing.' She straightened her shoulders and lifted her chin. 'I have been listening at the door. Although I could have listened from across the hall, Dev was so loud.'

'You never cease to amaze me,' the Duke murmured, the words softened by the look of love in his eyes.

'Well, I know the two of you don't get along. I didn't know why Dev was here, and I wished to be able to intervene if needed.'

Dev groaned. 'Mother.'

'Very commendable,' the Duke said. 'But 'tis true. We are not as close as perhaps we might be.'

Dev had thought the conversation uncomfortable earlier, but that was nothing compared to now. He and his father never discussed their differences. He didn't want to start now.

The Duchess grabbed one of the Duke's hands. 'Please, Rundell, say you will help.'

Her husband looked at her. 'Does it matter that much to you?'

'Yes,' she said quietly. 'I think the boy is innocent. Stubborn, but innocent.'

The Duke looked from one to the other. 'Then I shall see what I can do. But no promises. A man who is thought a traitor has very little sympathy from everyone else. Including myself.'

Relief washed over Dev. 'Thank you, sir. If anyone can get a postponement of the trial or get it set entirely aside, you are the person.'

'Don't set high hopes. Either of you,' the Duke said brusquely, looking from one to the other. 'This is very late to be interfering. I should be surprised if anything is changed.' As they both rose to protest, he held out one hand. 'Quiet. I said I will try, and I will.'

The Duchess grabbed his hand and took it to her bosom. 'I shall see that you are amply rewarded, my love.'

Seeing the amorous turn the situation was taking, Dev bowed himself out of the room. No one noticed him leave.

The next afternoon, Pippa returned from a ride in the park with the Marchioness of Witherspoon to find her grandfather sitting morosely in the library. The drapes were pulled and the only light came from the fire. A tumbler of liquor, held loosely in one hand, threatened to spill its contents on to the rug. The Earl was oblivious.

Pippa knew immediately. He hadn't been able to get anything changed. Her heart sank.

She went to stand behind him and draped her arms around his neck. 'It was no good.'

'Wellington would not hear of dropping the charges. Nor would the Prince Regent settle for allowing Philip to renounce his rights to the title and go to the Continent. I fear the results of his trial. I do not believe anyone thinks him innocent.'

Pippa hugged him tight, inhaling the scent of his soap and the citrus bite of the snuff he used. He looked ten years older than he had this morning.

'The trial before his peers starts tomorrow morning,' he said.

'We will contrive something,' Pippa said, kissing him on the cheek. 'But right now you need to get some rest.'

Mindful not to spill the liquor, she took the glass from his unresisting hand and put it on a table. Next, she helped him stand and led him from the room. If she weren't very careful, this trial would be the death of her grandfather. She couldn't bear two such heavy losses.

With her arm around his waist, they mounted the stairs. She tucked him into bed for a nap and turned to leave. He grabbed her wrist.

'Pippa, you should know. The Duke of Rundell was before me. He asked for the same leniency as I.' His eyes held her for a long minute.

'Thank you,' she murmured.

He released her hand, and she hurried away. If the Duke of Rundell had asked, it could only be because Deverell had requested him to. What did this mean?

Agitation sat on her shoulders like a bird of prey. Had

Dev decided Philip was innocent? Did he regret bringing Philip to trial? She didn't know what to think, but found herself softening toward him. He was trying so very hard to change the wrong he had done.

Perhaps there was a chance for them. How wonderful it would be to marry the man she loved. Their child would be better for it, too.

If only she could truly believe Dev regretted his actions. Everything would be perfect, or as nearly perfect as possible under the circumstances.

She spent the rest of the day in a haze of hopeful anticipation.

The next morning was cold, damp and eery. Pippa entered the courtroom with dragging feet and a heavy heart. She was to testify in Philip's defence. Character witnesses were considered almost as important as those who gave evidence about the supposed crime. Aunt Tabitha was to testify as well.

Grandfather walked beside her, his head held high and his shoulders back. His ruddy complexion was paler than usual. He stared straight ahead, ignoring the few curious glances.

Pippa looked over the group of peers who were to decide her brother's fate and recognized all of them. At one time or another, she had danced, talked or ridden with each one. The Marquis of Witherspoon was one, his face with its usual sour expression. She knew how he would vote before the trial even got under way.

Aunt Tabitha beckoned to them. She had two seats set aside. They took them, with the Earl between the women. Pippa had noticed that Tabitha seemed able to calm the Earl when nothing else could.

Shortly after, Philip was brought in with chains on his

wrists. The sight was nearly more than she could stand. To
see her proud brother treated like an animal was unforgivable. She heard a soft moan of pain from her grandfather.
She reached for his hand and held on tightly.

The expanse of the room separated her from Deverell,
who sat with his mother. The Duchess smiled at her. Pippa
did her best to return the gesture, but knew her effort was
weak. Dev stared at her. She turned away from him, all of
yesterday's softness erased by her brother's plight.

If not for him, Philip wouldn't be facing a death sentence. Bile rose like acid to eat away at the love she still
had for him.

The rest of the day did nothing to change her opinion.

Wellington stated what he thought Philip had done.

Pippa squeezed her grandfather's hand. Together they sat
as still as though they expected to be pounced upon if they
made the slightest movement or sound. On the Earl's other
side, Tabitha's face was as white as a sheet. Pippa knew
she looked the same.

Then Deverell was called to present his information.

As much as Pippa didn't want to watch him, she could
not take her gaze off him. He sat stiffly, his eyes looking
straight ahead. He spoke dispassionately, neither adding nor
deleting anything they had found out in Paris. The only
things he didn't tell were her part and what she had done
here in London. Even to her, the evidence he presented was
damning.

The tightness in her chest increased until it seemed she
would expire from lack of breath. But it wasn't over yet.

When Dev was thanked and told he could return to his
seat, he asked, 'I would like to add something more.' When
no one objected, he continued. 'While I brought Viscount
Staunton in to stand trial for treason, I would like to caution
that we have no absolute evidence. To condemn him to

death and the abeyance of the LeClaire title is severe punishment if there is any doubt as to his guilt.'

A chorus of suppressed gasps sounded around the room.

'I am not saying he isn't guilty,' Dev said. 'Merely that we have no unarguable proof.'

Pippa's mouth twisted into a bitter smile. Too little, too late.

Tabitha leaned around the Earl and whispered, 'He has tried, Pippa.'

Eyes brittle, Pippa hissed, 'He would have done better to have second thoughts before being responsible for Philip's incarceration.'

As Dev returned to his seat, his eyes sought out Pippa's. She stared stonily at him, refusing to acknowledge the regret in his. Head held high, she looked away, going so far as to turn her shoulder to him.

Aunt Tabitha was called next. 'Philip is one of the most honourable men I know. He would never betray his country. What would he have to gain?' She continued in this passionate vein until asked to step down.

Pippa glanced around the room. The closed faces on the people present told her louder than words that her aunt's testimony had done nothing. Her hands clenched so her nails bit into her palms. She was next and had nothing to say that Tabitha had not already said. Still, she was closer to Philip than anyone—except, possibly, the Marchioness of Witherspoon.

Pippa glanced at her twin as she made her way to the stand. He nodded at her, his eyes full of encouragement. She fought the tears his confidence in her brought.

'Philip is my twin,' she started. 'I, more than anyone else, know him, and he would never commit the acts he is being charged of. From the moment we were old enough to understand our place in the world and what it meant to be English, Philip has been determined to help make his country strong. He is the eldest son of the eldest son, heir to the title and lands. He joined the army to protect that heritage, not destroy it. He would never spy for Napoleon.'

She said more, but could tell by the bored looks on several of the faces and the pity others did nothing to hide, that she was failing. Her voice trailed off, the catch in her throat threatening to become a sob. She would not cry. She would not show such weakness to a room of people determined to destroy her brother.

She stood and glared defiantly at anyone who met her gaze. 'He is innocent. If you condemn him, you will be condemning a man who would have died for his country before betraying it. You will be making a mistake.'

She walked back to her grandfather and sank into her chair. The Earl's hand sought hers and squeezed. Tabitha gave her a smile of understanding. The gestures were nearly more than she could take. Her vision blurred, and she blinked rapidly to keep the tears from falling. The trial was not over yet, and she had to be strong—for Grandfather, for Philip, who was called on last.

He rose, his chains clinking clearly in the silence. Loudly and clearly, he stated, 'I am innocent of treason. However, I have no way to prove that. I believe the real spy is in this room…' Shouts and anger met his words and it was some time before it was quiet enough for him to continue. 'You don't like what I say, but the information the French spies had could only come from someone privy to government policy. Who else? Since no one will stand and claim responsibility, I am the scapegoat.'

With a contemptuous curl of his lip, he sat. His gaze roved boldly over the assembled peers. Most met his stare.

Silence followed as Philip's peers deliberated.

Soon afterwards the sentence was pronounced. Philip

was found guilty of treason and to be hung and then drawn and quartered. The LeClaire land and title were to revert to the Crown upon the death of the present Earl.

Pippa felt as though someone had given her a mortal wound. It took all her resolve and strength not to crumble to the ground. She blinked furiously to keep the moisture filling her eyes from falling. The knuckles of the hand holding her grandfather's were white. The other hand shook under cover of her skirt.

Every eye in the place turned to them, some with pity, some with righteous gloating. She ignored them. Somehow she would stand up and walk out of this room. She would make her legs support her and her heart continue to beat. She would draw one ragged breath after another. She would show them the pride of a LeClaire. Then tonight she would take justice into her own hands.

She had forgotten her grandfather.

A sharp intake of breath, followed by a low moan were the only warnings. He collapsed to the floor.

Forgetting all her resolve of a haughty exit, Pippa fell to her knees. Fingers clumsy and frantic, she unloosened his cravat and shirt and slid her palm over his heart. She could feel it beating, swiftly and erratically. His face went from flaming red to the white translucence of a turnip. His breathing was laboured.

Across his chest, her eyes met Tabitha's. Tears streaked the perfectly applied powder on the older woman's high cheekbones.

'Is he…will he…' Tabitha took a deep breath '…live?'

Pippa fought off her own tears. She needed to remain calm. Just for a little longer. 'I don't know.'

A commotion drew her attention. Philip was struggling with his gaolers in an attempt to get to them. The Duchess of Rundell went to the scuffling group and, with an impe-

riousness that was magnificent to watch, demanded that he
be allowed to attend his grandfather. The guards, too taken
aback and unused to dealing with aristocracy of such rank,
fell back.

Pippa would have risen and thrown herself into Philip's
arms if a hand hadn't dropped to her shoulder. 'Pippa,' Dev
said calmly and authoritatively, 'you have got to help your
grandfather.'

His words penetrated the fog of pain engulfing her. She
reached for her reticule and the small vial of foxglove tincture she always carried in case her grandfather had an attack. The midwife she had helped used it for many things,
from dropsy to falling sickness to apoplexy. Pippa had seen
with her own eyes that it helped. Her hands shook uncon-
trollably as she tried to open the strings of her reticule.

'Let me,' Dev said calmly, taking the bag from her. He
opened it and withdrew the vial. 'Is this what you want?'

By way of answer, she grabbed it from him and wrested
the cork out. Tipping her grandfather's head back, she
poured the liquid in his mouth and prayed.

In a loud voice, she demanded, 'Everyone stand back.
He needs room to breathe. Someone find a litter. He must
go home.'

It seemed to Pippa that they waited an eternity. Philip
knelt beside her and they joined hands with Tabitha. Without thinking, Pippa even took Dev's hand and held it tight,
thankful for the sturdy comfort of his presence. She didn't
even think of what a contradiction to her earlier feelings it
was. All that mattered was his nearness in this most awful
time.

Tabitha's tears fell freely. Pippa sniffled, but refused to
give in to the grief welling inside.

In guilt-riddled pain, Philip said, 'I've done this to him.
I am so sorry.'

Pippa's agony increased, for there was no honest answer to Philip that didn't agree with his self-condemnation. 'Don't make it worse, Philip. He would never blame you.'

Suddenly, miraculously, she felt the Earl's right arm move. 'Grandfather,' she said softly.

His eyes opened, the right more than the left. His lips moved but she couldn't hear what he said. The words were slurred.

'Tabitha?' he whispered, the effort closing his eyes again.

'I am here, Julian,' she sobbed, laying her cheek against his. 'Always.'

Grandfather and Aunt Tabitha loved each other. Awe and happiness held Pippa motionless. If only it weren't too late for them. She smiled through her tears.

Just then, several men arrived with a litter and carefully lifted the Earl on to it. He slipped into unconsciousness during the procedure, but Pippa noticed that his breathing seemed to ease. Tabitha stayed by his side, never once releasing his hand. A carriage waited outside. They settled him inside and Pippa turned to Philip.

She wrapped her arms around him. 'As soon as Grandfather is comfortable I shall come to you,' she said. 'Be prepared.'

Understanding momentarily lit his features as he kissed her forehead. 'Take care of him.'

'I will,' she promised, entering the carriage.

Through the window she saw Deverell and his mother. They stood near Philip, who was once again being held by his guards. She smiled sadly at the Duchess and waved. Deverell she ignored, although she couldn't forget the sense of security his nearness had given her during the first moments of her grandfather's collapse.

The coach moved forward, the wheels clattering on the

cobbles. Increasing the distance between her and Deverell did nothing to dampen the depth of her reaction to him. It seemed that no matter what he did to her family, she could not stop loving him and depending on him.

It was a curse she would spend the rest of her life trying to overcome.

# Chapter Sixteen

Pippa and Tabitha took up opposite sides of the Earl's bed. Pippa monitored his pulse and breathing while Tabitha bathed his forehead and spoke softly to him. The Earl went in and out of consciousness.

Finally, in the small hours of the morning, his eyes slowly opened and he focused on the room. 'Tabitha?'

She leaned over him until she was in the field of his vision. 'Yes, Julian?'

He smiled, the left side of his mouth not quite as high as the right. 'I love you.'

'Oh, love,' she murmured, burying her face in the crook of his neck.

He tried to raise his right arm to her shoulder. Seeing that he couldn't, Pippa did it for him. His eyes thanked her.

'Why did you leave me?' he asked, his voice hoarse and barely audible.

Tabitha lifted her head and wiped at her tears. She glanced at Pippa then looked at the Earl. With a sigh, she said, 'Because it was the right thing to do. Mary had slept in your bed, and you had made love to her.' When he opened his mouth to speak, she put a finger over his lips. 'Hush, love. I know you were drunk at the time and that she disguised herself as me, but that did not change the act, only the intent. She loved you so much. To do so desperate a thing was unheard of. And you are a gentleman. You had to marry her after that. I knew it. So did you.'

'Yes,' he muttered. 'And I did my best not to hate her for it. Although I often felt I failed.'

'Hush,' Tabitha said. 'Do not fret yourself. She was happier with you than she would have been without you. I knew that, and that is what made it bearable for me to let you go.'

'So many years,' the Earl rasped, exhaustion drooping his eyelids. 'So many wasted years.'

'But no more,' Tabitha said. 'I will never leave your side again. I promise.'

He smiled before drifting into a sleep.

Over his gently rising chest, Pippa said, 'Grandfather was the lover you let go because of honour.'

'Yes, and while I missed him horribly and had bouts of anger over the pain of losing him, I never truly regretted my decision.' Her eyes met Pippa's squarely. 'I had no other choice.'

'You could have run away with him.'

'No. Neither one of us could have lived with ourselves if we had done so irresponsible a thing and hurt Mary like that. Nine months later she birthed his child. Your father. No, it was better to go through life without him than not to be able to live with myself.' She looked down at the Earl, longing and love softening her features. 'He would not have been happy either.'

'Honour,' Pippa breathed.

'Sometimes it is all we have,' Tabitha said.

'A cold life.'

Tabitha caught one of Pippa's hands. 'Think well on what you just said.'

Unable to meet Tabitha's gaze any longer, Pippa pulled her hands free and turned away. 'I have things to do,' she said over her shoulder. 'He should sleep for a while and, unless something else happens to upset him, I hope for a nearly full recovery.'

'If he has some paralysis, it will not matter,' Tabitha said. 'I will care for him always and be thankful for every day we have together.'

Such love and devotion. It made Pippa's heart ache for what she did not—would not let herself have.

'I will check on him as soon as possible,' she said, moving to the door. 'But I will be gone for a while. Maybe several days. If he relapses, give him the contents of the bottle on the table.'

'Be careful, Pippa,' Tabitha said, the solemnity of her voice making Pippa pause. 'If you are caught, you may well suffer Philip's fate, and then where would your grandfather be with both of you gone?'

Pippa swallowed hard on the fear that rose up in her throat. 'I have no other choice. I cannot leave him to be executed.'

'I know,' Tabitha said quietly.


Dev stood in the shadows, watching Earl LeClaire's town house. It was a position he was becoming too accustomed to. Behind him, his horse whickered. Absentmindedly, he reached behind and petted the gelding on the nose to quiet him. The last thing he needed was for a restive horse to reveal his position.

A cold wind blew off the Thames. There was no moon so the stars shone more brightly than normal, their glitter the hard sparkle of diamonds. He shivered and pulled the collar of his caped greatcoat up around his ears.

Soon Pippa would be creeping out on her way to the

Tower. She had no other choice. But how would she break Staunton out? That remained to be seen, for he had no doubt she would manage. The only real question was whether or not he would stop her.

It was just hours before dawn when he saw a figure slip from around the back of the house. She paused as though listening, then motioned behind her. Another figure, draped in an all-encompassing cape, hurried up to her and stopped. The second person was taller than Pippa, so he knew it wasn't the Marchioness. Probably a servant. Two horses followed.

Dev began to suspect what the plan was. He wondered when it would occur to Pippa that arriving at the Tower at such a strange time would be suspicious.

Quickly the two shrouded figures mounted their horses and headed in the direction of the Tower. Dev waited until they were well on their way and the sound of hooves on cobbles had died away. Then he followed more slowly, always careful to keep a silencing distance between them. He knew their final destination.

Dev reached the Tower in time to see Pippa hand the guard something. A bribe most likely. The two figures disappeared inside, and Dev settled in to wait. He didn't have long.

Three figures stood silhouetted in the light from the door. Pippa, the tall person whom Dev thought was now Staunton, and a much shorter individual. He wasn't surprised to see the Marchioness of Witherspoon with them.

Dev shook his head and agonized over his decision. Did he stop them, or let them escape? It seemed the guard didn't realize that his prisoner had taken the place of one of the late-night visitors. Or, if he did, the gold he'd received was adequate to make him deny any such knowledge.

The three shadows moved swiftly to the horses and

mounted. He had allowed them to make their getaway. Nor was he completely sorry. In his heart, he believed Staunton was innocent. He was even beginning to wonder if the Viscount was protecting someone. But if so, he was paying a steep penalty.

He spurred his mount onward. From now on, he would have to keep close behind them. His guess was that they were headed for a seaport. If he were doing this, they wouldn't go to Dover or another large port. They would go to a small fishing village and arrange to be smuggled across the Channel to the coast of France. From there, they could quickly lose themselves on the Continent. He quickened his pace.

Pippa thought she heard hoofbeats behind them, but couldn't be sure. They were travelling too fast for her to safely look behind. Philip was in the lead, planning on taking them to a small village where he knew a fisherman who did smuggling on the side. But it was a long ride, and they had to be well away before daylight and someone came to check on Philip.

Their capes spun out behind them as they raced toward the rising sun. Blood-red light crested on the horizon when they stopped at the first inn. They changed horses and kept on going without a rest.

It was mid-morning when they cantered through the quiet main street of the tiny village. Philip deposited them at the single tavern and left.

Pippa hunkered down over a pine table in the darkest corner of the public room. Jane sat across from her. Fatigue lined their faces and dulled their eyes. Neither spoke for a long time.

Finally the Marchioness spoke, her accent more pronounced than usual. 'Were you surprised to find me with your brother?'

Pippa looked dispassionately at her, noting a smear of dirt that dragged across the other woman's cheek. She probably looked worse.

'No. I was only taken aback when you pleaded to come with us. You're giving up everything for my brother and without benefit of marriage.'

She shrugged and a sad smile tugged her lips. 'I love him. It is something I never expected when first we started, but it happened. It changed everything.'

'How?'

Pippa's sixth sense told her there was something the Frenchwoman wasn't saying, something that was important. She remembered Dev saying Jane had taken a paper the night they rifled through the Cabinet member's desk. Why?

Jane's gaze slid away, wandered the room without ever coming back to Pippa. 'Perhaps some day I will be able to tell you, but not now. It is better this way.'

Suspicion, only a hint before, flared in Pippa. But there was nothing she could do. All she was certain of was that the Marchioness loved Philip. Anything else didn't really matter. Not now.

The same sixth sense that had warned her about the Marchioness made her turn her head in time to see the edge of a beaver hat and the black greatcoat of a man walking by the single window the tavern boasted. She didn't see enough to be sure of who the man was, but she knew. Dev had followed them.

But why didn't he do something to stop them?

She rose and headed for the door with the intention of confronting him. Before she could turn the handle, it opened and Philip stepped inside. His eyes looked hunted as his gaze darted around the murky room. Danger emanated from him.

If he knew Dev was here, he would kill him without giving Dev a chance. They were too close to success for him to do otherwise. Pippa couldn't bear the thought.

'Where are you going?' Philip asked harshly. 'I thought I told you to stay put until I returned.'

Pippa bristled. 'I'm not your servant to do as you order. I wanted a breath of fresh air. The smoke in here is making me cough.'

His eyes narrowed, but he said nothing. She brushed past him. Outside the sun was bright enough to make her squint. A quick look in all directions showed no one who met Dev's description. For a moment, she wondered if she'd been in error, her heightened nerves making her see things that weren't there.

The skin between her shoulder blades itched, and she knew she was right. Dev was here somewhere, watching them. She hoped he would be cautious as much as she hoped he would not interfere with their plans. Philip had to escape.

She took several deep breaths, seeing no reason to waste her time in the clean air, then re-entered the dark, smoky room. Philip sat at the table with Jane, his arm around her. She leaned into him. Pippa sat opposite them.

Philip's face was expressionless as he watched her. She imagined this was how he looked when he was on a mission, cold and unemotional. His only weakness, that she could see, was Jane.

'I have a room for us. We need to get some rest.'

Pippa nodded. Jane sank deeper into his embrace.

'I have arranged for us to leave tonight with a shipment of wool. If all goes smoothly, Jane and I will in France before the sun rises tomorrow.'

Pippa breathed a sigh of relief.

Philip rose and drew Jane with him. Pippa followed them up a set of rickety stairs to a small room tucked into the eaves. The single window looked out on the only street that went through the town. Philip would be able to watch anyone coming into or going out of the village.

She and Jane stretched out on the two pallets. Philip pulled the single chair to the window and straddled it with his back to the room. She noted the pistol he took out of his pocket and sat on the sill. A shiver chased down her spine.

Her brother was serious and would stop at nothing to escape. She was doubly glad she hadn't said anything about Dev. Still, sleep eluded her through the chill hours of the afternoon and early evening. Beside her, Jane tossed and turned. Philip sat motionless.

Well after dark, Philip rose. 'It is time,' he said quietly.

They left the tavern as unobtrusively as they had entered it. A light, salt-laden breeze fanned their faces. Clouds skipped across the sky, obscuring the sliver of moon. Within minutes they walked on the rock shingle of the beach. A single lantern glowed in the distance, outlining a small boat. Figures scurried around it. Philip led them toward it without hesitation.

Pippa shivered. Everything was going too smoothly. Why was Deverell letting them escape? He had followed them this far, surely he meant to stop Philip. Unless…

Hope sprang in her heart. Perhaps he was here only to see that she remained safe, like he had in London. He'd tried to keep Philip from being condemned as a traitor, it wasn't unreasonable to think he might let her brother go. If that were so, then maybe…just maybe they could finally be together. Her heart longed for him, had done so even when he was convinced Philip was a traitor and should be punished. She might be able to forgive him.

She stumbled on one of the larger pebbles and her foot slipped out from under her. With a muffled shout, she twisted her ankle and went down. She flung her arms out to break her fall and ended up scraping her palms on the rocks and shells. Sharp, burning pain shot up her arms and up her leg. Very likely, she had a sprain.

Philip turned back with an impatient grunt. He extended a hand to help her up. Pippa took it and stood. She gasped as her ankle buckled and she nearly went back down.

'Are you hurt?' Philip asked.

'I have sprained my ankle,' she managed to say through teeth clenched against the discomfort. 'But I shall be all right. Just give me a minute.'

'I don't have a minute,' he said. 'Stay here and I'll send one of the men to help you back to the tavern. You will be safe there until you can send word to Grandfather.'

She stood shakily with her weight on her good leg. Reason told her his suggestion was the only sensible one. And if Dev were here, he would find her.

'Ah, a damsel in distress,' a French male voice said, the words seeming to originate from a nearby spit of rock.

Pippa twisted around, suppressing a gasp of pain. She felt Philip tense beside her. Jane rushed to their side, not stopping until she was in the circle of Philip's free arm.

The clouds chose that moment to clear. The hard light of the waning moon combined with the harsh glitter of stars to show the small, slight figure of a man stepping away from the rock. He moved toward them with an economy of motion that spoke of control. He held a pistol aimed at them.

'Grimod,' Jane whispered, the softness of her voice doing nothing to disguise her fear.

He made a mocking, disdainful bow. 'Jacques Grimod, spymaster extraordinaire, at your service. Or should I say, your demise?' His lips split in a cold, hard smile.

'How did you find us?' Jane asked, her voice trembling as she moved even closer to Philip. 'I thought you were in Paris.'

His smile disappeared. 'That is what you were supposed to think. You are stupid to think yourself my only spy in England. I knew about your affair with Staunton. When I heard through my other contacts that the Viscount was accused of treason, I knew you would run with him.' He levelled the pistol on Staunton. 'You are a flawed tool, Jane. One I can no longer afford to use or let continue to exist.'

Staunton released Pippa's hand and pushed Jane behind him. 'Let her go. She can't harm you. If you must kill someone, kill me.'

Grimod laughed. 'How noble. I intend to. And then I will kill both women. I won't leave any loose ends. That is why I am Napoleon's spymaster. I never take anything for granted. The lovely Jane can recognize me, something not many can do.'

He pulled back on the pistol's hammer, moving slowly as a gloating smile of anticipation transformed his face to that of a mocking demon. Pippa stared in horror. Her brother's death was writ all over the Frenchman's countenance.

'Stop!'

The order momentarily distracted Grimod, who looked for the man behind the word. In the seconds following, a figure darted forward and in front of Staunton. Realizing his mistake, Grimod shot.

The sound reverberated in Pippa's ears. Her heart stopped.

Oh, God, not again. First Philip, then Grandfather and now Dev. She flung herself at him, ignoring the protest of her ankle and mindless of the second pistol Grimod still aimed at her lover. She had to cover Dev's body with her own.

She fell down on Dev, only to have him push her away and roll to one side. Another shot pierced the air, rising above the pounding of the surf. The soft thud of impact was barely audible.

Grimod folded, a rag doll that has had the stuffing pulled out. Red spread across the chest of his shirt, creeping ever further until almost no white showed. His eyes glazed over.

Frantic with worry, Pippa crawled over the sharp stones to Dev. His breathing was loud and rapid.

'Where are you hurt?' she demanded, running her hands over him. 'Tell me. We must staunch the flow. Oh, Dev, how could you be so reckless?'

Tears soaked her cheeks and desperation lent her the strength to push his fingers away when he tried to interfere with her search. She couldn't lose him now. Please, God, not now.

'Shh,' he said, finally capturing her hands in his. 'I'm fine. Just a graze to my shoulder. More painful than dangerous.'

Relief rolled over her and she collapsed against his chest, her tears soaking through his shirt. 'Oh, Dev, I thought you were going to die. I couldn't bear it.' She clung to him, burrowing her face into the hollow of his shoulder.

He held her tight, his free hand rubbing the tight muscles at the base of her neck. 'It is all right, love. I'm fine.' He kissed her temple and released her hands to smooth the hair back from her face. 'Everything is fine. Calm yourself.'

Slowly his words penetrated her terror. Clutching his shirt, she lifted her face to look up at him. There were no lines of pain around his mouth and eyes such as she remembered from when his leg wound was fresh. He even smiled. The tightness in her chest began to ease.

'I owe you a thank you,' her brother said, drawing her attention momentarily from Deverell.

Dev rose, drawing her with him. She gasped and clung to him for support. 'Are you hurt?' he demanded.

'Only a little sprain. Nothing.'

He frowned at her, but turned to Staunton. 'I owe you a debt. It seems I had the wrong traitor put in the Tower.' His gaze shifted to the Marchioness, who was still sheltered against the Viscount's chest.

'*Merci,*' she said, her voice a husky whisper. 'I am so sorry. So sorry.' She looked up at Staunton, her lashes wet with unshed tears. 'I never meant to endanger you. I swear it.'

'I believe you,' he said.

'Then why?' Pippa demanded, all her anger aimed at the Marchioness. 'Philip nearly died and all along you were the real spy. You even pretended to help me hunt for the "traitor".'

Dev cut through the accusations. 'Was there something on the sheet of paper you took from the library the night I caught you and Pippa?'

She nodded. 'It had information on Napoleon's imprisonment that I thought Grimod would be interested in.' Her gaze slid away from Dev's hard stare. 'I had to spy for him. He had my mother.'

'Ah, love,' Staunton said tenderly, wiping a tear from her cheek.

She caught his hand and kissed his palm. 'If I did not spy for him, he was going to kill her. I could not let him do that. So I did as he ordered. To the bitter end. Please forgive me.'

Staunton brought her fingers to his lips and returned her caress. 'There is nothing to forgive. You had no choice. I knew that.'

'What?' Her shocked eyes met his.

'One of my informants knew about you. He warned me.'

'You knew?' Pippa demanded, furious at her brother and hurt by what he had done to her. 'Then why did you send me all over London looking for the traitor?'

'I'm sorry, Pippa,' Staunton said. 'I knew there was another spy, but not who. I wanted to find him and implicate him, hoping that would be enough to clear me and keep suspicion away from Jane. We still don't know who he is, since Grimod will never talk.'

For the first time since Dev shot the man, they looked at the Frenchman. He lay motionless.

'We'll take his body to London,' Dev finally said. 'It should be proof positive for Wellington that you aren't the spy we're looking for. I'll tell him Grimod said there was a spy in London. Hopefully, the information will be enough to clear your name, but I'd still go to the Continent right now. This may take time.'

'You're letting us go without a fight?' Staunton asked.

Dev stiffened and his arm that held Pippa tightened. 'You're innocent and, no matter how guilty she is, I can't condemn a woman to a traitor's death.'

But instead of watching them get into the boat, he turned away. Pippa thought she understood. His loyalty to his country told him not to let the Marchioness go, but the gentleman in him couldn't punish her as his honour demanded. By letting them go, he did the thing he considered the lesser of two evils.

'Thank you,' she said after the boat pushed away from shore and disappeared into the black night. 'You'll never know what this means to me.'

He grinned his crooked grin that never failed to make her stomach do somersaults. 'Oh, I think I know. Remember, I'm the man who travelled with you all over France and chased you around London as you did everything in your power to find and then save your brother.'

'I'm so sorry I misjudged you,' she said.

'You didn't misjudge me. I intentionally broke your trust and used you to find your brother. I put my sense of duty and honour before my love for you. My only excuse was that many of my friends died fighting Napoleon. I believed, and still do, that anyone who betrayed England for France deserves to die.' He looked briefly out to sea in the direction the boat had taken. 'I just couldn't bring myself to turn in a woman.'

'You tried to clear Philip's name. I know you asked your father to help and you spoke for my brother at the trial.'

He tipped her chin up. 'I would do the same things over again, Pippa. Given what I knew at the time, I would apprehend your brother again and send him to the Tower without hesitation.'

She knew he meant what he said, but in the past few days she had learned that sometimes you must accept a person for what they are, even if they have done something you feel betrays you. It was a hard lesson to learn, but too many people she loved had seemed to betray her because of their love for her or for someone else. She hoped she had grown.

'It doesn't matter any more, Dev. I love you and want to spend the rest of my life caring for you and proving to you that what has happened in the past is forgotten.'

He caught her to him and buried his face in the wild curls of her hair. 'I love you, Pippa.'

With a grunt he lifted her into his arms and started back the way they had come.

'Put me down,' she gasped. 'You will hurt your leg. You don't need to do this. I can walk with help.'

He laughed at her. 'Are you trying to keep me an invalid forever?'

'No,' she said, tangling her fingers in his hair. 'I just want you able to perform other duties for me.'

He hugged her tight. 'Never fear.'

She pulled his face to hers. He stopped walking to devote his entire attention to her demands.

# *Epilogue*

*Rundell Abbey, Boxing Day 1815*

Dev looked around the dining table. Everyone was present: his brothers and their wives, his parents, Earl LeClaire and Tabitha and Pippa. Pippa, his wife of one week. She looked at ease amongst his family. The emeralds his mother had given them as a bridal gift were draped round her long neck and dripped from her ears. They were considered the finest in the land, but they were no more brilliant than her eyes which returned his study. He smiled at her and rose to propose a toast.

He lifted his wine glass. 'To marriages of love. May they always prosper.'

His brothers rose and seconded his proposal.

'And may my bride always be glad she gave in to me,' he added, his gaze fixed on Pippa's rosy face. They had made love before coming down to dinner and her lips were still swollen from his kisses. He grinned at her.

Earl LeClaire rose and raised his glass. 'May everyone find a second chance in their life.' He took Tabitha's hand and raised her for his kiss. The room exploded in applause.

Looking very pleased with himself, the Earl added, 'Even my scapegrace grandson, who I hear is in Rome with the woman he loves.'

Lastly, the Duke of Rundell stood up. 'I propose a toast to my lady. Without her gracious meddling, we would not all be here tonight. Nor would I have learned that marriages can be more fulfilling and satisfying than anything else in life.'

Everyone stood and raised their drinks high to the Duchess, who sat looking pleased and embarrassed. When everyone was seated once more, Pippa caught Dev's eye. He nodded so she cleared her throat.

'I…that is, Dev and I have an announcement.' Every face turned her way. Many had a knowing look. She blushed. 'Yes, well, it seems most of you know what I am going to say, but I must say it anyway.' A smile of blinding happiness lit her features. 'Dev and I are to be parents.'

Pandemonium broke out.

The Duchess jumped from her seat and rushed to hug Pippa, scant steps ahead of Tabitha. 'My dear child, I am so delighted.'

Tabitha took the Duchess's place. 'Pippa, darling, nothing could make me happier. Come to us when it is time. I very much want to keep you safe and care for you.' She gave Dev a devilish glance. 'And I am sure your new husband will be frantic and grateful for the calming effects of Julian here.'

At so patent a misrepresentation of the Earl, everyone burst into laughter.

Just as things settled down, Samantha came up to Pippa. 'I am glad we are sisters-in-law.' She glanced at Dev who smiled at her. 'I am even more glad that Dev has found someone he can love with all his heart.'

Pippa fought down the urge to cry from happiness. She

put her arms around Sam and squeezed. 'Thank you. Our babies will be within weeks of one another. I hope they will be good friends.'

Sam wiped away her own tears. 'I know they will.'

A commotion at the door announced the arrival of the nursery bunch. Liza's baby was given to her by the wet nurse. Stephen and Amalie came in, both of them excited at attending a very adult gathering. They moved quickly to Sam, who still stood by Pippa.

'Mama,' Amalie said, 'Stephen says we are all to go riding tomorrow. Is that true?'

Sam smiled and pulled both children into her arms. 'That is what your papa says, and he is always right.' She gave her husband a mischievous grin.

Watching the small exchange, so redolent of love and caring, Pippa was achingly glad she had found Dev. As though sensing her thoughts, he came around the table to her and put his arm around her waist.

'Is it time we went to bed?' he asked softly.

She looked around the room. Everyone was caught up in conversation with someone else. No one would even notice they were gone. 'Yes.'

Arm in arm, they left the room. Tabitha and Alicia watched them before turning to each other. Tabitha winked. Alicia lifted her glass. Both women beamed.

Upstairs in the suite of rooms set aside for their use, Dev turned Pippa around until her face was a breath away from his. 'I love you, Philippa St Simon.'

'And I you.' She burrowed into his embrace, inhaling the scent of bergamot.

He scooped her into his arms and carried her toward the large bed. 'Stop,' she protested. 'What about your leg? 'Tis not good for you to lift me.'

He chuckled. 'It is the best thing for me. Without you I

would not have the thing. Without you I would be wallowing in self-pity.' He set her gently on the feather duvet. 'Without you I would be lost.'

She drew him down to her with a murmur of love and desire. He went willingly.

'I love you more than life itself,' he said.

'I finally know that,' she replied, turning into his arms. 'Nothing will ever part us again.'

'Nothing' he said, meeting her lips with his.

\* \* \* \* \*

# MILLS & BOON®

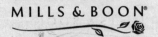

# *Makes any time special*

## Enjoy a romantic novel from *Mills & Boon®*

*Presents...*    *Enchanted*™    TEMPTATION.

*Historical Romance*™    ⊣ **MEDICAL ROMANCE**

**THE Regency COLLECTION**

*Where rogues find romance*

Look out for the seventh volume in this limited
collection of Regency Romances from
Mills & Boon® in November.

Featuring:

*The Cyprian's Sister*
by Paula Marshall

*and*

*A Compromised Lady*
by Francesca Shaw

Still only £4.99

**MILLS & BOON®**

*Makes any time special™*

*Available at most branches of WH Smith, Tesco, Martins,
Borders, Easons, Volume One/James Thin
and most good paperback bookshops*

## books and a surprise gift!

We would like to take this opportunity to thank you for reading this Mills & Boon® book by offering you the chance to take TWO more specially selected titles from the Historical Romance™ series absolutely FREE! We're also making this offer to introduce you to the benefits of the Reader Service™—

- ★ FREE home delivery
- ★ FREE gifts and competitions
- ★ FREE monthly Newsletter
- ★ Exclusive Reader Service discounts
- ★ Books available before they're in the shops

Accepting these FREE books and gift places you under no obligation to buy, you may cancel at any time, even after receiving your free shipment. Simply complete your details below and return the entire page to the address below. *You don't even need a stamp!*

**YES!** Please send me 2 free Historical Romance books and a surprise gift. I understand that unless you hear from me, I will receive 4 superb new titles every month for just £2.99 each, postage and packing free. I am under no obligation to purchase any books and may cancel my subscription at any time. The free books and gift will be mine to keep in any case.

H9EA

Ms/Mrs/Miss/Mr ...............................Initials...................................
BLOCK CAPITALS PLEASE

Surname ...........................................................................................

Address ............................................................................................

.........................................................................................................

................................................................Postcode.................................

**Send this whole page to:**
UK: FREEPOST CN81, Croydon, CR9 3WZ
EIRE: PO Box 4546, Kilcock, County Kildare (stamp required)

MILLS & BOON®

# MEDICAL ROMANCE™

### A FAMILIAR FEELING by Margaret Barker

Dr Caroline Bennett found working at the Chateau Clinique with Pierre, the boy she'd adored as a child, wasn't easy. It didn't help that his ex-wife was still around.

### HEART IN HIDING by Jean Evans

Dr Holly Hunter needed respite, and the remote Scottish village was ideal. Until Callum McLoud turned up accusing her of treating his patients!

### HIS MADE-TO-ORDER BRIDE by Jessica Matthews
*Bachelor Doctors*

Dr J.D. Berkely had a good job in ER, a delightful son Daniel, and a truly good friend in nurse Katie Alexander, so why would he need a wife?

### A TIMELY AFFAIR by Helen Shelton

Dr Merrin Ryan sees that widowed Professor Neil McAlister needs nurturing and she falls in love! But Neil is aware that he could damage her career...

## Available from 5th November 1999